The Tale of the Dream Seller

Minority

By **S.Farzpour**

Title: The Tale of the Dream Seller: Minority

Author: Saeed Farzpour

Publisher: Supreme Art, Reseda, Ca, USA

ISBN: 978-1942912187

Library of Congress Control Number: 2018903342

CONTENTS

CHAPTER ONE
THE BANISHED

November 21, 2059

The old man was standing among the tall pine trees in a dark forest. He raised his head to the gloomy clouds while a disturbing thought was swirling in his mind. With sad eyes, he kept on walking on a backroad, along the snowcapped hillside, which ended at a lake.

Passing through the rough and rocky terrain, he could see the lake at the foot of the mount. Each time that he reached a mound, he stopped by to watch the still body of water, and after a short pause, he continued on his way.

Though it had been raining and occasionally snowing for days in that area, the old man's cloak, without getting wet or even muddy, was protecting him from the bitter cold like a magical cape. Eliminating his footprints in the snow, it concealed his quiet and ghostly wanderings from others.

He had been walking for a while when he reached a small bare area. He looked around, as if he had been waiting for someone and then sat on a rock. With a slight movement of his hand, a big roaring fire appeared in the middle of the bare land, and he stared at it with a sad look in his eyes.

The flames were playing with his mind, dragging him into the maze of the memories. He could see the faces of children, sitting on wooden benches in a small classroom, looking at him cheerfully and free from the thoughts of a war-torn future waiting for them.

Among their childish laughter and commotion, a girl with golden locks was standing in a corner, looking at the man inside the memories. The scenes were parading before his eyes, and among them, the image of children was more vivid. Adam looked at each of them with patience and let his thought loose. Looking at their happy faces and delighted smiles, mixed feelings of trepidation and hope invaded his heart.

Deep in his thoughts, he felt the presence of someone among the trees before him. A shadow was crawling towards him, just like a discordant mist in the wind, getting closer. It became tall and changed into the shape of a robust middle-aged man in worn, frayed clothes. He had long sloppy black hair and looked more like a gypsy in his threadbare pants. Walking barefoot in the muds, he got close to Adam.

The old man wasn't surprised; as if he was awaiting him. The ragged man was standing under the rain without getting wet, just like Adam. His face showed rough and bitter days which he had been through.

He called Adam loudly: "No one lights a fire at the heart of mountains these days unless he is lionhearted." Torching his beard, he stood there in silence and waited for Adam to answer.

Adam smiled while he was doodling some shapes on the ground with a twig. Adam: "You don't need to be brave, knowing what and who you are looking for suffices you to start a fire in the middle of the night and wait for banished dream wanderers. But it intrigues me when even a tiny light in such a vast mountain, is not concealed from your eyes."

The ragged man: "How are you doing man? Are you still dreaming of doing favors to this world? Aren't you tired of constant failures, all this darkness, deceits and delusions that even bends the mountains, let alone the humans? One day you will understand that there is nothing to do but to accept the truth and to put up with the harsh fate of this world. But apparently, you are not ready for retirement yet."

Adam: "I still have unfinished businesses that do not let me leave at ease, Kisan."

The ragged man looked around and said with open arms, "Anyway, Welcome to the territory of exiled. Regardless of the old feud between our ranks during all these years, I always have wondered how a weak and small group like yours is still standing. How come weren't they able to dry up your limps yet?"

The old man answered in a calm manner: "Maybe our roots are so strong that they are not easily dried."

Adam looked around; he could see the creeping of banished among the trees who were attracted to the growing fire and were listening to the conversation between their leader and him. Although Kisan words seemed to be friendly, Adam felt threatened by it due to their profound discrepancy and the reasons they believed were behind their unjust exile.

Kisan took one step forward towards the old man; though it was just a small move, the air between them tensed up. An aura of force formed among them and encompassed Adam, so he continued doodling with peace of mind. The banished leader stretched forth his hand toward the old man and moved his finger before Adam's face, along the horizon. As he moved his finger, the air beneath it burned with a dazzling light, and black liquid was poured on the ground.

Kisan furrowed and stepped back, and at the same time, the beam of force disappeared. Adam raised his head, smiling and said, "It was strong, wasn't it?"

Kisan: "It was strong, but not friendly. I believed you have more trust in us, but maybe, if I were you, I would somehow protect myself in such gloom and loneliness."

Adam stood up with his common serenity and glanced at Kisan with penetrating eyes. He came closer, put a hand on his shoulder and said softly, "I need your help."

Kisan gave him the cold shoulder and said, "What kind of help?"

Adam went close and whispered in Kisan's ear: "I have to find a way to the Gaalve."

Kisan kept his eyes focused on him: "Inside Gaalve? You must be kidding me?"

Adam: "I'm very serious and also it's vital to me. I know your rank were key holders to the dream gates since ancient time until you were exiled, and that's because of the specific nature they have. Therefore no one knows its complexities better than you..."

Kisan interrupted him harshly: "And that's why Glidaar has sent us into a torturous exile since seventy years ago!? Moreover is that after Karapan's -the dark king- downfall and according to the agreement between Andium residents and Gaalve, nobody is allowed to pass through the gates of this realm between the two lands where its borders were always watched by Guardians of Dream. After my people's exile, it has been watched and guarded even more."

Adam lowered his head: "I know that the Great Glidaar, the Guardian of Dream, has persecuted you and your people. I know that our ranks had been engaged in mighty conflicts, but my old friend, the time of neglect and loneliness is over. Together, we may be able to find the reason behind your exile, and I as well will gain my desire."

Kisan, heavyhearted and sad, replied, "I didn't even have the chance to talk to Glidaar about his decision and to defend my people's right. One of his great advisors, Andowlin, drove us out of the land which we belonged to."

Adam was aware of the torment they were going through, and Kisan's words strengthen it.

Adam: "Kisan, no matter what, I have to enter Gaalve, reach the main hall and talk to one of my imprisoned fellows. My only hope to give her vital information is there, in Gaalve. If I don't communicate with her, all my efforts for saving her will fail. I am in critical condition and can't even contact her via local resistance. I've thought a lot about it, but don't know anyone other than you for entering Gaalve in secret; my information about that dark place is limited to the handwritten documents in Limora's great library."

Kisan turned his back to him with arms akimbo on his stout hips and stared at the overcast sky. He said with sadness in his voice, "there's nothing I can do, Adam. We have been forgotten for such a long time that even our return would not help. Knowing the reason behind our banishment also will not change anything, and we would still be deserted in abandoned mountains. My people had been backstabbed in a dastardly and villainous way."

Disappointed, Adam sat on the rock. Kisan moved his hand in the air and signaled the banished to leave as it was time to go and they disappeared among the luxuriant forest. Kisan walked slowly towards the mountain, but after a few steps, he stopped. He was struggling with his inner conflicts, feeling of hatred and revenge was clawing at his soul. By helping Adam, he could take a revenge from the great leader of Guardians of Dream as he was filled with rage and frustration.

As Kisan stopped, Adam raised his head and glanced at him, knowing the deep hatred in his mind caused by ruthlessly betrayal to his people and hoping this would spur Kisan on to his aid.

Kisan looked over his shoulder: "A big willow tree; when you reach it take the eastern path, you will arrive at the great abandoned gate, through northern backroad."

Adam stood up enthusiastically: "Yes, that's right. I know where you are talking about, but there isn't any gate at the end of this road. I have checked there several times."

Kisan smiled bitterly: "You have to be a half dreamer like us or use the power of the jewel you have to find the breach. All five jewels of the guardians can reveal Gaalve's hatches. Using it, take the road ahead of you and pass through the darkness of the limbo's borders. When you get to Gaalve, the great trove is specified. I can't help you more, just remember, fire is the key. Good luck Adam."

Then he left and disappeared without leaving any trace behind. Adam was conscious and alert now, knowing how to step into the dark latent world.

Once again, the children's laughter and their commotion filled his mind. He looked at the cloudy sky and determined about his decision, went towards the lake. As he left, the fire also went out, and a hideous shadow raised from the lake and went up into the sky.

The old man kept walking through the dark forest, and his pace slowed as he reached an old hut; Smoke was coming out of its chimney, and a faint glimmer of light could be seen on its single small window. He stood before the house and cleared his throat; then knocked at the door gently and constantly.

The Voice of a middle-aged woman could be heard: "Who's there?"

Adam: "an exhausted old man, dear Mariana."

Though the woman recognized his voice, she asked him to stand before the window and say the password. Adam did the same, so the woman could see his face and said, "The Lake's night."

She moved towards the door and opened it immediately, a thin and tall woman, holding a golden dagger in her hand.

Seeing the old man, she heaved a sigh of relief and put the dagger back in its sheath on her waist.

Adam smiled at her and entered the hut.

Mariana: "Many strange things happen these days that I don't dare to open the door without caution."

Adam: "That's a wise choice. Weird and hallucinatory things happen around us."

Mariana: "Would you like anything to drink?"

Adam answered with exhaustion: "I would appreciate a cup of forest tea."

Mariana smiled with eagerness and went to the kitchen.

Adam also went to a small room at the back of the hut. He pushed open the wooden door and looked inside, moving his hand, he made another fire and pushed it towards the fireplace, and the firewood inside it burst into flames.

After a few minutes, Mariana was standing at the door with a cup of tea in her hand. She knocked at the door: "May I come in?"

Adam: "Oh, of course. Who could keep Mariana waiting with that pleasant tea?" and laughed.

Mariana entered that simple room and placed the cup on the table: "The cold outside could freeze ones to death."

Adam took the old metallic cup between his hands and had a sip; fresh wild herbs warmed him.

Mariana: "During these days that I had been waiting for you, I didn't have good feelings. The local people living beside the lake say this place is haunted. Evil spirits and people who resemble the shadows wander among the trees, coming and going mysteriously. Tonight was horrifying. I was scared, thinking that I could hear footsteps on the snow outside. They were many, moving in a group. I was not brave enough to look out the window and could only think about you and Philip somewhere out there, thinking what might be happening to you… you know, just silly thoughts."

Adam gulped his tea and said kindly, "It's so nice of you to think of us. Your gentle soul could attract anyone Mariana; Philip must be proud of you. You know it better, many dreadful happenings had occurred to our world, which were inevitable; disease, poverty and at the end, that Great War which defaced our world. Now, fifteen years have passed since those days, and I have to accomplish an unfinished mission. I have to pass through this road in order to find peace. With a little bit of patience and steadfastness, we will put these harsh days behind, and I am sure that you and Philip would see better days in a better world."

He put the cup down and asked Mariana to sit at the table. Looking at her black eyes, Adam could see constant intolerable anxiety deep inside them.

Adam: "I don't think that Philip would face any difficulty and I hope that he can fulfill the task I have assigned him. You would better be more patience and stop being worried and restless."

Mariana could not hide her most profound feeling from a man who had been accompanying them for more than thirty years. To her, Adam was not only a leader but also a kind, older brother who had always tried to awaken those around him and warn them about incidents happening in their surrounding in the time of chaos.

Mariana, who was deep in thoughts, pulled herself together and said, "I'm filled with apprehension. I can feel how distressed Philip is these days; he had never been this way before. Wounds, caused by loss of his family has not healed yet, and his soul is still in turmoil, especially about his twin sister, Rita; He even calls her in sleep. I am perturbed about his health condition."

Adam went closer to Mariana and took her hand: "Don't worry, everything will be alright. I think I know the reason behind it; keeping the Taarnaar for too long will lead to such weird behaviors. When the enormous power of the Taarnaar overcomes the will of humankind, it gradually leads his mind towards a world of hallucination. It is time to take it back from Philip, as staying in touch with the Taarnaar for longer is not rational. He will be all right, I promise. He must have finished his mission by now and will be back to us soon. Anyway, we have to tolerate all adversity we are facing with for the time being. Dear Mariana, you were a young girl; many years have passed since then, and I have always been proud of having companions like you. Without your iron will, I could never pass through this road."

Adam and Mariana kept talking and recalling good old days, soothed Mariana. It was midnight when the old man felt sleepy, "I want to write down something which has just come into my mind before forgetting them; in private if you don't mind. Old men like me tend to forget things quickly…"

Mariana: "Not at all, I'll leave you alone. Just let me know if you wanted anything." and left.

Adam took out a black, leather-bound notebook from his pocket and started writing under the oil lamp's light.

"21st November, 15 years after the war;

My efforts to infiltrate the authorities of the northern alliance has failed. What they expect of me is to be a fail-proof weapon for conquering the world, which in current circumstances would lead to a destructive war between the three world powers. I don't want my resistance against the sovereignty and pressure to be misjudged in the future. I would do my best to leave my remaining forces to the Life Council. Today I met the banished; nothing much was achieved, only vague directions towards Gaalve. I have to solve the problem of entering there on my own. The risk of losing my companions down there is high, but this is a vital turning point, and I have to sacrifice some for the greater good as I have begun my last effort to form the Life Council."

Then he looked at his manuscripts and brooded deeply. What he could not mention in his writings, was finding the children whom he was thinking of from beyond the flames in the forest; Helena, Robert, Nadia, Alexi, and Peloma.

Adam closed his notebook and lied down in his bed in the corner of the room. His thoughts were jumbled inside his head while he was facing many hesitations.

Struggling with his doubts, he fell asleep and entered the world of dreams. After a while, when he was in a deep sleep, he felt a hand on his shoulder and woke up with anxiety.

CHAPTER TWO
THE TWINS

The pale light of autumn passed through the cell's hatch and fell on the skinny young girl's face, warming her battered figure. A guard rapped harshly on the cell's door and Nadia, cringing, tried to push herself back into the wall. The small hatch opened, and the guard pushed in a dirty tray with a small bowl of soup and a piece of moldy bread on it as her portion of the day.

She rushed forward and swallowed the soup, then crawled back without touching the bread and lied under the ray of life, which was shining through the steel bars on the ceiling. Autumn's sky, though cast down and grey was a pleasant view to her eyes. Tree years in prison, dreadful Alucine prison, three years of loneliness and darkness, without even a day off or a fresh air outside her cell in open air. The only time she could see the sky above, was a thirty-minute- break when they opened the hatch above her so that she wouldn't rot. Nadia was tortured mercilessly, and the only hope she had for surviving was seeing Alexi whenever he was dragged to the interrogation room. They did it deliberately as they believed seeing the tortured body of her brother may lead to revealing of the secret laying in her heart. Nadia and his twin brother were among many victims of Neo-Nazis gaining power in Europe. They were sacrifices of their parents' pacific activities, who were murdered brutally upon their return to Poland. The twins were nine years old when they lost their parents and lived with their grandfather in Crooked Forest, before being arrested.

Everything started with weird dreams. Nadia felt an odd sensation about natural elements; Water rolled in her hands and she was able to warm Alexi's face only by touching him. Rumors started spreading among the neighbors and soon after, United Europe's security police under General Heinrich Adler leadership, arrested both and imprisoned them in Alucine.

It was tolerable in the beginning, but harsh interrogations started after just two weeks. When their true identity, attributed to their parents regarding their activity in UPNO[1] before the war, was revealed, investigation gave its place to torture. That UPNO was the place where the great Adam Heber was last spotted. After being tortured physically and mentally, weird devices were placed on Nadia and Alexi's heads to break through their minds. Under the chief of staff's of the united Europe Army strict order, the twins should be kept alive, so whenever their health condition was in danger, due to harsh tortures, they would be left alone for a few days to recover. Interrogators were looking for information deep inside their minds, while the twins themselves were not fully aware of it.

Nadia could guess what they were looking for and was doing her best to keep that valuable information away from their reach. But Alexi was losing the battle under constant pressure and wished he were dead each time they took him to the interrogation room. The last time he had communicated with his twin, Nadia warned him: "Don't let them break through your mind…" Their cells were in one row, but far from each other. In the past three years, the twins had been kept in solitary confinement constantly.

After thirty minutes, the steel hatch was closed, and darkness descended on Nadia's cell. She stood up with difficulty and turned her back to the door. A voice was resounding deep in her mind. "Don't give up…"

---

[1] United Peace Nation Organization

Half awake, she had felt a dazzling light twisting around her face several times, but opening her eyes, she saw nothing but absolute darkness. Hallucinations would not leave her alone for a moment and closing her eyes; she stepped into the darkest nightmares, which kept on repeating, consuming all her energy like a vicious round.

Concentrating on her fingertips with the last remaining amount of the energy inside, a small flame flickered right above her finger, shaking like candlelight without burning her. The more focused she became, the bigger the flame grew, covering her palm. It was as red as the flames of a wood fire, and among it, she noticed the presence of someone who was looking at her from afar.

Nadia could never go any further. Though the stranger tried to communicate with her several times, she couldn't perceive the meaning as the sound was unintelligible. The stranger among the fire, reminded her of the good old days when she was a kid in the Douala Base of Cameron. She thought about Helena, Robert, Peloma... They had a strong bond with one another and with their affectionate teacher, Adam.

She had mixed feelings; thinking about them would warm inside her heart and sad at the same time, not knowing what was going to happen and her part in it. She felt a strong insurgent force, getting ready to burst.

The shaking flames grew and lighted up the walls of her small cell, but the stranger inside it was gone when she heard footsteps behind her cell, so she shook her hands hurriedly to vanish the fire.

They opened the door violently. Two guards were standing there, for taking Nadia to the interrogation room and of course for more merciless tortures.

Nadia had to resist.

If only she were more concentrated, maybe she could understand incomprehensible voice among the fire. Sometimes she thought she is out of her mind due to long solitary confinement, and all she could see was nothing but some illusions to comfort her wounded body and mind. However, she could not deny the presence of a dominant feeling inside. The hope for salvation was far to reach, but not impossible.

The guards went close and beat her so harshly that she stopped breathing. Finding her condition critical, guards dragged her body out of her cell.

A few meters away, a tall guard with pale skin and bright eyes was looking at them. He was hiding in the shadow of stairs, watching how Nadia's battered body was dragged on the floor. Guards dropped her down in the corridor: "I guess she's dead. Look, she's not breathing…"

The second guy kneeled on the ground and put his ear on Nadia's chest to check her heartbeat. He nodded with dissatisfaction due to what just had happened: "Let's take her to the infirmary. They may be able to save her."

The tall guard could not stay for much longer in that section. The wing where Nadia and her twin brother were kept, was off limits; no one could enter there, but trusted guards. The only chance to check on the twins, was when the guards changed their shifts.

The man hurried back to the locker room. No guard was around, so he opened his locker, carefully, pushed the bunch of clothes back to search for a small transmitter and a bomb with the shape of a tray. He had to hurry before anyone would notice him. He turned the transmitter on to communicate the sad news, but he paused; not knowing what to do. Leaning his forehead on transmitter's antenna, he felt helpless and desperate. Finally, he changed his mind, turned off the transmitter and hid it under the cloths again.

They had an important mission ahead. He was not sure whether Nadia was dead or alive, and could not risk the operation to one loss, so he decided to wait for the night to fall and to find out about Nadia's condition in any possible way.

CHAPTER THREE
SHADE OF POWER

A tall man was walking slowly in deserted and narrow alleys of the town, constantly looking over his shoulder and then continuing with caution. He wanted to make sure that he is not being chased. After a while, he quickened his pace, took the first turn on his right and stepped into another maze of alleys. He had covered his face with a piece of cloth, and in the dusk, his mind was focused on the mission at hand. He put his hand in his long, black overcoat to touch the jewel around his neck, which gave him peace of mind. Being assured of the necklace's safety, he hurried on and passed the alleys one after the other until he reached a dead end where a red wooden door, looking old and creaky could be seen. He took a deep breath and walked towards the door. Stopping just before it, the man hid the necklace under his tunic to make sure that no one could see it at all. Then he knocked three times at the door. After a few seconds of silence, an old voice was heard from behind the door: "I'm drunk..."

The tall man answered: "But you have your wits about you..." Without delay, an old man with a bent back opened the door; holding a lantern in his hand, he raised it with difficulty to see the newcomer's face. The tall man uncovered his face; his big, blue eyes were glinting in the dim light of the lantern. The old man recognized him immediately: "Oh, Sir Philip, long time no see. Please come in..."

Philip entered the house with utmost caution. They passed through a long, narrow porch, reaching a staircase connecting the porch to the upper floor. They stopped there, and Philip looked at him. The old man signaled him with a head gesture, confirming that those who Philip had come to meet are already upstairs, waiting for him. Philip looked above and went up the stairs. The narrow and dark corridor of the next floor was lit with a small lantern, showing a door at the end standing ajar.

The tall man could hear the hum of some men speaking inside the room in Spanish and laughing from time to time. Philip cleared his mind and stood before the door with a determined look. Standing in the doorframe, the three men inside fell silent and looked at him.

One of them, with a muscular body and a cigar hanging from his mouth, signaled the other two and then left his old chair to inspect Philip in person. His look was cold and uncaring: "Do you have the money we asked for?"

Philip: "Yes, but you will see it once I see Robert Delmar."

The muscular guy pointed with his hand and said: "Follow me…"

The other two readied their guns and waited in the room. The first guy went to the next room and asked Philip to enter. There, a middle-aged man, clad in expensive garments, was seated on a fancy chair and a golden gun was at hand on the desk before him. The man touched his hat and said: "I believe we have what you've asked for, although that beast was not making it easy. But, they call me Delaponte for a reason and in this wild world, I could do almost anything, provided that its cost could be paid…"

Philip, disregarding Delaponte's words, said: "I want to see Robert."

Delaponte stood up, touched his golden gun and with a swift move, armed it. Then said: "I don't want bloodshed. I'm the law here, and I say what to do or not."

Philip didn't back off, keeping his face determined. After a pause, Delaponte said: "Why isn't the old man here? He's nicer than you, or at least he seemed so when dealing with us; the last time he was here I made him a cheesy ID card."

Philip: "Your deal is yours and mine is mine. He believed me to be suitable for this trade. Otherwise, he wouldn't send me here."

Delaponte smirked and said: "heh... first I have to see the Platium."

Philip took out a black leather purse from the bag hanging on his hip, dumping its contents on his palm. Four rectangular pieces of shiny metal appeared before Delaponte's greedy eyes. He looked at them with such intensity and greed as though he was ready to swallow them. Delaponte was suspicious about him, but couldn't resist Philip's unshaken determination. So he turned to the muscular guy and said: "Bring the boy over."

The man exited hurriedly, and Philip returned the Platium to the purse, standing on a side. It didn't take so long that all three men returned with a prisoner who was dragged on the ground and his head was covered by a mesh hood. Without struggling, he sat on a bench. Philip pulled out a picture from his pocket, holding it before the prisoner. It was a picture of a child with a long forehead, round face, and bright, angular eyes. It was time to reveal the truth.

Delaponte was rubbing his hands in a show of greed and impatience. He turned towards Philip and looked at the picture in his hand. Philip removed the mesh hood with his right hand; there was a weird device on the prisoner's head, and some wires were running from it to his body. Delapbonte was delighted: "Yes! It's him! It's him!"

As their eyes met, Philip saw a shattering look deep in prisoner's eyes. He felt like being scrutinized by someone behind those eyes. Robert was quiet; a twenty-year-old boy who had not changed much comparing to the kid in that picture. But his pale face was devoid of any emotions.

Delaponte was delighted: "Here you are, the guy you were looking for! The damned boy doesn't eat or drink and is creepily weird. Okay, I don't want to keep him forever, so give me the Platium and take him."

Philip, dispassionately, said: "There is one thing left to do."

Then he bent down a bit and took out the necklace. At his movement, all three armed men in the room aimed their guns at him. Showing his fingers, Philip said: "It's nothing, only a necklace."

He opened the necklace from around his neck. The chain was made of platinum with a green jewel floating at the heart of its pendant; it was Adam Heber's treasure, and Philip was ordered to protect it at any cost.

The jewel had a dazzling beauty, which belonged to a place beyond the human horizons; a secret and tempting feeling was within its green stone, which could possess the hearts of all mankind.

Delaponte, who was staring at the green jewel with his wide eyes, stammered: "I... I... I would... pay forty Platium for it."

Philip glanced at him; he could feel Delaponte's greedy soul was craving for the jewel. He took a needle from his pocket and pricked Robert's fingertip with it. A drop of blood dripped from his finger; though it was abnormally black, Philip couldn't notice it in that dim light of the room.

Philip drew Robert's finger closer to the jewel and let the blood drip right at the heart of the medallion. It absorbed the blood and started to illuminate.

Sparkles of delight and satisfaction appeared in Philip's eyes. He wore the necklace around his neck and walked instantly towards Robert to remove the device from his head, but suddenly rejecting the blood; the jewel stopped shining.

Philip was confused.

Delaponte asked anxiously, "What the hell is going on here?"

Philip stepped back: "How did you catch him?"

26

Delaponte looked at the muscular man and asked in Spanish: "Edwardo, how did you catch this boy? Hah?"

The guy stammered a bit, then said: "We crossed the Mexican border and entered the New Life City, where the old man had told us. We had been watching the house for two days until he showed up. He left in the morning with an empty bag and returned in the evening with the bag full. As he left on the third day, we broke into the house; it was around midnight when he returned and emptied loads of money and jewelry on the desk. Right, Khorkhei?"

The thin, sleazy man, who was standing there with a gun in his hand, nodded. Edwardo continued: "I aimed the device that the old man had given to us. When I pushed the button, the boy jumped, and at the same time the ajar window was opened with a wind blow, it hit my head, and I was blacked out for a second. But as I opened my eyes, I saw him on the ground with that device's wire, attached to his chest. Khorkhei, Gaspar and I went over to him and attached the device to his head just the way the old man had told us. Then we left and brought him straight here."

Philip was calm: "This is not the right guy."

Delaponte was freaked out and filled with rage, not knowing what to do: "Cut the bullshit you son of a bitch. He is the guy in that damn photo. I want the money we agreed on, now; then you can take this asshole to whatever you want."

Philip: "I guess you didn't get what I've just said. I am not going to pay a penny for him. You are a fraud Delaponte and only wasted my precious time."

Edwardo grasped Philip's neck and pushed him hard against the wall. Khorkhei and Gaspar went towards Philip to seize the leather bag. But Philip touched Edwardo's waist, and as if being electrified, the muscular guy froze and dropped on his back. Khorkhei and Gaspar were shocked and quickly retreated. Delaponte aimed his gun at Philip, but all at once, series of events happened rapidly.

With an incredible speed, Philip reached him, and as Delaponte pulled the trigger, they both collided with a massive impact; the bullet from his gun hit Robert's head. He fell on the ground, staring at them while a dark, foul-smelling tar-like liquid was gushing out of his head.

Khorkhei and Gaspar were terrified and tried to reach their guns, but Philip lifted Delaponte with his enormous power and threw him at them.

He ran towards the window, had one last look at Robert and then jumped over the neighbor's roof. Delaponte reached the window and started shooting aimlessly just to realize his rage, but it was too late; Philip had disappeared among the shadows of the night.

According to the southern confederation law, the curfew would affect from early evening, and no one was allowed to commute without army permission during the night. This law was implemented and followed for nearly fifteen years right after the end of the third world war, when General Marco Monte Corrales came to power, and all the countries under his command had to obey this rule; the ones which were once independent and by the end of the WWIII, under a united power, had created the Southern Confederation.

Philip left that dark and silent town empty-handed and headed towards the mountains. All the way back home, in that harsh terrain, he was agitated and could see creature's creeping in the dark or maybe they were just illusions, made by severe exhaustion. In the morning, worn out and wounded, he found himself in front of the hut. He brought out the necklace, kept it before the door and entered. Mariana was asleep on the chair beside the fireplace. He went towards her and kissed her forehead.

Mariana opened her eyes; seeing Philip beside her, she stood up and embraced him tightly. Philip whispered, "I love you dearly, my northern star…"

Mariana just kissed his lips and held him close to her heart.

Philip: "Is the old man back?"

Mariana: "Yes. He's sleeping in the next room…"

He went straight to Adam's room.

The old man was sleeping. Philip touched his shoulder gently and shook him awake.

Seeing him, Adam got up and looked at Philip.

Philip shook his head: "I don't know what to say. Delaponte brought someone identical to Robert, but the jewel didn't accept him."

The old man rubbed his eyes and said: "It's not possible," brooding deeply, he whispered: "It was not Robert, or he must have played a trick on us."

Philip nodded sadly: "I saw him being shot right in the head. But instead of blood, a tar-like liquid gushed out."

Adam closed his eyes for some moments, whispering old incantations, then said, "No, the one whom you saw was not Robert. This is an old trick, but can't fool an old man like me. Dear Philip Remember that sometimes, even eyes can lie to us. Robert is still alive somewhere out there."

CHAPTER FOUR
THE JOURNEY BEGINS

An old bus was crawling along a dried out desert. Everywhere was filled with the wreckage of bombers, artillery machines, and tanks belonging to the Great War. Adam and Philip were sitting next to each other inside the yellow bus. They were on the way for two days, and in a little while, they would reach the border between Mexico and the former United States. Today, both countries were parts of the vast territory of Northern Alliance, bordering Siberia on the north and reaching Panama in the south. The autumn was halfway through, but the day was hot and stuffy. The war had changed the world so much that weather forecast was not easily possible anymore.

Philip had covered his face with a red-checkered handkerchief, and Adam was dozing, with his head hung in exhaustion. It was the only bus in the long desert road, which its dust trail could be seen, from miles away. The deafening sound of two supersonic bombers, passing overhead, startled both awake. Philip, who was near the window, removed his handkerchief and moved his head closer to see outside, the bombers, belonged to the Northern alliance air force, flying at low altitudes.

Philip looked at Adam: "Where are we?"

Adam: "probably near the old Mexican-American border." Then he lowered his voice and said, "Right in the enemy's territory."

Philip looked at the surroundings for a little while, then hid his face under the handkerchief and resumed his nap. In the past few days, they had been on the constant move, using fake IDs.

The IDs were made by the fraud Delaponte that had proved its efficiency before reaching the main border near Panama.

A few hours later, the bus arrived at the border. The second crossing point within the northern territory was swarming with fully armed soldiers and huge traffic scones, which stopped anything and everything for inspection. Even after fifteen years, there were tensions and this part of the world, in particular, was always troubled. The bus halted with the screeching sound of its brakes.

Adam, shaking Philip awake, said, "We're at the second crossing point."

A long line of yellow buses was ahead of them. They could feel that something was not right as big, black cars had surrounded the post and soldiers wearing uniforms with a big 'N' on their chests, made their ways through vehicles to inspect the travelers and their luggage.

Adam pointed to the driver with his eyes; Philip got up immediately, went towards him, and spoke to him in Spanish. Then he returned to his sit: "He says that soldiers had never inspected the cars this rigorously and the checkpoint had never been this crowded" he paused and then said, "I guess we are in trouble Adam."

Adam: "why?"

Philip: "what if Delaponte has betrayed us as we yanked the deal."

Adam: "I don't think so, we passed Panama's gate without any trouble; moreover is that Delaponte doesn't know our real identity unless he has disclosed some vague information in exchange for some money. But If anything happens to me, you must continue the mission. At least one of us would reach Robert. When you arrived at the Eagles Nest town, go to the railway station and take a train for New Life City." He brought a paper out of his cloak and handed it to Philip: "This is the address. Although I doubt you can find him there, no thanks to

Delaponte's mistakes, but do your best. If you didn't locate him in three days, go to the city's water supply reservoir and wait for me. I'll try to catch up, but if you didn't get word on me for two days leave the city for the White Pasture. Still, I hope this inspection proves to be nothing, and we could pass it together, though we should be careful just in case."

There were many buses still waiting for inspection. People inside were tired and complaining. Some young men got off the bus, followed by an old lady and her daughter, so It was the best time to take the chance for escape. Adam signaled Philip, and they both got off. People were making a long line while soldiers were everywhere. Making a run for the desert was impossible. They waited for an hour, but nothing changed. Philip: "I guess it's better to part ways." But Adam took his hand: "Follow me. I will go first, and if anything happens, you wouldn't be suspected." He paused, and then added with a graver tone, "You are not allowed to use my training. Under no circumstances should you use them. Is it clear?"

Philip: "Okay."

It was their turn, by the sunset. Soldiers got all the travelers down to inspect the bus. A humanoid robot was at the gate to scan travelers' eyes. After passing the scan stage successfully, they had to hand over their certificates to a soldier seated before a computer, which belonged to the pre-war world.

Now, it was Adam's turn. He showed his eye to the robot, and after a short pause, the light on its head turned green. Apparently, it was a system to filter criminals and prosecuted suspects; Philip also received the green light. Adam showed Delaponte's forged ID to the soldier.

His ID card was held up before a laser scanner, but a red warning sign appeared on the monitor. The soldier showed the card once more, and the same warning emerged. He was bewildered: "It shows you're passing this gate and the northern one on the same day. It's impossible!"

Adam: "I came in from Panama's gate two days ago…"

The man tinkered with his computer: "There should be something wrong with the system then, but you must go to the inspection office, they will probably solve the problem." Then pointed to a door behind the counter. Meanwhile, Philip had passed the computer verification and was waiting for Adam on the other side of the gate.

Adam stepped into the room. Three officers with two soldiers were there, and a man with formal clothes was sitting on a couch arrogantly, playing with a device in his hands. Adam, in his long cloak, went ahead and waited there. One of the officers who seemed to have more authority, looked at Adam and put his pen down: "Mr. Garcia Pernie, Where are you coming from, where is your destination and what is the reason of your journey?"

Adam answered calmly: "I'm coming from Salta, a small industrial city in the south. I'm going to Canada for a better life. I have an acquaintance there who has found me a job."

Officer: "The name of your acquaintance?"

Adam hesitated a bit and then said: "William Atkinson, in Port McNeil. It's a small town in the west of former Canada."

The officer entered the names on his computer and confirmed their authenticity. But it seemed that he was not convinced yet, so he stood up and said: "Unfortunately, I cannot let you pass. Something happened here this morning, which made us more cautious with cases like yours. The record before me shows that two people have passed two crossing points, both using the same ID numbers. Time and place-wise, this is impossible; unless one is using the other's identity. I hope you get what I'm saying."

Adam: "You mean one of us have passed the gates with a fake ID?"

Officer: "Exactly. According to the court law of Northern Alliance, I have to keep you here for the time being to determine your true identity."

Adam: "It's alright. I only need to get my baggage from the bus."

Officer: "Of course." He signaled to one of the soldiers: "Escort Mr. Pernie."

One of the officers also followed them. When the door was closed behind them, the first officer glanced at the high-ranking agent seating on the couch. He had arrived on the special copter of the North's Security Corps just a few hours ago. The officer cleared his throat: "I believe it's him, Mr. Jones."

Jones massaged his temple with his finger, comparing Adam's appearance with the documents he'd just received. He said thoughtfully, "Despite his name, he doesn't have a Spanish accent, so I agree with you, Mr. Jackson. But first I have to make sure since I'm not keen on wasting the energy of my forces on wrong people.

Jones: "Keep an eye on him for now, and I'll see what I can do." Then he got up and went to the opaque window. The darkness had fallen, and large projectors were the only source, illuminating the patch behind the gates. Jones pressed his hands together and whispered, "I think we have trapped the kingfish."

Jones's eyes were following the two and Adam who was going towards the bus until they disappeared into the crowd.

Adam noticed Philip standing back at one side, looking at him. It was clear that he was not going to intervene without his permission. The officer, who was one-step ahead, was looking for the driver to come and open the bus's luggage compartment while the soldier was standing behind Adam. For a brief moment, Adam touched their hands, and both of them fell into a deep sweet sleep.

It was then when Philip joined Adam.

Adam: "That charlatan, Delaponte, has given me the ID of another guy without changing its number. The real Pernie has passed through the northern gate today, two days after we did in the south. This is the worst possible situation, which can ruin everything. Probably they stopped him from doing investigations and found out that he was the owner of that ID." He paused for a second: "Philip, we have to hurry before it's too late, they will come for me at any moment, so it's better that you go forward alone; I'll go to the desert and try to catch up with you later. See you there and good luck."

Adam went towards the desert and after a while disappeared in the darkness beyond.

A few minutes later, Jones noticed soldier and officer's absence, so he decided to check the situation in person. When he found them, his eyes popped out. Both of them were unconscious. Jones took out his radio and ordered the guards to start the search and hunt operation. The gates were closed instantly and the sirens and emergency backup lights added to the chaos.

Philip's bus had just left a few seconds before the lockdown, and he crept in the corner of the bus and focused on his mission; facing mighty Robert.

CHAPTER FIVE
ROBERT'S STORY

Robert was walking towards Fifth Avenue anxiously, and reaching a crossroad, he stopped to check his surroundings. He had to make sure that no one was after him.

Delighted people were only in this part of the town; as usual, wealthy families were out there for fun and shopping. Robert took a deep breath and looked at the clouds above him. He took great pleasure in looking at them and finding shapes since he was a kid, but now he was too weary to see imaginary shapes among the clouds. Moreover was that instead of puffy white clouds of the summer sky, a grey layer had covered the firmament. He pulled his cap down and started walking again. The main road of New Life City was always crowded. Every few minutes, military's urban patrols passed through the streets without grabbing attention, as they were still worried about the potential threats, those concealed ones from ordinary people's eyes.

This times Robert was aiming at Tropical Brothers' jewelry, where he could for sure, find some pieces of precious Platinum. In front of him, there was a billboard, which its message could be perceived from afar; it was showing a semi-nude woman, lying on the ground and winking. Beside her, there was a big pillbox; Robert narrowed his eyes to read the sentence beneath it: "Make Your Dreams Today."

Robert had seen this company's ads in the suburbs and slums of New Life City as well, though it was different and pictured sexual desires, directly. Manufacturer of this pill was a big, multinational company, which was founded after the Great

War to cure the post-war spiritual wounds. Most of the target consumers were from the poor level of the society, who couldn't make their dreams come true in the real world. The military government of Northern Alliance was advocating this project, to suppress the protest against poverty and low quality of life. The authorities of Northern Alliance could deprive the poor majority of the society of taking the real joy of life by selling fake dreams to them and keeping them quiet and hopeful to the coming days. Those pills made dreams to satisfy people beyond boundaries of mind and fancy.

He had been tempted several times to try one of those pills, but an invisible hand always prevented him. The company name, EL Corp, was meaningless to him but rang a bell to Robert at the same time. Having large amount of financial resources and workforce at hand, The Company used them to provide electricity, clean water and temporary accommodation for the war refugees; while its worldwide reputation was affected by some rumors.

A few months ago, an underground group distributed unregistered pills in the black market, which caused brain hemorrhage for the poor consumers and led to their death within a few hours. It was then when baseless rumors spread out, and after that, no one trusted unregistered pills and the black market was closed soon after.

Robert didn't want a dream in hallucination, but a glamorous reality; just like all those rich people walking around him and could afford pleasure in the real world.

Mulling over these thoughts, Robert walked until he reached the street where his target jewelry was located among luxury shops, covered with a glass roof and secured with guards in both ends. Only the known, affluent customers were allowed there; those living in the triple Moon Towers could show their residency card to enter the Stars Alley, while the rest had to bring documents verified by the bank, which showed a minimum of 5 million dollars or 100 Platiums deposit.

A couple of muscular sentries in black suits were standing before the main gate of Stars Alley where people were standing in a queue behind the gate, to show their documents. Robert held his breath for a moment, hoping that his supernatural power would assist him once more. He pulled himself together and stood in the line.

Right then, one of the guards who had been watching him pointed to him and said, "You, sir. Could you come here, please?"

Robert: "Why? What's wrong?"

The guard answered with a smile: "Only a security check."

It must have been Robert's appearance since his clothes didn't resemble a well-off persons'. He didn't expect them to be this strict without even giving him time to wait in the line. He tried to be at ease: "I don't get your point. The line is here, and I'm waiting for my turn."

Putting a hand on his gun, the guard said, "Sorry sir, you have to step out of the queue." Then he signaled to another guard who was behind Robert. Their conversation had scared other people, so they all stepped aside; now Robert was all alone there.

The second guard went straight to Robert: "either show me your documents or leave this place immediately." Robert shook his head with regret: "Such poor customer relations. Your behavior is rude and unacceptable."

Guard: "We're sorry, sir, but there are certain security protocols which could not be ignored. I hope you understand that our main objective is customers' satisfaction."

Robert was sure that they had sniffed him out because of his clothes. That morning before leaving home, he thought about putting on something better; but living in one of the slums wouldn't let him go out and show expensive clothes which would reveal his identity and destroy the loose safety of living among low-level scums. Though he had earned great amounts of money through his past robberies, he couldn't live where wealthy people used to live as reach people were under the close supervision of mighty government of Northern Alliance. Being troubled, he was furious with himself as he had no choice but doing what they had asked him.

He planned to incapacitate only one guard and to slip in among the chaos. But now he was trapped between two guards, and couldn't continue according to this plan.

He took out his third-grade residency card. Seeing the yellow of the card, both guards stared at him with wide eyes and then started laughing. "You must be kidding us boy? You really want to get inside with this?"

Robert: "No. My documents are there on the table right before you."

Guard: "I saw you the moment you stepped in! You didn't get close to this table."

Robert: "I was here earlier, but I had a parcel that I couldn't bring along with me. So I gave my documents to your coworker and put the parcel back in the car. When I returned, it was so crowded that I had to wait in line. Why don't you ask your friend?"

Both guards looked at each other, and the first one said: "Wait here. I'll go and check."

Robert: "You'd better do so. Mr. Penfield is one of the close acquaintances of my father, and I hope you have a good reason for such rude behavior."

Guard: "Mr. Penfield, as the head of security?"

Robert: "Yes, Idiot!!"

The guard panicked: "What's your name, sir?"

Robert: "Peter Melvin. Hurry up; I don't like my time to be wasted on you."

The guard took a step back as if he was scared to be punched by the tall, well-built man before him. He went to the gate and asked for a check on Peter Melvin: "Hurry! We're in trouble. He says Mr. Penfield knows him. Look for his documents, hurry! Look at his face, don't you recall him being here before?" The guy sitting behind the desk tilted his body so he could see Robert behind the gate's bars. Shaking his head: "Not sure if I have ever seen him. Maybe I've forgotten. But there are no documents with that name."

The first guard was furious. "There is nothing here!"

Robert put on an angry face and got closer, swearing: "Are you blind? There it is!"

He took out a card randomly from those stacked on the table, mumbling: "Hurry up, damn it, hurry and touch me!"

The guy sitting behind the desk tried to stop him, but Robert caught his wrist in the air. All the guards were confused, not knowing what was happening. The two other guards also tried to pull him back; then he unleashed his unstoppable power. Just like a dragon, awakening from a long long sleep, the force pounded all three guards' will and put them on the ground unconscious.

Robert stepped back and looked for some patrols passing in the street: "Hey, help! Something is wrong here!"

The street descended into chaos. Robert was lucky; before new patrols could see the happening, he snatched his backpack, disappeared in Stars Alley, and walked fast as he knew he had just a few minutes to rob the jewelry.

Inside the street, sweet scent of perfume was wafting in the air. Robert didn't slow his pace down, but could not resist the urge to look at some long shapely legs and getting warm inside. Here was a separate part of the world, somewhere safe from carnage and war, standing with glory. It was one of the most beautiful cities in the post-war world, only second to City of God in Europe.

Petrol and oil were plenty, and the new energy of Platium was running in the veins of uptown areas, which cost many lives. New Life City and its triple towers were one of the few places in the world, which still enjoyed the nightlife while most of well-offs had transferred their wealth to there at the break out of the war.

After long wars and downfall of capitalist, communist and religious regimes, a new world order had been created based on absolute power and racist fascism; Those who survived the mass destruction of the war, all around the world, could inhabit in New Life City- thanks to their wealth. Where could be better than here for a young boy who had lost all his family in the violent raid of UN's last Peace Lookout by the Neo-Nazis? A boy who had lived in filthy slums of New Life City, filling his stomach with the leftover of the rich and surviving on his mental capabilities.

The target jewelry was relatively large, usually full of the nobles who spend their wealth, buying ornamental pieces of jewelry, all day long. Robert took the last few steps before entering the shop, confidently.

He pushed open the door and entered the shop without anyone noticing him. He turned the 'closed' sign on the door and just then one of the clerks asked: "What are you doing sir?"

Ignoring him, Robert locked the door and closed the thick curtains behind it. One of the customers raised her arrogant voice and said: "What is the meaning of all this, Mr. Storige?"

Storige, apparently the shop manager, bowed slightly and used his low and polite tone to answer: "I will immediately look into it, Lady Sonya."

Then he turned towards Robert with rage, but it was too late. Robert raised his hand and said: "Aaaaaalll Downnnn......"

His powerful mind, impatient as an untamed wild horse to break free, surged forward to rule the will of those in the shop. Their mind and consciousness crumbled, and all fell to the ground. Storige hit the ground with a sick sound, like a melon being dropped, his wide eyes were staring motionless at the ceiling. Robert stood over him and bent to shake his head with a smirk: "Stupid ass."

The security alarm didn't trigger. Robert started from the nearest glass box and put any piece of jewelry, which caught his eyes into his black backpack.

Robert came to know his supernatural power many years ago; when he was young, he could penetrate into people's mind simply by touching them. As time went by, his power grew stronger and he no longer needed physical contact for affecting the others. Still, when he needed to incapacitate selected target among a crowd, he had to resort back to the old way of touching.

Calm and at ease, humming a song from his childhood, Robert picked the most expensive pieces. Now, it was time for the last part. He had to find where Platiums, that priceless metal which was the reason for bloodshed in the world, had been stored.

He could feel it close. It was probably stored in the main safe. The problem was that he couldn't access the safe since it was in a small room behind the shop. Robert was enraged, cursed loudly and wondered who would know the password to the security system. But even knowing that, would not change anything, since everyone was unconscious and he was not capable of awakening a specific one among the crowd, yet. Disappointed, he returned to the main gallery. Suddenly Robert saw a girl lying on the ground. The muscles in his stomach clenched; she resembled Helena, his childhood friend and his first love when he was still too young to understand what love meant and long before it was mixed with the dirty notion of adults' world.

He sat on the floor next to her and caressed the girl's cheek with the back of his hand. He felt a weird sensation in his heart. All his life, Robert had dealt with anxiety and lack of comfort. Since

43

the night Delaponte's people had tried to kidnap him, he was sure that there were enemies on his tail. That night, as he sensed the presence of Delaponte's people in the room, he swapped his place with a shadow, tricking them into believing it was Robert himself, while he was hiding in a corner, leaving them with an empty shell of him.

Many years ago, exactly one year after the beginning of the war, he lost his parents. It was a terrifying night; he could still remember vaguely, how his parents had tried to protect him from some people in black. Robert never knew what happened to them eventually, but someone called Benjamin saved him and put him to flight on a cargo ship heading towards America that sinister night. Without knowing the destination, Robert started his journey. It was then when he began to discover and develop his supernatural powers, which was a rebirth to him. Each time, he derived a new power which was unimaginable for ordinary people.

He went closer to smell the girl's face and neck, mumbling: "Seductive." A rebellious temptation was rising inside him. He was about to kiss the girl's lips when suddenly a stronger power intervened and cut Robert's strong will; Everyone was awake now.

He was shocked and with confusion, tried to find a way out without anyone noticing him. The main door, which he closed it himself, was out of the question since getting close to it would reveal everything. Robert wished that someone would make a move so he could leave as well.

Mr. Storige was touching his head as if being stricken hard. He commanded in French and one of the guards went forward and stood before the door. The fat manager stood up and ran his eyes to the confused crowd of customers. Robert stepped back and tried to hide himself among the crowd. Most of the people had fallen unconscious on the ground before even realizing what had happened to them, but now, searching their bags and pockets, they found out that they had been robbed. Robert was terrified and tried to urge his power a few times, but to no avail. His mind had shut down. His backpack was abandoned a few meters away, and it made trouble when an old woman noticed stolen goods inside.

Lady Sonya, the one who had seen Robert before, noticed him and shouted: "It's him! That shameless thief…"

Storige and two guards pounced on Robert and tackled him to the ground. Without the aid of his tremendous power, Robert could not fight them off. Voices could be heard from behind the door, and he was screwed. It seemed that guards at the gate were also awake and were searching for a possible thief in Stars Alley. As soon as the door was opened, they recognized him. "So Mr. Penfield knows you! When we're finished with you rat, you won't even remember your name."

They handcuffed and kicked Robert in the stomach, dragging him outside half conscious. The uproar resulted in locking down both ends of the street and in a few seconds, the head of security, Penfield, arrived hurriedly.

Robert's hands were tied behind him. He sat beside gallery's wall and leaned against it. His mouth was bleeding. He felt dizzy and was scared out of his skin. A large crowd had gathered around, watching him as though Robert was a rare wild animal in a circus. Some were shaking their heads out of pity, and some were cursing him. A short, old man was standing closer, holding his young lover in his arms. He said insolently: "I would pay 20 Platiums for this beast who has passed the security and reached here. What do you say, darling? We can cage him in the house."

Everyone burst into laughter. Batting her eyelashes, his lover answered: "No dear, he wouldn't be a good pet for us, and he doesn't worth that much. Let's forget about him and do our shopping."

The old man looked at her and whispered: "And you think you worth more little whore?" He smacked her bum and said: "Go do it yourself. I still have business to do here."

The girl walked away calmly; his teasing words didn't even bother her a bit. Both knew that money is the reason she was there. She just turned her back and went over to the shops on the other side of the street.

Glancing at him delicately, the old man came closer, squatted before Robert and lighted a cigar, but Mr. Penfield jumped ahead and said: "Mr. Walton, sir, he could be dangerous. Please don't get too close to him."

Walton narrowed his eyes and silenced him with a finger, gesturing to Penfield to sit beside him on the ground.

Walton: "How long have you known me?"

Penfield: "Many years, sir."

Walton: "So you should know that I don't do anything without reason."

Penfield: "You're right, sir. Sorry, sir."

Walton: "Send these people away. I want to talk to this young man alone for a few minutes. Then you'll understand what I have in mind."

Penfield: "As you wish, sir."

Gary Penfield called the guards, and they began driving the reluctant crowd away from the spot.

The old man puffed out smoke and looked directly into Robert's eyes "How did you do it?"

Robert didn't answer and turned his face away to ignore him.

Walton: "How did you knock out the guards?"

Robert didn't want to answer, but it was getting scarier by the moment. The man before him was asking about his powers, and he couldn't concentrate since that unknown, mysterious force had paralyzed his power and turned a wrathful dragon into a tamed animal.

He tried to think. Maybe this old man was testing him. He couldn't bring himself to look at his face but was eager to sneak glances at the old man. Robert thought to himself: "He had seen me at the gate, is it possible?"

Walton was impatient. He grabbed Robert's chin, forced him to look him in the eyes and said: "I saw you. I admit it was by accident, but I saw you knocking them out and walking away as if nothing had happened. I want to make a deal. As you see, there's no escape from this hell. I need your power, and you need my help. Either you accept and leave here with me, or they will hand you over to the police and then you would be tortured to death and confess to things you haven't even done before. Works for me, works for you? It's your decision."

Robert mumbled: "What do you want to know?"

The old man snapped his finger: "That's it! I don't want to know anything. I just want you to do something for me, a deal with a great profit. If you make it, you'll get reach overnight."

Robert: "I don't need your money."

Walton; "Even if your share would be 5,000 Platiums?"

Robert couldn't believe it. He doubted this much Platium could even exist. "5,000 Platiums, just my share!" He thought to himself. ! He could live three times a luxury life and still have Platiums to spend.

Walton: "What do you think?"

Robert: "What is the job?"

Walton: "Now this my lad, is a good question."

His old face was lighted up with satisfaction. Robert didn't want his identity to be revealed and accepting Walton's offer could prevent it. All he had to do was to stay away from the police.

Walton: "I don't know what happened inside the shop that you couldn't make it, but I saw how you swept away guards. That suffices me. I'm not saying you were great. Otherwise, I would be one of them myself. Anyway, I need someone like you for a top-secret job. If you're for it, I'll call my driver, and we'll leave here together."

Robert said desperately: "I don't even know what the job is!"

Walton winked at him. "It's better than pickpocketing."

Robert was not in a right situation. It was clear that he had no other choice. Suddenly, he remembered what his father had told him many years ago: "If you did something wrong, and no one punished you for it, beware that you are a fish in trouble." Robert was sure that it was not the best decision, but he had to buy sometimes.

Robert: "Okay, I'm in."

Walton: "Wise decision."

Walton looked around in search of his young lover, but then he shrugged and asked one of his bodyguards to prepare the car. A few minutes later, New Life City police arrived at the scene to take away Robert. But Penfield and Walton intervened, forcefully appeased the shop's owner and managed to prevent Robert from being arrested. Then Walton and Robert got in a black SUV and left.

Inside the car, Walton uncuffed him: "Now listen carefully boy, I'm the head of EL Corp's branch in Northern America and have some problems with my partners. I've decided to earn their promised interest myself, in another way." He smiled wickedly and added: "You know what I mean..."

Robert, rubbing welts on his wrists, said: "Yeah, I got what you want. I can't believe I've met the head of yellow pills' company in person. Is it true that they damage the brain?"

Walton: "Have you ever used them?"

Robert shook his head no. Walton was overjoyed. "That's good! You remind me of a younger me; ambitious, but not wretched to exchange reality for a dream. I'm getting to like you more and more, boy. But, as for your question... it's better not to be so curious unless you would be perished."

Walton Looked out the window and said, when the time comes, I will send my men to you. Give me your address, since you can't reach me. I'll start working on this project tonight and explain everything later. You must be prepared for the operation, maybe in one or two months.

Then he took a dollar stack out of his pocket and offered it to Robert. "Take it; this will hold you up in the meantime."

Robert: "I don't like waking up in the middle of the night, with armed men standing beside my bed. Give me your address, and I'll come to see you in two months."

Walton paused for a moment: "I'm not used to not having things my way, but this time I let go. Then visit me next month."

Robert: "Where?"

Walton rolled down the window on his side and pointed to the triple Moon Towers: "There. Go to the security and say you're the Black Swan. They'll escort you in."

As they were talking, Robert realized that he had regained control over his force and the mysterious blocking power was gone. He smirked and put his hand on Walton's knee: "How do you feel?"

Walton, confused and paled, mumbled: "I can't feel my legs as if they have been in a freezing river for so long."

Robert: "Ask him to stop the car! Now!"

Walton stuttered and called his driver to stop the car. Robert got off the car, not forgetting to grab the money. Before closing the door, he turned his head and said: "Thanks for saving me. See you next month."

And before Walton could comprehend what had just happened, he was gone. Robert felt that a boundless force was bestowed upon him as though he was floating in the ocean of powers, Stronger than ever… Recent incidents had damaged his confidence, but still, he felt something enormous inside. Limping along, he turned towards the main square; the sculpture of a huge eagle with open wings was at its center, the Salvation Square.

He was both furious and anxious, about the stronger will, which had cut off the flow of his mind. Many things could be revealed, his identity, what he was looking for and how he had earned money through robberies. However, it was not time to think of all that happened to him today.

A question came to his mind. "Can I incapacitate more people at once?"

The answer laid at the heart of Salvation square, where hundreds of people were passing by.

He reached the square, climbed up the statue, grabbed the eagle's wing with his powerful hands and went to the top.

Standing over the statues, 6 yards above the ground, he looked at the triple moon towers. A sphere, shining as the second moon at city nights, connected the three skyscrapers on top.

He thought about Walton's offer; 5,000 Platiums, worth 250 million dollars. The temptation was burning him. It was time to unleash the beast within. His mind-blowing power, spread out, immersing people like a raging sea.

The crowd was falling like autumn leaves, and then, an eerie silence filled the air. He started to shout, out of joy and felt like walking on air.

He looked around; everybody was lying down. Everyone but a man.

Adam Heber was standing there!

CHAPTER SIX
HEALING

The sound of the massive explosion had filled the space. A family of four was working its way among the rubble and burnt remaining of firebombs, rushing towards one of the underground shelters, in fear. Helena's hand was in her father's while the gunpowder smell was hurting their lungs. Mother was holding their younger son in her arms, covering his small face with a wet cloth to help him breathe easily. The city had turned into a pile of rubbles; tall buildings seemed like floating shadows, succumbing to massive bombs one by one. Thick smoke had covered everywhere, and only the occasional wind allowed them to breathe and to survive.

A large bomber passed over their heads, and Helena looked at it with wide eyes. It was so close that she could see the military sigils on its flanks. People were flooding into the streets, which were filled with debris. The silence ruled for a while, then the rumbling of an enormous chopper, mixed with the cries and shouts of the people, took its place.

The chopper was coming over the ruined buildings, moving towards the fleeing people. Its boom was the sound of death, clawing the people while everyone was running for his life. In the crowd, Helena's hand slipped over her father's grasp; Astonished, Helena looked at the chopper, and it was then when two large rockets were launched from it towards her. The last image was pictured before her troubled eyes when a tall man shield her from the blast. The earsplitting explosion was heard at a close distance, and high pitch ringing echoed in her ears...

A broken down image of her family and the people in blood was before her eyes. Helena was speechless, standing at a short distance from the scene and holding the tall man's hand; she was in utter shock. She looked at the man; his face was silhouetted by the faded sunrays behind him. Helena, wounded and bewildered, could not recognize him.

The man: "We could do nothing for them. Let's go, Helena."

But Helena cried: "No, no… no…"

Then an absolute silence filled her mind, and Helena woke up startled. She was confused and lost, looking at the bare room. An old wooden ceiling was above her, and a small grilled window let in tiny light.

Helena sat up, pulled back her golden locks and remained motionless for a few minutes on the bed. She felt dizzy and wasn't sure if she could walk or even stand up. Eventually, she got up and left her small room.

It was a small and green village, upon the hills facing a rich plain. Men were busy working in the surrounding farms and orchards; younger ones tended the livestock and women, sitting in the shade of village's ancient elm, were making ropes from roots of old trees that had covered the mountain all around the village. They were sitting in a circle, singing happy songs in their mother tongue, and the intimacy among them was tangible. Their melodious voice was carried by the wind; their song was full of old mysteries, their ancestors' way of life before them and how they were connected to the green paradise in the best possible way.

Helena had been among them for a few years, but she was still treated as an honorable guest who should be respected and kept safe.

As she left the room, a middle-aged women noticed her and with a smile and tiny gesture, invited her to sit with the rope-weavers. Helena joined them with a smile.

The woman: "Did you have a nightmare again?"

Helena: "Yes, Hong. It's an old nightmare which bothers me from time to time."

Hong: "I know. When you came out of your room, I felt you are restless. Then she opened a round basket and offered Helena some fresh bread and honey: "eat something, you will feel better."

Helena took them with thanks. Putting small pieces in her mouth, she asked: "Where is Mamalan?"

Hong turned her head and answered: "Last night she went to the lower village with my brother, Tuan. It was urgent, and she didn't even wait for the morning to leave."

Helena frowned: "Is it about the Green Hats?"

Hong: "Yes, I think. It's rumored that they have made an outpost near the northern pass of the mountain and are looking for certain people…"

Helena: "Certain people?"

Hong: "Yes, certain people like you. They are looking for healers to treat their wounded soldiers and if they find out about you and how you treat people with herbs, they will come for you. But it's all rumors; that's why Mamalan went to the lower village to get some information and their true intention. I've also heard that they enlist men forcefully and do some other dark things; things which talking about them would only ruin your beautiful morning. Let's hope they don't appear around here."

Helena, anxious and restless, asked: "You're scaring me. What if it's all true?"

Hong took Helena's hands in hers and said: "Don't worry. First, we don't even know if these rumors are true. Second, even if the Green Hats are here, the villagers won't let them hurt you."

Helena took a deep breath, then looked at the farthest point of the village, where people from the mountainside and other villages always gather and wait for her to heal them.

Helena: "It seems that today, we have more patients. I'd better go to them. Otherwise, it would not be finished by the nightfall. Will you come with me?"

Hong: "You go grab your stuff, and I will join you shortly."

Then she put a 'Non-La' straw hat on her head: "Some of them have been waiting for you since last night."

Helena took her hand-made box from the room and went to the cottage where she worked. She heals them in various traditional ways; giving wild nettle to some, berries and the gum of fig tree to others. Hong usually stood beside Helena to learn the diagnosis and proper treatment for each disease. Often, she would be her interpreter, since in spite of Helena's long presence among the native Vietnamese, she still, got confused by the accents of the locals. Hong was a worthy assistant to her. Sometime between the patients, Helena found a little time to rest and then, her mind wandered back to the difficult years when Mamalan, the old matriarch of the village, had taught her traditional medicine patiently. Until recent years, she went into the forest with the old woman to learn about the herbs and their usage. But now, Mamalan was too old and feeble to climb the mountain and Helena had to use Hong's helping hand for gathering the necessary herbs.

In the evening, Helena sat down in her room, staring at the small bowls of rice and vegetable stew. Hong slid her head in, smiling. "May I come in?"

Helena welcomed her with a smile. Hong sat beside her and opened a small wrap of fresh bread. The smell was heavenly.

As they were eating supper, Hong said: "I guess today was a tiring day, right?"

54

Helena wiped out the sweet on her brow: "It was just like any other day. I don't care how hard the work gets; I'm just wondering why everything has spoiled."

Hong: "It's not too bad for us. Don't let what I said this morning worries you. It may be true that the Green Hats are powerful, but we won't let them touch you. They're unwelcome like a green curse, and people will resist them; they are just a bunch of brainless brutes who are looking for an easy catch in this chaos."

Helena: "I'm not worried about myself, I fear for the people here. I have always been a burden for the village. I came here as an orphaned child, and without your care and attention, I wouldn't make it. You know that I lost all my dreams in that damned war."

Hong looked at her with kind eyes: "You know we count you as a member of our family…"

Helena interrupted her: "Yes. This… this is my concern. If the Green Hats are really looking for people like me, your life, which is dear to me, will be in danger. They are ruthless and armed. They won't think twice before destroying anything on their way. I would better leave you, even for a short while."

Hong: "We have the same idea, not because of our safety, but because of you. I think you shouldn't worry; maybe their presence would be just a rumor. They usually do it to spread fear and panic among the people."

Suddenly the turning wheels of a cart outside grabbed their attention. Hong jumped to the door and looked out: "They are back, Mamalan and Tuan."

Both left the room and went towards the cart. One of them took the old woman's hand, helping her down. Tuan jumped down. He was a young, sturdy man with shaved head and trained muscles. He looked at Hong, shaking his head disappointedly. Hong felt her heart stopped for a moment. Apparently, the rumors were not just rumors. Mamalan, tired and dejected, started walking towards Helena's room.

Helena was bewildered, not knowing what was going on. Tuan went closer: "The situation is not good." Just then, Mamalan raised her head, pushing her bend figure forward, signaled Helena to enter the room.

Mamalan sat down. Hong and Tuan were engaged in an agitated whispering, and some of the villagers were looking at the wise woman in silence.

Mamalan looked at Helena: "Last night, my nephew brought disturbing news from the lower village, so I went there with Tuan to investigate in person. My brother was there, saying that the Green Hats have been spotted in these parts. We sent over Tuan and my nephew to lower parts, and they brought word of the weapons and forest warriors at the base of the mountains."

Tuan nodded: "I guess they had camped for the night only to start their search in the morning. They will reach here shortly. We have to find a solution."

One of the men said: "It's better to hide her in the heights."

Mamalan: "Yes, I agree. It's better to send Helena to the north with Tuan. They can hide in the old hunting huts for a while." Hong and Helena looked at each other.

Helena: "But Mamalan, what about you? I'm worried about the people. Perhaps the spies have already informed them, and they could be here to catch me at any moment. If they don't find me, the condition will worsen for you."

Mamalan was calm. "Don't worry about us. The rest of elders and I will find a way. Just pack your things and go with Tuan." The meeting was short; in a few minutes, Helena and Tuan were ready for the journey. Meanwhile, Mamalan had gathered the elders to think about all the possible ways of protecting the village.

Helena embraced Hong and whispered: "I hope to see you all, fine, when I come back. I don't want any of you to get hurt because of me."

Hong looked at Helena: "Nothing is going to happen to us, Just move. Mamalan asked me to give you this note; you have to open it only when you reach the huts."

Helena was puzzled. She put it in her old backpack: "Where is Mamalan?"

Hong: "She is talking to the elders. You cannot wait for them…"

Then she looked urgently at Tuan and said: "just go and… be careful"

Helena and Tuan started their journey on the warm, sultry evening, leaving the village without being seen by unwelcome eyes. They stepped on an old, narrow path behind the last cottage and moved up the mountain. After climbing for a while, Helena stopped and turned to look at the village. She could see that the patients were scattering. When they passed the last turn in the path, the village was lost from her sight. They had to keep going, so Helena walked alongside Tuan without saying a word.

After a while, she broke the silence and asked: "When do you think they'll reach the village?"

Tuan, struggling to open a path before them, answered: "They could be already there. Last night, in the lower villages, people said they have made an outpost at the base and would climb the mountains soon. It seems that they want to make another post in the heights. Then they could cover more parts, or at least that's the rational thing to do."

Helena: "Do you think they would come over to the hunting huts?"

Tuan stopped and breathed heavily: "they will if they have enough motivation. But you see how hard it is to climb there. I don't think anything could convince them to do so."

Helena, passing Tuan slowly, said: "I hope so. Are you going back after we arrive?"

Tuan: "No. Mamalan asked me to stay until they inform us."

Slowly but steadily, they got closer to the hunting huts. It was dusk, and the sun was sinking behind the western ridges when they reached there. A light rain was wetting the ground, and Tuan sped up to reach the furthest hut sooner.

Seven huts were built there, in a place far from the local residents and on the mountaintops. In the past, hunters used them in the hunting season. But when the war started, they stopped coming, and the huts were abandoned. Six huts were placed closely, each with a slight distance from the next one. The last one, at the back of the rest, was 130 feet away. Tuan chose that as their resting place, thinking it would be the safest one.

He opened the door of the hut, checking inside it; then he started moving the old furniture and piling them outside with a skilled hand. In a matter of minutes, he created a cozy hut for their indefinite stay.

Both were thinking about the village, wondering what the people were doing and if they have escaped the trouble without any difficulties. When night fell, Tuan started a small oil-burner which he had brought along, and under its faint trembling light, they sat to pass the first night of their escape. After a light meal, Tuan lied down on a piece of goatskin. Helena was eating much slower, still sitting by the light.

Tuan: "Where did you live before coming here? Where is your family?"

It wasn't a pleasant conversation; Helena chewed on her food slowly. Before this, none of the villagers had asked such questions. But then, she said: "I'm from France. My father was working there for the Peace Lookout."

Turn turned on his side, putting his hand under the head to see Helena better.

Helena continued: "I spent my childhood in Toulouse and the Peace Base of Douala in Cameron. It was the last hope for peace when the European Fascists came to power again. It was a large base, something like a camp for employees. I lived there with my family, playing with other children and going to school. When the war broke out, we returned to France. Then Neo-Nazis began bombing European cities."

Tuan asked in surprise: "Why would they bomb their own towns?"

Helena, shaking her head with pity, answered: "They believed that Europeans are too mixed with the immigrants; the nouveau-riche Fascists thought that the foreigners are responsible for the poverty and economic crisis. I was too young back then, but I listened to my parents' conversation after the dinner, when they thought we were asleep and they could discuss things freely. Useless methods were used to separate Europeans from non-Europeans, and then the extremists from both sides found the chance to slaughter one other. They killed each other with no mercy; bombed cities kidnapped people, tortured and butchered them. The world was changing, and people had gone wild. They could no longer distinguish between soldiers and civilians; the gangs were on the rise, and this went on until the actual war started."

A lump was growing in her throat, but she ignored it and went on: "I lost both my parents and my little brother on a gloomy day. I still can see it happening in my nightmares. Then a stranger brought me to Mamalan. After the world changed, I didn't make any effort for my life and decided to forget my dark past and instead focused on what Mamalan had taught me. I decided to stay in your village, believing happiness is at hand. But…"

Tuan: "It is a sad story which has not ended yet. I didn't experience the world before the war; I was born here, raised here, and learned to tend the animals and gather firewood", then continued with a serious look on his face: "Why don't you look for your family? Maybe they are still out there?"

Helena said sadly: "No one is left and there is no way to look for them. I just want to have a normal life."

The last sentence was in utter conflict with her inner feeling, getting stronger at each moment. She knew that a normal life is impossible now. She could feel something driving her towards a lifetime adventure. She stared at the small, half-open window and looked at the darkness outside. Suddenly, she remembered the note –Mamalan's note- that Hong had given her before leaving the village. She hurriedly opened her backpack and took it out.

Tuan also sat up with great excitement. Helena looked at the folded paper and then, with shaking hands, opened it slowly. It was time to reveal mysteries.

CHAPTER SEVEN
THE LIGHTHOUSE

Peloma checked her pockets for the fourth time. Anxious and tense, she came down the stairs once again and looked around. She had lost a very important photograph, a picture showing Peloma and her sister Sarah standing behind little Hana's wheelchair. Now that Peloma couldn't find it, she just hoped that no malicious hand would ever touch it.

She walked back and sat behind her desk in total despair. Peloma had been working in an office, located on the fourth floor of the tallest building in San Sebastian city, overlooking the Bay of Biscay. Due to its beautiful beach, San Sebastian was one of the few cities survived the war and turned to a popular resort for the new rulers of the world.

Juan Almonte was Peloma's department head. As he was browsing through documents on his desk, Almonte glanced at Peloma who seemed to be distressed. Then he pushed his thick glasses up his nose and resumed his work.

Later that day, Jose Martinez, the supervising officer of "Endless Blue" agency of beach tours, affiliated with Spain's army, entered the office and went straight towards Almonte. He took something out of his pocket and showed it to Almonte. Peloma could feel her heartbeat rising inside her chest; her lost photo was in the officer's hand. What made him suspicious was the person sitting in a wheelchair in the picture. Almonte pointed to Peloma and Martinez walked up straight to her desk. Stopping before her, he looked at Peloma's appearance and asked: "Is this yours?"

Peloma tried to be calm: "Oh… yes. I guess it must have fallen from my bag."

Jose Martinez, supervising officer of Administrative Bureau of United Europe's fascist, handed her over the photo: "The girl in the middle, what is her relationship with you?"

The resemblance between them was so much that Peloma couldn't deny they were sisters, but Martinez wanted to make sure. "She was my sister. The other one is also my elder sister."

Martinez: "Was? You mean she is no longer your sister?"

Peloma wore a sad face and replied: "No. she fell sick with seizures and was taken to the hospital two years ago but passed away later that night."

Jose Martinez nodded. "Right. It's better to take care of such a valuable memento, then. Wearing a fake smile, he turned to go. While his heavy steps in those jackboots were breaking the silence, he left the office and went back to his room on the upper floor. Peloma took a deep breath, but she was still worried. Putting the photo inside her bag and pulling herself together, she tried to focus on her job.

Another routine working day was coming to an end, and everyone was leaving. Peloma also gathered her stuff and went towards the house, which was located in the southern part of San Sebastian. On her way back home, she thought about her little sister, Hana. Her only concern was to find a way and send Hana to one of the cities in South America, the last Free State that hadn't joined the antihuman convention on elimination.

It was dusk when she got home. A feeble light was flickering through the window. Seeing that beam, meant everything is under control, and they still have another night to spend together in peace. It always wiped away her weariness.

Peloma entered the home joyously. She hugged her mother, Astera who was baking a chocolate cake and hurried upstairs. Sarah had recently found a job in the fishing harbor and was not back yet. Their father had gone to Mundaka the day before to see one of the dealers for transferring Hana to a safe zone.

Plume went to Hana's room, the girl whose existence she had denied that very morning. According to the convention of elimination, the population had to be purged from the handicapped to those suffering from terminal diseases, literally being eliminated.

As Peloma opened the door, Hana turned towards her with her angelic visage and innocent eyes. Sitting in an old wheelchair, she was reading Animal Farm; even the book was a forbidden one, just like the life she was deprived of. The war of grown-ups opposed her to such an undesirable state. Unable to talk, Hana wore a smile that was lucid only to her family.

Peloma hugged and kissed her, as if they hadn't seen each other for ages, maybe she was feeling guilty for the life she denied its existence that morning.

To Peloma, Hana was an ephemeral being who could be carried away at any moment by the elimination squad of General Adler.

She said kindly: "Dear, pretty sister. My only delight is to see your bright face .And you know what? Tonight is our weekly night out!"

She winked at Hana: "Mom is baking chocolate cake for us. We'll go up that hill which faces the lighthouse. Pack your things while I dress up. We have to hurry!"

Hana didn't answer, only smiled back at her. It has been a long time since she last talked. She was struggling with deep mental problems, while Herbods were trying to get her away from the fascist butchers. They were looking for a way to move the family to the free continent, far from their motherland and among the towering mountains of Andes; the land of Golden Eagles.

Before the war broke out, they moved to Spain where Mr. Herbod began working for the UPNO[2]. They lived in Douala, Cameron, in the base of UPNO employees for a while. After the war ended, they went back to Spain, a neutral country that its impartialness was thought to be accepted by Europe's Neo-Nazis who came to power under General Heinrich Adler's leadership, but that was violated later on in a disgusting manner. After War of Europe between the racists and extremist-immigrants of the green continent, Neo-Nazis groups overcame democratic states and created United Europe with no barrier to harness their unrestrained madness. Their ideology also created deathly violence, which was storming the people.

Her passion for pleasing Hana was boundless. Peloma changed her uniform, wore a beautiful white Sarafon and took her to the garage where an old blue Van was parked. It was so old and rusty that not even thieves would look at it twice. She put Hana on the back seat of the car, pushed the wheelchair in the front and headed towards the hills overlooking the Bay of Biscay

The city was not lightened up as before. Resources were scarce to be wasted on city illumination. Only a silhouette of the good old days could be traced in that dim city. Herbods took Hana out once a week, Sometimes Sara or their father, but Peloma always took her to the hills.

It couldn't be denied that their nightly ventures were risky. If Neo-Nazi patrols found them, nothing would stop the disaster. Peloma chose empty roads and took a narrow track, which continued to the top of the hills. The gigantic lighthouse, the symbol of Spanish fascist's authority, which was constructed only in two years, could be seen with all its glory. This

---

[2] United Peace Nation Organization

lighthouse was the only reason for Hana's presence there. Now Hana was here, in peace and far from greedy eyes.

Peloma took a basket out, handing a piece of homemade chocolate cake to Hana. The Night wind was blowing in her curly black hair, and she could feel the breath on her bare shoulders and arms. Peloma put a red shawl over Hana's feeble shoulders: "Soon we're going to leave here. We'll go somewhere safe to live without fear and oppression. Dad is taking care of everything darling…"

As if she was flapping, Peloma opened her arms: "The Land of Eagles…"

Hana looked at the lighthouse and felt the beauty of the quiet night, which was passing smoothly, but Peloma knew it could be the calm before the storm and if they couldn't find a way to leave, difficult days would be ahead. She began massaging Hana's thin legs, trying to make her feel better. The disease was spreading throughout her body, slowly but surely. Everything seemed to be normal in the first few years of her life, but then a form of palsy had emerged in her legs. Sometimes Hana complained of having problems with moving her hands, and after a while, all of her tiny body was stricken.

While the two sisters were enjoying their beautiful night out, they heard some vague voices from afar; It was a sound of laughter which turned that peaceful night into a nightmare.

Three soldiers, drunk and tipsy, were climbing up the hill, roaring racist songs. One of them spotted Peloma: "I see a pretty chick up there…" and all three howled with laughter.

Peloma hurried and pushed Hana's wheelchair back into the van, and hid her under an embroidered blanket. But she was not fast enough, and before sitting behind the wheel, the soldiers reached the car.

One of them who seemed to be more alert, cocked his gone and said: "What are you doing here?"

Peloma said in terror: "Nothing... I just came for some fresh air..."

Soldier: "Show me your ID."

Peloma took the documents out of the van's sunshade and handed them over to him. One of them shouted: "An immigrant... in our country?!"

Peloma hurried and explained: "But I've been living here for more than twenty years since I was four."

The third one who was losing himself in lust went near and said: "She smells sweet..."

Then put his nose on the girl's neck and sniffed. Peloma tried to back away, but he grabbed her hand harshly and pulled her closer. The other soldier, chocked the rest of liquor down and threw the bottle away, then pounced on Peloma. Drunkenness had taken over the third soldier's mind, and he didn't know what's going on. Peloma was trying to fight and push them back. The smell of alcohol and sweat made her sick with disgust and panic.

Suddenly a fourth guy appeared from behind them and hit one of the soldiers in the head with the butt of his gun. The other sobered up immediately, standing face to face with the man who had grizzly hair and dark eyes. The epaulet on the new comer's shoulder showed him as an officer of higher rank. His serious face and thick eyebrows indicated that he was a Spanish man, serving in the army. He pushed back the other soldier harshly, shouting: "You drunk bastards! What the hell are you doing far from your posts?"

The soberest soldier answered anxiously: "Sir... we were patrolling..." But seeing his accusing look, he shut his mouth and lowered his head.

Soon after, a motorcycle arrived and stopped beside them. It seemed, that the senior officer had been witnessing them from afar, and decided to catch the soldiers red-handed. He ordered his adjutant: "Jot down their names and posts. Tomorrow I'll kick their sorry ass." His last sentence scared the shit out of them.

The man turned to Peloma and helped her tidy her clothes. Peloma was scared and didn't know what to do as her condition was getting more critical. Juan Pablo Alvarez, a high-ranking officer, was there, fully conscious and had arrived at the scene by chance. Hana was crouching in the back of the van, not knowing what was happening out there. Alvarez looked Peloma's documents over and glanced at her, clearly surprised. He returned the documents to her: "What do you have in the back of the van madam?"

He walked and reached the van. Peloma felt like dread had turned her legs into jelly. Their address was in the documents, making it clear who they were. And then, that horrifying moment arrived. Juan Pablo was looking inside the van with wide eyes. Inside, Hana's frightened eyes were staring back at him. Her thin legs and the old wheelchair left no doubts in his mind; she was handicapped, an easy prey, found with a bit of luck and enough to bring rewards or even promotion to any officer by being loyal to the new regime's anti-human rules. The adjutant asked: "Is everything alright, sir?"

Juan Pablo: "Yeah. You take these three idiots back to the base, but crawling..." He shouted: "You heard me? Take them crawling."

All three got down on the ground, blaming each other, but it was too late. They were far enough when Alvarez turned and looked at peloma's frozen and Grief-Stricken face. He asked calmly: "What is she doing here?"

Peloma began shaking her head, not knowing what to say.

Alvarez lowered his voice: "Her sentence is certain death; don't you know that?"

Peloma sobbed, and tears ran down her cheeks. She felt frozen inside, and her heart dropped. All at once, the Bay of Biscay turned restless and tore its long waves to the rocky shores.

Alvarez closed the car trunk and ran his eyes on the surroundings. Brooding deeply, he reached the driver's side, opened the door and glanced at Peloma. He took his army hat off while beads of sweat on his forehead showed his distress: "Hurry up, leave here immediately."

Peloma was caught off guard and looked at Alvarez's big, black eyes. He handed her over the documents; looked around and whispered calmly: "Long live free Spain!"

Juan Pablo glanced at Peloma and disappeared in the dead of night.

CHAPTER EIGHT
THE OLD BONDS

With his eyes wide open, Robert was staring at the old man in front of him. Everybody was unconscious on the ground, but the old man.

Adam's white cloak was dancing in the wind, and when he started walking, Robert's surprise turned into fear by facing his great foe. He was panicked and jumped down the statue, but slipped and was about to fell on his face but just before hitting the ground, a force stopped him.

Floating in the air, Robert turned and looked at Adam, who was coming with his right hand stretched forth towards him. As Adam came closer, he rolled his hand back, and the force disappeared, letting Robert land safely on the ground. Robert couldn't mask his wonder as the man before him was far more strong. He was confused, didn't know whether to run or stand his ground and face what fate had brought him. He got to his feet and stepped back.

The old man looked so familiar to Robert, but he couldn't place him. He ran his eyes on the people around, and a thought came to his mind. Maybe he could try waking them up and then escape in the ensuing chaos. He focused and commanded them to wake up, but nothing happened. The same force interrupting him in the jewelry was back again, stopping people from being awake. It all made sense now; the force had come from the man approaching him with calm and confidence steps. Robert must turn his back to the situation and escape for the second time in one day; he had no other choice; suddenly the old man called him by name.

"Robert, stop! We have to talk."

Robert assumed it another trap and yelled back in terror: "Don't come any closer! I'm very strong, and if it's necessary, I'll put you in your place!"

The old man stopped and stared at him. Robert knew how stupid he seemed, but lying was his only way out.

Adam: "I have no doubt in your strength, that's why I came for you in person. But let's be realistic, none of your power would work right now. It's better to stop this swordplay before attracting too much attention and talk instead."

Robert: "Why should I trust you?"

Adam: "Let me come closer, and you will understand."

Robert hesitated. Then said: "You'd better do nothing stupid…"

The old man left him no choice, but at least Robert could face him prudently. Adam walked gently, and with each step forward, old memories were evoked in Robert's mind. Four feet away from each other, all buried memories were before Robert's eyes vividly.

Now everything was as clear as a sunny day; He was Robert's old teacher, in the last years of peace in Douala Base of Cameron. In total shock, he whispered: "Mr. Heber?"

Adam nodded and smiled. "You've grown up so much, you naughty boy."

He noticed the bruises on Robert's face; which were left from Stars Alley's guard punches.

Adam: "What's happened to your face?"

Robert glanced at the triple Moon Towers in the distance and said: "Don't worry. I'll make money out of these wounds…"

Adam: "Although you seem beaten up, I'm glad you're alive. I've never forgotten you all these years."

This struck a wrong chord with Robert since those long years were full of poverty, misery, loss of his family and all his belongings. He had felt forsaken, full of rage and a sense of injustice. He clenched his fist with anger and regret.

Adam shook his right hand, and the pounding force was removed from everyone. People started to wake up, looking around in confusion.

Adam: "Standing here for longer is a risk; I hope no one has traced us. Let's move; we need to talk. By the way, I wonder if you could guide me to the city's water supply reservoir. I'm looking for someone who unfortunately does not trumpet his powers as you do, so he is harder to find."

Then he flashed a bright smile like a treasure hunter satisfied with his finding. Robert: "My condition is not better than yours. Some people are still pursuing me, as you see..." Pointing to his face, added: "I doubt they would leave me alone. But the reservoir isn't far from here; today is your lucky day."

Still suspicious and hesitant, Robert wanted to know the reason behind recent incidents. He knew something must be linking them. In the past, Adam was a kind and patient master, amazing his young fellows with marvels that he pretended them to be illusions and tricks. But as time went by, they all realized his tricks should be something beyond a childish deception.

However, good old days were gone, and neither of them resembles the people they were in the past.

They passed through the crowd who were awakening in Salvation Square. Police sirens could also be heard from afar. Robert led Adam to their destination. Adam focused his mind on tracing Philip, and as soon as they entered the street, going up to the tank, he felt his presence.

Philip, far from all the chaos going on, was lounging in the shadow. As a disguise, he wore gypsy clothes and as usual, he covered his face with a red handkerchief.

Adam: There he is!

71

Robert felt a sense of relief; such person in rags could not harm him.

The order's members could feel the presence of their leader mentally, as they were bind to guardians' soul. Adam could share his ancient knowledge among them considering their inner capacity. So Philip as well sensed that Adam was around. He removed the handkerchief and looked around. At the same moment, Robert's eyes met his. Robert recognized Philip since he had seen him before, through the eyes of his shadow and Philip, had felt the buried look deep down that shadow.

Robert's blood ran cold; His friend and his enemy were both in the same front. It was clear; Adam was his foe, as well. Adam stopped: "Let me explain to you. I guess you've met before. Your trick was interesting, but not powerful enough to distract my senile mind…" He smiled. "It was just an old one, and you played it well! I knew catching you wouldn't be that easy for them, so I stepped forward myself. "

Robert said: "So you were behind it!"

Adam: "I was sure you would escape, but then you made a shadow of yourself. When Philip was describing the eyes of your shadow and the shattering look in it, I made sure that you're safe and sound, playing scary games with us."

He paused, then said: "Eventually, I took a risk and stepped into the heart of my enemy's territory, where they are craving to catch me. It all seems to be a twist of fate; today I was going to meet three people. You, Christopher and an imprisoned friend, and…"

Robert interrupted him: "Christopher who?"

Adam: "Christopher Gray."

Robert: "What would you want from a murderer like him? All the security forces are after him."

Adam: "They made you believe just the way they do. He's not a murderer, nor even dangerous. How do you dare to judge him when you have never met him? Christopher is the leader

72

of America's black people. Fascists have oppressed them like never before. They're not even included as the second class citizens. You, yourself must have seen this racism in New Life City over and over. After black people's genocide, Christopher had no choice, but to migrate."

He shook his head with regret and continued: "I have to teach you many things all over again. Robert, you don't have to live this way. Just realize that your true gift is your common sense and intellectual power. No matter how strong you are, you always have to rely on your rational mind. How could you see black people's miserable life and still believe the fascist's propaganda? I know what you were up to! And I have always realized, you are different. You're so noble and worthy at the bottom of your heart. So you'd better stop petit larceny and thievery."

Robert interrupted him in rage and yelled: "What do you know about me, you old dotard? I've struggled this far. My life is a bitter nightmare, just like those black people you're defending. I lost my parents, lived and survived in filth and mud, all alone, with no one protecting me. Now you're standing here, calling me pilferer?"

Robert restated loudly: "Pilferer? Pilferer?!" Swirling his both hand, he sent a pile of compressed air, like a white orb towards Adam's chest. But Adam deflected the orb with a flick of his finger, disappearing it behind them. Robert was fully aware that Adam is stronger, but he hadn't realized its grandeur yet, though he, himself, was the God of War to the old man.

Robert retreated, stared at Adam's eyes. Philip was looking at him in the distance, trying not to worsen the situation. Adam said quietly: "I did what I had to do, little Bob. In all those ruthless years, there were other people, desperate and in need of my help, more than you were. Though we all are from a big family, I was sure you could save yourself."

Robert shouted: "It's all lie! You abandoned me, and I can't figure out why you came to me after all these years."

Adam: "I never abandoned you, but I had to take care of others; Helena, Peloma, Alexi, Nadia and of course you. Philip and others could look after themselves, but Helena was the most fragile one."

That name echoed in Robert's mind, and he felt all warm inside. Helena was alive, just like him. He continued in aggressive tone: "But, I was your last priority!"

Adam: "No, you were stronger than the rest. I knew you could fend for yourself. I sent Benjamin, one of my trusty companions to your rescue. After your parents got killed, he took you to the ship. You just remember this part, but tell me, do you know what happened to him? To Benjamin whom you called uncle? Of course, you don't. Those who were looking for me found him, before boarding that ship. He stood against them and was killed cruelly just to make your scape. I lost my closest friend in the altar of sacrifice, to save you. I paid the price for others salvage, but for yours, it cost a life. I fully understand it, you weren't aware of all these things, yet being incognito and living in poverty was far better than being arrested by those who wanted to turn you into a war machine and serve their greed through you. They would have used you for conquering more countries and turned you into a bloodthirsty weapon, killing your race."

Robert was impressed by his words and calmed down when suddenly he felt a hand on his shoulder. It was Philip holding his robust shoulder warmly. He nodded and said: "The time of solitude is over. I know you have many questions, but give it time. You'll understand everything, I promise. Now that we have found you alive, we have time to start piece de resistance."

Robert: "Are we leaving? Where to? When?"

Adam answered: "Africa."

Robert felt empowered, accompanying Adam again, recalling his astounding childhood memories, when he was a seven-year-old lad. Adam taught him how to move the pencils on the desk just by looking at them.

Robert: "Alright, but before leaving I need to grab some valuable stuff, and I must do it alone. Oh, I can't go along with you now, cause I've found a new business partner and could earn good money, cooperating with him."

Adam smiled with affection and asked the reason why. Robert explained with cautious how he met the man behind El Corp in North America and mentioned briefly what was offered to him in exchange for doing the job.

Hearing El Corp's name, Adam's got more interested in it. He was eager to know more about this mysterious company, but tactfully, convinced Robert to accompany them for now. He talked about possible dangers of staying there and promised to help him with the offered job. Adam could not lose the chance to infiltrate El Corp.

Robert: "Ok then, I go and pack my stuff. I can't leave my valuable Platiums here while I'm on another continent."

Philip looked at him scrupulously.

Adam: "When will you be back?"

Robert: "Around sunset, I'll meet you here."

Adam nodded: "We'll wait for you. It's better to head out in the dark."

He turned back without a goodbye and said: "See you at sunset."

Robert retraced his steps, thinking about his treasure, Platium, the most valuable substance in the post-war world.

When he was gone, Philip turned to Adam and said: "I'm glad to see you alive."

Adam: "As I am. I guess you couldn't trace Robert by yourself, right?"

Philip: "Yeah. When I arrived, I figured out New Life City is bigger than what I had imagined. As you suggested, I was cautious and didn't use my powers. I was sure you'd make it through."

Adam: "You can't rest assured. I have to grant this power to its true owners. Meanwhile, I'm not allowed to use it; so I'm just an ordinary person like any others. I may be able to put a few of them to sleep simply by touching them, but surely, I can't face an army."

Philip: "Do you think Robert will be back?"

Adam: "I guess he will. But right now I'm worried about beyond the ocean; the twins and especially Peloma; they are under severe pressure. Time is flying so fast. I guess Northern Alliance and fascists of Heinrich Adler have signed a confidential agreement to catch me before I could reach the five kids. I was thinking about Gustave disappearance right before the war, or the reason why I never found that black suitcase. I guess, valuable information in that suitcase must have fallen into enemy's hand, and that's how they found Alexi and Nadia. Probably they don't know their value. Otherwise, they wouldn't keep them alive during these past three years. But our destiny is hanging by a thread. If they smell out about their real identity, they would kill them without hesitation and put us in big trouble. We will set on our trip tonight if everything is prepared. We have to find a middleman in the suburb to get a P1 and go to White Pasture, yet our journey must be concealed. I do not doubt that security agents are still looking for a trace."

Adam looked at the horizon, and after a while said: "Three nights ago after my escape from the second gate, I went straight to the mountains around there, I was about to be arrested. Very soon, they sent around twenty supersonic jets and chopper after me. The desert was crawling with soldiers, and I spent the whole night in a cleft like a dead body. As luck would have it, I met an old local woman the next morning who gave me a ride to New Life City on her old van. The last few days were not really fine. I'm no for sure they're after me, just like before the break out of the war. I suppose they have access to confidential information about my meetings and conversation with the state's senior officials. They know that I'm alive and what I'm after. If I gather the five kids, they can hardly restrain us. That's why they are doing all they can to prevent this from happening."

"Let's go," said Adam. "I have to meet Christopher and Nadia. Poland's resistance branch considers tonight a suitable time for connection. If Nadia proves brave enough and follows the message relayed by the resistance, we will have the chance to talk to her and provide her with vital information on her escape. We have to make it to Gaalve tonight, or we would lose Nadia. I can take no risk in her life and put her in Jaws of death with my own hand. It's time to unveil the truth."

CHAPTER NINE
THE DREAM SELLER

Helena took Mamalan's letter close to the light and started reading it. Mamalan had begun her letter with gentle words:

"My dear daughter, now that I'm writing this letter, I'm sitting here and recalling the past. Everything is so vivid in my mind as if it had happened only yesterday. I'm an old woman at the end of my adventure; as I look back at my life, I can see the long road behind me. More than ninety springs have passed me by, and I know that my time is almost up. There was something that I had planned to share with you someday but never had the chance to do so. With recent happenings, I don't want to risk having the truth buried with me. It's time for you to know a story; the story which started with a living legend among us, the Dream Seller…

When I was younger, life was unkind to me. I'd lost my chance at having a childhood when the misery of not having a family found and forced me into the life of an abandoned child. One day, when I was nine and living in an orphanage, a well-off couple came and took me away. I thought they're taking me to a better life, but it was just the start of an endless nightmare. It had tortured my body and soul since I have been carrying its shadow with me all my life.

Where I used to live before adoption, was not an orphanage but a trade house for future sex slaves. Having some clothes and my raggedy doll with me and not knowing where the destination was, I was taken to the red district and sold to a brothel. They sold my fresh soul, my dreams and my future in exchange for money."

Tuan raised his head and saw Helena's eyes in tears. She kept on reading:

"There, I was locked up in a small room, so called my 'workplace', and I wasn't allowed to leave, while seconds were long and heavy like years. Men got there to eliminate their thirst for lust, like pigs. My wretched life was so dark that I could not even imagine a gleam of hope, just like a dying light beneath the gloomiest nights. Even now, I find it hard to think about those days and write them to you.

As days were passing by, a guy came to my room; at first, I looked at him in disgust, thinking he's there just like any others, to satisfy his inner beast by rain blowing my shattered soul, but he was different... He sat beside my bed and caressed my hair, told me the words that still ring in my ears. Looking at me with his kind and calm eyes, he said he wouldn't hurt me and had come to save me.

He was called the Dream Seller.

Years later, when I was much older, he said he'd heard my little heart's plea which guided him to my rescue. I'll never forget the moment he took my hand, and we left that room forever. I could see the wrath behind those grey eyes. Anyone who confronted him in that brothel was burned in the flame of his rage. By touching them, they turned into frozen statues and were dropped down one by one. I felt the pain they were suffering, unleashed by the Dream Seller.

I remember, walking through still bodies, their wide eyes were filled with terror. Moving their lips slightly, not being able to utter a single word, just like they were struggling with eternal nightmares. Later, I heard that they had remained in that condition for the rest of their miserable lives, mumbling to themselves like maniacs, being tortured inside their minds. It was small retribution for what they had done. Dream Seller had given them a taste of their own medicine, which would tear every inch of them apart, until their last days. He took me to a big fortress somewhere in Africa, called the White Pasture."

Instantly, Helena remembered the name; when they lived in Douala Base, there was a mountain close by, called Mount Cameron, which her parents said the White Pasture was located close to it.

"It was like nowhere I'd seen before. The fortress was located in a rain forest at the mountain foot and couldn't be seen, except by those who had permission from its master. They gave me a room on the highest tower, and from then on, sometimes Dream Seller took me to the height of the mountain. There, I sat and looked at the clouds beneath my feet which had covered everywhere right up to the horizon. Their purity soothed my grieving spirit. There and with Dream Seller's care, the wounds in my soul were gradually healing.

Few people lived there, and even Dream Seller wouldn't stay there for long. He used to go on long trips, and each time, he asked the kind people in charge of the fortress to take care of me. It was hard to live there alone which reminded me of the dark life I endured. Solitude cast a shadow over me and shook me in terror.

Finally, on a fine spring day, I asked him to take me back to my homeland. While I thought he'd oppose me, he respected my decision with a smile on his face. He knew a family here who honored him deeply. Most probably, they'd come to realize how special he was through another story. Whatever it was, they accepted me willingly.

I grew up under the tender care of my stepparents. I got married, had children and built up this village, but still, I missed him each and every day. I didn't have the chance to meet him again, until the day the Dream Seller came back to our village. It was fifteen years ago. I had turned into an old woman, but he hadn't aged a day. The only difference was that he'd cut his long hair, but his compassionate grey eyes hadn't changed a bit. He came here, holding you in his arms.

I had mixed feelings, happy to see him once again before death, and scared to see you as it reminded me of my dreadful childhood. Wondering if you had the same story as mine. He told me all about your life and promised to come after you in the future.

He believed you would be safe here and insisted that I teach you about the traditional medicine. It was then when I realized that he had been observing my entire life from afar, knowing exactly what I had done during these years."

Helena was confused. The mysterious Dream Seller was supposed to come back for her, but when? It might have already been too late, or the Green Hats presence could have prevented this. Her mind was opened up now and all those years were passing before her eyes. Mamalan's patience and kindness in teaching her oriental medicine was upon that enigmatic man's request, who had brought her to this village.

"I kept my promise until today. But the harsh days are coming, and I'm afraid I can no longer keep you safe. I want you to do anything in your power to find him as your past and future, all traces back to him. He can answer all your questions and show you the way. I don't know where he is, even seeking White Pasture is in vain, as I told you, finding this place is up to their will. The best option available is to stay in the area and rely on the local people until Dream Seller shows up, but you have to find him, even by calling him in your dreams. When he comes, you have to trust and follow him wholeheartedly. You belong to the heroic path, which he leads.

I think that's all to it. Writing this letter, I'm in the lower village, waiting for news from the mountain base which probably wouldn't be any better. Somehow I'm sure the Green Hats' advance is not a baseless rumor. Darling, the storm is coming. Disappear and avoid contacting anyone but Tuan.

Helena, make sure to burn this letter as you finished reading it and do not let anyone know about its content. Be strong; you'll be in Mamalan's heart forever…"

Helena looked at Tuan in surprise. He didn't know what was going on since Helena had read the letter in silence. Knowing the secrets, she could feel a heavy weight on her heart now. Then she burnt down the letter just as Mamalan had desired.

Tuan: "What was in the letter? Why are you burning it?"

Shaking her head, Helena said: "I can't tell you, but I need your help to find a man called the Dream Seller…"

CHAPTER TEN
DRUMS OF WAR

Peloma was driving back home in utter shock, thinking about what just had happened to her and Hanna; she could see it all so vivid before her eyes. Juan Pablo Alvarez, the voice was echoing in her mind: "Long live Free Spain!"

The meaning was obvious, "Down with fascist" when anyone using this slogan could be executed to death squad without a military court trial.

Hana's lips and body was still trembling in terror. Time was passing so fast; Peloma's mind was so busy that she didn't realize how she arrived home. She entered the garage and closed the door behind so hastily that brought Astera to the back door. Seeing Peloma's troubled face, she asked: "What happened?"

Peloma: "We are in big trouble, we have to leave. Mum, an army patrol spotted Hana and me."

Astera leaned against the wall as it felt like every attempt they had made to save Hanna was in vain. Just then, Sarah who was the backbone of the family in the past few years came to the garage. She was a tall, beautiful girl, with long black hair. Seeing Sarah, Peloma hugged her and burst into tears. The Bay of Biscay was restless again, crashing waves after waves into the shore.

Sarah caressed Peloma's hair, raised her chin and asked: "What's wrong?"

Peloma relayed briefly, what had just occurred earlier that night. Astera was agitated; it was a terrible incident, but more hardships were on the way.

Peloma: "We have to leave before it's too late."

She couldn't risk and trust Alvarez; even though he had rescued them from those three drunks, she just couldn't risk Hana's life. "We cannot go right now. It's almost ten, and the curfew will start soon." Said Sarah in a calm tone and continued: "Mum, gather Hana's stuff and hide them in the cellar. Peloma and I will take care of the rest."

Wiping away her tears, Astera went back to the second floor.

Sarah: "We'll check the situation tomorrow. They won't find the hidden cellar, but if the condition gets worst, I will take Hana to Martin in the Cantabrian Mountains, don't worry."

She opened the van's trunk and brought down Hana in her wheelchair. Before going inside, she said: "Check the car, get rid of any pieces of evidence and then come to my room. We need to talk."

A thick fog had settled down on San Sebastian City, reducing the visibility to a few feet. Darkness and despair had embraced the town, and Herbods' spent that sinister night with restlessness until the dawn. Astera and her daughters waited for the morning without batting an eye.

Fatigue along with sleeplessness made such an illusory mixture that even affected Sarah who was standing by the window. Each time she looked out clandestinely, she saw eerie figures gazing at the house in the mist and pale light, which vanished just the way they had appeared. As the night was over, Peloma trusted more in Alvarez, but not as much that she could risk Hana's life over it. He could be one of the few remaining people who, hundred years after the WWII and the ruin in its wake, kept fighting the fascists in Europe. Otherwise, he wouldn't let them go!

The next morning, Peloma went to work more exhausted than any other day before. The fog still existed since last night, strengthened by the grey clouds. Staffs arrived one after the other, and everything seemed to be normal, but suddenly all hell broke loose.

Juan Almonte's phone rang. He summoned Peloma to his desk and without looking at her, in a cryptic manner said: "Go upstairs. Mr. Martinez wants to see you."

Peloma breathed deeply. It must have been something important. Otherwise, the military supervising officer wouldn't call her that early in the morning. She touched her long curly hair and went to the fifth floor.

Almonte's insidious look followed her to the door, and when Peloma left, he pushed up his thick glasses and went back to check his lists.

It took forever for Peloma to reach the next floor. On the fifth floor, there was a large conference table at the center of the room, and a young janitor was dusting it. The door to Jose Martinez's room was ajar, and as Peloma went closer, she could hear two men speaking. One of them raised his voice as if he was trying to prove something. It was Carlos Pontes, company's records and archive manager, who was standing at Martinez's desk and trying to clarify a subject. Martinez couldn't see Peloma was standing behind the door because of his desk location, but Carlos saw her and turned his look hurriedly before Martinez could notice it. He took heavy loads of documents from the desk and said: "That's all I know, Mr. Martinez." and left the room. Before Peloma could enter, he leaned towards Peloma and whispered: "Be cautious about that rabid dog girl…" then he shook his head in sorrow and went downstairs.

Peloma knocked on the door and entered, Martinez's cigarette smoke burned her lung. The man seemed beside himself with rage, but was trying to regain his control. A bunch of documents was on his desk.

He looked at Peloma with a fake, deceptive smile and said: "You know, one of my duties is to consider all security and administrative aspects. Your family was among the Jewish immigrants who left their country and settled here many years ago. Your father, Mr. Herbod, worked for the UPNO" And added with hatred "an organization founded for those seeking their own benefit. When the war broke out, your father moved the family back here, to a haven after storm…"

He picked up his expensive fountain pen, which was on his notebook and tarried for a moment. Peloma was quiet.

Martinez: "Winning states have a set of simple principles; do not tread our rules, and in return, we won't tread your neck."

Peloma: "I don't get you."

Martinez raged: "Don't interrupt me, Miss. Herbod." And continued: "We have always ruled this country with our regulations and strength, applied to everyone including you. Disobeying them means violating the authority of the country, the legitimacy of its ideology and its worldview which would never be accepted by the mighty government of Spain and Europe Neo-Nazi."

Peloma: "I don't know what you are talking about."

Martinez raised his voice: "Elimination law, one of the most important and at the same time human-centered rules which were applied even to our dearests. You are not an exception either. Yesterday, when I found your photo, I saw a girl sitting in a wheelchair. Do you remember what you told me about her?"

He paused and stared at Peloma's face with his particular eyes in silence to find traces of distress in her.

Martinez: "You told me your sister died two years ago in the hospital because of seizures. In other words, you have been living in a family of five, just two years ago. While, you mentioned four family members in the application, including yourself when you were hired here, five years ago. You're hiding something from the law."

Martinez narrowed his eyes and said: "It's better to confess unless you would be an accomplice."

Peloma was furious: "Is that it? It's just a simple mistake while filling the form. Moreover, I didn't know I had to include myself as a family member!"

Martinez hit his pen on the desk and said: "It's noted at the end of this form that family members have to be named, something you didn't do at all!"

Peloma: "You cannot accuse me of ignoring such an inhuman law like elimination, with a single clue!"

Martinez stood up, shouting with wrath: "You're an immigrant, a second-class citizen, how dare you talk to an army officer rudely?"

Then he picked up the phone, yelling at the operator: "Dial the central hospital." A few seconds later, the call was connected.

Martinez: "I want to know whether someone called…"

He lowered the handset and asked: "What was her name, your sister?"

Peloma: "Hana Herbod."

Martinez: "Someone called Hana Herbod has a medical record there or not?"

After a short moment, a voice on the other side replied: "Yes, sir. There is a record for Hana Herbod who passed away two years ago."

Martinez looked at Peloma calmly and said: "Cause of death?"

"Seizures and brain infection."

Martinez paused for a long moment until the voice on the other side called: "Sir? is everything all right? Is there anything else I could do for you?"

Martinez hanged up the phone and leaned back in his chair.

Peloma: "Are you satisfied now?"

Martinez paused and said: "You can go back to work. But remember, if you hide anything, you should pay dearly for it."

Peloma left the room without looking at him. Now she could breathe a sigh of relief. But two close calls in such a short period couldn't be accidental. One possibility was Juan Pablo Alvarez. "No, He saw Hana alive, they could have come to the house without playing games." thinking to herself, she had to be more cautious.

Peloma went back to her desk, where Almonte kept checking her with his goggle-eyes. The rest of that foggy day passed, not knowing about home and what was going on there. Contacting her family could reveal their secret, so she avoided any contact with them, at least for the day. The working day was over, and she left the building with other workers.

On the way home, she was thinking of how the thing could end in the worst way. When she arrived, everything seemed to be normal, like always. She opened the door and went in. Sarah was standing in the door frame of the dining room, she looked at Peloma but without a greeting turned her head, and said: "It can't be true. Is he ok now?"

An unfamiliar voice replied from the sitting room: "I don't know, but he's no longer there. He sent me a coded message, saying he's leaving and asked me to inform you. He had to destroy the radio station, which made contacting other resistance groups impossible, at least for now. He couldn't call your home either, fearing they might trace and arrest you."

Tears rolled down Sara's face. With a sob of despair, she whispered: "Poor Martin."

"We have been exposed, and nothing is like before. Well, I have to leave." Said the stranger.

He stood up and walked towards Sarah. Peloma went closer and reached them outside the sitting room. He was an old man, wearing a woolen suit, holding a wood carved stick in his hand. He had brought them news from Martin, Sarah's boyfriend. Despair and weariness were clearly featured on his face, as the Spanish resistance had been incapacitated badly.

The old man nodded at Peloma with courtesy and went towards the door. Before going out, he turned and put his fedora hat on: "I guess it'd be better if you move to somewhere else."

He left the house without a goodbye. Sarah's eyes were filled with misery, as though she had just realized how devastating the news was. When the man left, she threw herself on the old couch in the sitting room and burst into tears. Sarah had always been enduring, but sometimes even she, couldn't put on a strong face. The real danger was Martin being arrested and forced to confess under torture. Many were in danger of arrest and death by revealing their identities. It was even worse in Sarah's case. She was not only a member of the resistance but also hiding Hana from death at home.

They would be shot immediately.

They were Jews!!!

CHAPTER ELEVEN
A DREAM DAY

[Twenty Years Ago]

Yannic Lukas cross-court was so precise and quick that his rival, bending all the way towards the oncoming ball, couldn't reach it and the ball hit the last stretch of Wimbledon's grass court. Fans jumped in the air, shouting in ecstasy. For the tenth successive year, the young player had claimed the honor of world's tennis champion.

A guy who had gotten to the top at once, and eliminated his competitors one by one during all these ten sweet years. His wife and two young daughters were cheering him on. Yannic joined and hugged them tightly. Life could not be any better for him; being on top of fame and glory and above all these, being loved by a warm-hearted family that meant everything to him.

People were applauding him continuously. After a while, the court was prepared for handing over the trophy. A huge crowd was waiting for a chance to get his autograph. Fredrick Bigel, the director of the tournament, raised the microphone: "Ladies and gentlemen, the legendary Lukas, won his tenth world championship. Yannic, I'm sure you have so much to say, right?"

Yannic who was a bit shy took the microphone and said: "these years were like a sweet dream that passed me in a flash. I appreciate your ceaseless support and do my best to stay on top for another five years. My dear wife, Julia, thank you for being by my side through this tough road."

During the award ceremony, Yannic was exhausted and told his old friend, Abraham, who was also his coach: "I guess my blood pressure is low. I'll go to the locker room. Wait for me by the door. And please take Julia and the girls with you."

Abraham smiled and said: "No problem, bro, take a shower. We will wait for you in the VIP corridor."

Yannic grabbed his gym bag, turned to his fans and waved one last time on that glorious day, then smiled and walked towards the lockers. On his way, people shook his hands or congratulated him on the championship. Finally, he reached the end of the corridor and went inside. The sound of the crowd was fading in, and silence took its place as if no one has ever been there before.

Yannic locked the door, sat on a bench and lowered his head, thinking. He wasn't good at all, felt nauseous and dizzy. He tried to take a quick shower, but as he was heading for the bathroom, he saw a man standing before the mirror, looking at him. Adam Heber was there but looked much younger. Yannic was shocked to see him; as he remembered their forgotten deal, his extreme happiness turned into a surge of fear and cold.

He looked at Adam and said: "It's over, right?"

Adam nodded mercifully and said: "Yes, it is the certain end of all mortals Yannic. We had an agreement that ends at this very moment."

Yannic eyes were filled with tears and with a shaky voice, said: "Can I see my family one last time? Julia and my daughters..."

Adam was impressed, he came closer and said: "You know it better Yannic, they do not even exist. Behind that locked door, there's nothing but darkness. When you stepped into this room, everything ended, and as I leave, even this place will be gone forever."

Yannic didn't know what to say. He sat on a bench, lowered his head and said: "I'm grateful for all the things you've given to me, for the pleasure I had instead of my wretched life. For

94

someone like me, it was the greatest joy. By the way, you never told me your real name."

Adam lowered his head, touching his temple, answered: "I have many names, but I'd better remain the Dream Seller to you."

Then he winked at him and walked towards the door. There, he stopped and without turning his head, asked: "We still have our deal, right?"

Yannic stroke his chin and whispered: "Oh, Yes" After a pause, he asked: "Is it painful? I mean death… is it painful?"

Adam opened the door, and mere darkness started to slither, swallowing everything. Among this, Adam said: "I've never experienced death, at this very last moments, you have to think of all the joyful memories you made. In the world of mortals, there are things far worse than death. I believe you know what I mean. Things which could kill us over and over again and then come back for more."

He turned and had one last look at Yannic's pale face. They glanced at each other for a while:

"It's time to go… I appreciate the valuable gift you granted me. I'm sure posterity would be grateful for what you have left for them. Farewell, Yannic."

Then Adam disappeared into the growing darkness.

Dimness got closer to him. Yannic who was at the end of his road, kept going backwards until he reached the wall at the end of the room. Everything was over now, so he closed his eyes, while the darkness crawled and devoured him.

Right at that moment, beside the deathbed of a skinny man, his family and Adam were waiting, and a priest was reciting verses from Gospel, when a tiny ray of light, only visible to Adam, emitted from the man's mouth. Adam took out a necklace from his pocket. Yannic's soul, in shape of light, was absorbed to the green jewel, which was floating at the heart of necklace and rested there in peace.

When the light disappeared inside the green jewel, Yannic Lukas, who was suffering from lung cancer, stopped breathing. The Dream Seller's deal was fulfilled. Closing Yannic's eyes, Adam whispered: "Thank you, Yannic. Your precious gift would be much appreciated by the next generation."

His family gathered around in sorrow and grief when Adam left the building. He passed a wide street in Lille. Hiding the treasure in his pocket, he disappeared in the distance…

CHAPTER TWELVE
THE DREAM SELLER'S TRAP

Major Olivier Winoc was sitting behind his desk in a small and dim room, on the 7th floor of criminal department of Lille's police station, gazing at the radio and surrounded by piles of documents.

He took a deep drag of his cigarette while waiting for an important message to be transmitted via the police radio. Walls in his office were covered by the photos of a man who was tracked by France's criminal police. He had many names, but was known as "Adam Heber." According to the classified information given to France's DGSE by CIA, he was a dangerous criminal who must be arrested and handed over to CIA's representative in France as soon as possible. Winoc had reviewed his case many times which showed Adam Heber had mysterious relations with sick people who passed away after meeting him.

Winoc recalled old memories he had from Adam. Lighting a cigarette with one that is already burning, in a room filled with smoke, he was trying to find a way to redeem the previous mistakes he had made about Adam.

Suddenly an excited voice was heard on the radio: "Sir, he just left Lukas's house and is heading towards the main street. We're about 200 meters away from Solferino intersection."

Winoc held the radio in his hand, walking up and down his office; He touched his blonde hair and said: "Arrest him, Arrest him now."

Noises could be heard from the radio when a sudden, clear voice said: "Mission accomplished"

Adam Heber was at the mercy of France's police force.

Two hours later, Adam was sitting on a metal chair in the interrogation room, and his head was covered by a mesh hood. Then someone un-cuffed him and removed the hood. Adam rubbed his wrists while looking at the person who was sitting in front of him.

The guy had worn a classy suite. He grabbed a golden pen and wrote something down. He looked at Adam; "You have loads of criminal records, or at least this is what the documents show. Why you are back in France?"

Adam answered serenely: "To meet some of my friends."

"You mean those who died right after your visit? Is this your way of catching up with them?"

"Well, somehow all of my friends had terminal diseases with no cure. I was lucky to see them one last time before their death. In such an unkind world, it rarely happens to have the chance to be close to a friend whose time on earth is through."

"But according to their medical records, they could have lived for another six months or even more."

Adam scowled and said: "But they all died of natural causes…"

Interrogator leaned back in his sit: "Why did you come back to our country, Mr. Heber? Two years ago, on December 29th, 2041, you escaped France's security forces, and you're the most wanted man nearly all over the world. What the hell are you going to do here? Where do you plan to destroy and whom do you want to murder next?"

Adam smiled: "I'm sure the records are exaggerated. I'm not as dangerous as you imply."

"Your records are here, in front of me or I would better say the topic of your criminal history! You're suspected of killing, kidnapping and equipping organized criminals in many free states like the US, France, England, Russia, Poland and many others with weapons. When we're done here, you'll be handed over to security forces of the USA and do you know that in the end, electric chair is waiting for you?"

Adam smirked: "They don't have such power. But think twice before talking about free states. When you leave here, there will be no free states at all. The world is crumbling, and you know that. Neo-Nazis are gaining more and more power each and every day."

"It doesn't concern you… your crimes are not related to any of these happenings."

"You're calling me a criminal, just because of the case sent to you   by   my arch-enemies? Do you believe me to be a murderer?"

The interrogator stood up furiously and left the room. Outside, Olivier Winoc was surprised to see inspector Nicholas Simon who apparently had arrived at the same time. Simon was standing behind the one-way mirror of the interrogation room, looking at Adam Heber's calm and assured countenance. Winoc approached him and asked: "Did you detect anything, sir?"

Simon shook his head in negative and breathed out, in total despair. He had managed to arrest him after two continuous years of hard work, but he was sure he couldn't make Adam open up with common interrogation techniques. Frustrated, he said: "Don't let him sleep, put him under pressure until he talks."

Winoc hadn't forgotten what had happened two years ago when Adam was not as well-known as today, and only a confidential order for arresting him had been relayed to them. He thought about the talk he had with Adam back then, a more intimate conversation compared to the talk between a police officer and a suspect about a dangerous pending war. Winoc remembered all friendly advice Adam had given him. He deeply believed that Heber was not a criminal, at least not the way confidential reports show, he even didn't mean to sabotage there.

After two years, they were face to face again. This time, Winoc's position was considerably at higher risk, since he was responsible for Adam's escape. If anything untoward would happen again, he could be imprisoned because of betrayal. He had spent many sleepless nights recently, trying to remember why he had un-cuffed Adam that cold winter night, helping him escape by staging a suspicious scene. But today was Winoc's day to act. He had to go ahead and face one of the biggest fears in his life.

He opened the door to the interrogation room and entered. Heber looked up but didn't give any hint of knowing or remembering Winoc from the past. Winoc placed his documents on the table and sat with serenity in front of Adam. They looked at each other until Winoc broke the silence.

"During the past two years that I've been in charge of your case, I couldn't live a normal life, in peace. Not a single day passed without thinking of your detention, and now you've come here on your own as if the events of past were not enough." He touched his chin: "I can still feel the pain caused by your brutal punches to my face the night you escaped."

Adam smiled: "I apologize for leaving that way, you wouldn't let me go peacefully, so I had no choice other than being a bit harsh. Accept my apology for those punches, as well."

Nicholas Simon was listening to their dialogue from behind the window. Adam's words were contemptuous, but Simon couldn't put the finger on them. He was not rude nor sardonic as if he was saying them wholeheartedly.

Adam knew what Winoc was thinking about, and this conversation was nothing but a feint. He was waiting for a proper chance to talk to him alone. Maybe the temporary cell or even the lockup. But with the mess Winoc had made two years ago, they wouldn't be left alone even for a second.

A few minutes later, someone entered the room and placed a paper before the inspector.

Winoc stared at the paper, then said: "the last friend you visited, passed away a few hours ago. Just don't tell me it was due to natural causes. "

Adam said: "Sorry to hear that. He was struggling with lung cancer and eventually surrendered. He was too young."

"I know them all, just tell me why Heber. Why you appear by their side at that very last moment of their lives."

"I have nothing to say. It's better not to keep your American friends waiting. They are like hungry wolves, having a thirst for their victim's blood."

After hours of interrogation in vain, Winoc took his papers and was about to leave the room when Adam said: "Shagad."

Winoc turned back and said: "Excuse me?"

"Shagad... It is him. I have to be there to confront Shagad."

Winoc smirked, repeating: "Shagad!" and left the room.

Outside, Nicholas Simon was waiting. He said: "Who the hell is Shagad?"

Winoc was bored: "Nonsense. He has been repeating the same bullshit for two years. He's just a crazy bastard who projects all his guilt on an imaginary person. I'm done here; there's nothing left that I need to know about him. It's better to hand his case to the judge so that he could be transferred to the American side. He will be executed, and the world would be a better place."

Simon tied his collar and said: "thinking the same. This case is over. We will hand him over to the U.S government, and we will be done with it. I fancy a glass of champagne and a Cuban cigar. It's time to treat ourselves after all these troubles..."

Winoc nodded and left. But in his mind, he was looking for a solution. If American intelligence service has Heber, the chance for compensating the past will be lost. They wouldn't let Heber off before digging every bit of information out of him. He had to get rid of Heber tonight, but not like before. He had the best solution in his mind, to obliterate Adam Heber.

CHAPTER THIRTEEN
THE STEPFATHER

It was 2:00 am when Nicholas Simon's phone rang. He reached the phone half-awake and answered with anger.

The voice on the other side was anxious. Nicholas glanced at the clock and bobbed up like a cork, hanged the phone and sat up on the bed; wasn't sure if he was awake or still dreaming after last night's drunkenness. He dragged himself to the restroom, rinsed his face and looked into the mirror.

He was alert now; "Adam Heber is not in the lockup..."

This sentence was piercing in his mind; he couldn't believe, it had happened in such a short period. He started cursing, as usual, put on his clothes and rushed to leave. Simon called Lille's police station night shift and asked for further information, but nobody knew precisely what had happened.

When he arrived, the station was in chaos, as if a bomb had just exploded there and bitter, pungent smell had filled the air. He hurriedly called Olivier Winoc, but no response, so Simon rushed to CCTV control room.

A special team of DGSE was already there to check the record of cameras. At the very first moments of the attack, white smoke filled the station and knocked out the night shift officers one after the other. Then a guy wearing a police uniform and gas mask reached detention room. Apparently, the guard believed him to be a backup, waved to him while he was checking inside the cell. His little neglect sufficed the invader to hit him unconscious with his gunstock; then he opened the door to Adam Heber's lockup and dragged him out. Out of police station was commotion, but the two went to the parking,

103

got in a black van and left from the back door. As camera records showed, the van belonged to investigation's division.

The officers reported the van's information and the Patrol found the car soon after, but it was vacant. Simon asked to check entrance and exit of everyone, and the result showed twenty people hadn't left the police station that day; Olivier Winoc was among them.

Now everything was as plain as a pikestaff to Simon, though it seemed stupid, probably Winoc had put Heber to flight again. In the middle of the road, far from the police station, Winoc and Heber were driving in an old Peugeot. Heber was handcuffed in the backseat and said with his natural sense of humor: "I should thank you since you've put yourself in trouble for helping me scape once more."

Winoc yelled: "Shut up, you lunatic! If they find out it was me, dismissal and prison would be nothing compared to losing my one-year-old daughter's custody."

He mumbled: "I make mistakes after mistakes" Then shouted again: "I should get rid of you, you understand, get- rid- of- you…"

Heber: "Sooner or later, they're going to find out it was you, there are cameras everywhere and your absence in such an emergency condition, will remove their doubts. Getting rid of me won't solve your problem Winoc, I'm not a criminal neither a murderer and you know it. I have already explained to you the reason behind all that I do. The world is ending, and if we don't do anything, nothing will remain of it."

"Hell with you and your bullshits … I have important things to worry about…"

Heber interrupted him: "Those important things may not have the chance to live in safety. If I stop doing what I'm doing now, all the good stuff in your life will turn into nightmares, and you won't even have the chance to face them… Why don't you understand, Shagad is a real threat to our world."

104

"And the hell with that Shagad! I don't know why I'm arguing with you…"

"There's going to be a great war in the near future. No one knows the reason, but let me tell you. Discrimination, racism and financial corruption lead to a bigger gap in class difference. Fascists, religious and capitalists systems are turning people into slaves and plunder them each and every day. Technologies are widening the distance between people, intimacy and sincerity are gone, and money takes control of everything, even people. People, themselves can be dealt if you offer the right price. These regimes and their ringleader are leading the society towards individualism to shatter people in order to rule astray ones. Nothing could intensify the social gap but financial corruption. And the result is the formation of the worst nightmares. When everything tends toward corruption, any effort for regulation is doomed to failure. Right now, the world is like a gunpowder magazine; it would be blazed by the smallest flame into another world war. Fascists will be war's detonator and poverty will be its fuel."

"What does it have to do with you, bastard? Why should I risk everything for you? Don't you expect me to let you go, do you? Over my dead body!"

Heber whispered: "I'm so sorry Mr. Winoc, but your name is among the people I had to visit in France. You're the last on my list…"

Winoc turned to Heber astonished, but hearing the continuous horn of an oncoming car; he turned his look back at the road. He gazed at Heber in the rear-view mirror and said: "what do you mean? Are you threatening me, you son of a bitch?"

Heber looked at him in silence. Winoc shouted: "Say something! Why do you shut the fuck up?"

"Yes. You are not going to see the dawn, and I'm sorry about it."

Immediately, Winoc remembered his daughter and calmed down as if being in a trance. He kept driving for a while in silence, then started to talk in a soothed tone: "My wife was an utter whore. One of the worst things that can happen to a man is that his wife leaves him, but the worse one is to see her in his best friend's arms. They had an affair."

Tears dropped his wet eyes and rolled down his cheeks. Winoc rubbed his eyes. "My life and all its beauties were gone and all my effort to make a great life seemed to be in vain. The only thing left for me is my daughter, Nilsa. If I lose her custody, she has to live with that bastard."

Gradually he was believing it; that night his life would come to an end. He held the steering wheel with both hands and drove faster. Adam, who rarely got sad, seemed to be down and said despondently: "I know your life didn't turn out to be what you've expected, but it was not always this way. Life was meaningful until people came to know greed and selfishness. Everything was ruined since then."

"Why did you come to my life and destroyed it, I can't believe I'm gonna die tonight." Said Winoc desperately.

Adam: "All those people that I've met had already surrendered to death. Some had cancer or suffered from another disease, but all of them were at death's door. I made a deal with them; I gave them the chance to live their lives the way they wished, to live in their dreams, which I made in their minds, so they could enjoy what they couldn't be. In return, they bestowed me their souls willingly, after they are gone for good. The jewel, taken away from me in the interrogation room, accepts only those souls; the ones that dreams were given to them.

Winoc looked at his black leather bag in the front seat of the car. "What for?" he asked.

I have an order to store marked souls; we will need these essences of life in the future. That's all I can tell you.

"Damn liar! I'm not sick, nor asked for a dream! Then why should I be on your list?"

Even Adam didn't know the answer.

"The Taarnaar, my jewel, has chosen you," he said with hesitation.

"Look, Heber, I never thought of you as a murderer. I knew they all had terminal diseases, but still, I don't believe you are a Dream Seller."

"The last pieces of their lives are my treasure and will surely help me and those who will have a difficult road ahead in the future."

Suddenly, three stray dogs ran into the road, and Winoc turned the steering wheel without a second thought. The car smashed hardly through guardrails and fell into a shallow valley beside the road. Both of them were unconscious.

After a while, Adam regained his consciousness and looked around; he was in the back seat and still handcuffed. The fuel tank was leaking, and Adam could feel it on his face. He got himself out of the wreckage and looked for Winoc; he was lying down on the ground a few meters away.

Blood was flowing from the corner of his mouth, and his breath was coming in gasps. Adam dragged himself towards him, put Winoc's head on his knee and looked into his eyes. Winoc was looking at the sky, "The stars… they're beautiful…" then took out handcuff key from his pocket with difficulty. Adam uncuffed his own hands hastily, then wiped away the blood from Winoc's face. They stared at each other in silence. Winoc grabbed Adam's arm and said: "Do you have a dream to sell to me as well?"

Adam didn't know why a healthy person's name should be on his list. Moreover, Winoc had saved him twice. He shook his head: "No, I don't have any dreams for you, but I give you reality as a gift, not a dream. A mighty life for your daughter, Nilsa."

Winoc smiled; "I brought you the jewel they'd confiscated during interrogation. I had the feeling that nothing but your hand should touch it. I knew something beyond human comprehension and wisdom is within it."

Then he pointed to his black leather bag, a few feet away on the ground. Adam put Winoc's head on the ground carefully and reached the bag. Opening it, the green light at the heart of the Taarnaar lightened up the surroundings. Adam went back to Winoc immediately.

He looked at Adam's grey eyes under the green light and then turned his look towards the starry sky with wide, astonished eye, whispering: "ma petite fille…" uttering this word, the life force within him faded away.

Adam brought the jewel near Winoc's face. The green stone was shining beautifully, swallowing the last threads of the man's soul.

Adam looked at Winoc's body one last time heavy-heartedly, he still didn't know why Winoc's soul was stored in the Taarnaar as it only drains the souls which dreams were made for them.

Hearing the commotion of passers-by coming for help, Adam was forced to leave him, so he started walking and disappeared into the dark with the injured body and a broken heart.

CHAPTER FOURTEEN
THE MINORITY'S SIGN

[November 25, 2059]

Somewhere on the suburbs of New Life City, right beside the city's old water supply reservoir, Adam Heber and Philip Vince were standing before a big barrel, warming their hands on the flames of a fire burning inside it. Philip was restless, walking around the fire; but Adam was calm and quiet. Both were waiting for Robert to return as he had promised.

"Do you think he'll come back?" asked Philip.

"I hope so. He was a little scared at noon and a little furious about the past." Said Adam.

"Who's not?"

"He thinks others are responsible for all the hardships he had been through. He lived in poor condition, and we couldn't do anything for him. Despite our expectations, not everything went as it was supposed to. I'm sure that Northern Alliance and European Neo-Nazis are united."

"Southern Confederation doesn't show any interest in following these two, but it won't last for long. They will join that filthy union in greed of plundering Africa. What matters now is all three powers are ruled by the military and moderates do not exist as they did pre-war. We have to hurry; I told you before why they're looking for the five kids, due to impart of the classified documents that Francis Verache lost. Though he tried to burn the list of people in touch with me, before his detention, many names fell into enemy's hands."

Philip nodded and stared at flames, recalling the dark years before the war.

Some gypsies were wandering around. Seeing the fire, they came forward. One of them offered his tea to Adam gently, and he accepted it with a smile.

"The message was true; the famous Dream Seller is here..."

Adam smiled without looking at him. "And you reached us, Chris." Said Heber.

Philip didn't hear their conversation as they were whispering without attracting any attention. The broad-shouldered man in gypsy's clothes, towering over the others, had covered his face. Adam informed Philip about Christopher Gray's presence: "Let's get out of here. The enemy would be grateful to arrest us all, at once."

A few streets away, they entered an abandoned warehouse. A group of homeless people was reposing in the corner. Adam could see how miserable their lives were, even families of six were living in a worn out tent. Mothers whose only dreams were to see their children's well-being.

The three went up iron stairs, reaching a room full of old, useless furniture. Philip pushed aside some boxes, and Adam made a small flame in the air, by moving his hands. The flames illuminated the room, and their shaky shadows started dancing on the dirty, damped walls. Adam sat on the floor and asked Chris to join him.

Adam turned towards Philip: "You know where we are. Bring Robert here, as he returned."

Philip nodded in obedience and left.

Christopher removed the shawl from his face and under firelight, Adam could see a deep scar on his face, an old one inflicted by a sword, running from his left eyebrow down to his chin.

"I'm happy to see you alive, Chris." Said Adam.

"My people are not fine, Heber" Gray continued with grief; "I tried to contact the Northern resistance several times to pass refugees through the ocean to Africa, but each time my request was rejected due to the same reason; "It is not possible yet!", until I received your message. It was the best chance to see you again and share the difficulties of black banished people. I even doubt in the Northern resistance; wondering whether they relayed my messages to you or not."

Adam: "Actually, each time I talked to them, they shared your requests with me. I will explain the reason and obstacle to you later. Now tell me more about your people. I want to hear it directly from yourself."

Gray: "When it was obvious that the new government is totally a fascist one, we decided to leave the country, but the worst decision we made was to go towards the north instead of the south and Latin America. Back then, I didn't have enough influence on black community leadership, so we headed towards the northern lands with this wrong decision. You know that after the Great War, many people were killed, regardless of their color or race. In the first few months, our sixty million population was reduced to less than ten million. We hoped that things would change gradually, but when fascists came into power, rays of hope were all gone. People started going to the north, Canada, and Alaska, no matter how even on foot. Some left America to unknown destinations, maybe to Brazil and Africa, but the majority headed towards the north. Most of us settled down in the North of Canada and residential parts of Alaska, but you know, accommodating and managing this crowd would be extremely difficult. The hardest part was supplying enough food to them. Many died in the north due to the cold weather and food shortage. It was an awful condition. They started hunting each other and resorted to cannibalism. Finally, that million-strong population was dispersed, and each went their own way. What we went through is so tragic, only a few followers were left, maybe ten thousand who could get along with the existing situation."

Adam: "That's why the central government didn't come for you; you were not a threat to them anymore."

Gray: "What we did to ourselves was exactly what they desired. Later, we created a close leadership to manage the remaining population and divided people into smaller groups. We did our best to supply necessary food and medicine to them. Though they still live in poor condition, in abandoned warehouses, old power plants, empty docks, anywhere that has minimum requirements of living, I'm sure they will come for us; they will come to massacre all of us. They're monitoring the southern borders and margins of the Atlantic and Pacific oceans. Therefore we can't ask for help from the south. They have imprisoned us in a natural jail and wait for our gradual and painful death."

A sad look appeared on Adam's face: "But right now, we can't transfer you..."

Adam's words shattered Gray. He didn't expect the resistance's great leader to overlook the lives of thousands black people that easily; to him, Adam was the last ray of hope in the outside world.

Adam: "I'll discuss your problem with the North America resistance as soon as possible; we may be able to send you food and medicine, but currently we can't move the people. If you were in Europe, we could, but it's not feasible here. We are surrounded by the ocean, and the Northern alliance air force notices every permanent, planned move with its eagle eyes. Any action will lead to a mass suicide of your people."

Adam put his hand on Christopher Gray's shoulder: "Bear with me Chris and be strong, I'm going to outflank the enemy. We may not be able to move your people, but..." He paused and preferred not to continue.

"But... what?" asked Gray.

Adam: "I'll tell you at the right time. Just trust me and my words…"

Chris looked into resistance leader's gray eyes, stood up and pulled down his on the collar so that Adam could see the tattoo on his chest. It was an "M" in a circle -the minority's sign- which also stands for all the people following the leader of Half-Dream Order who believed his attempts are made to change the chaos in the world. The sign of deep fondness to the Great Adam Heber and his minority people, the sign of resistance against the dark powers rising after the great war. If the enemy found anyone with this tattoo, he would be executed on the spot without connivance.

Gray bend and looked into the old man's face and said: "I will serve you wholeheartedly and I'll wait but not so long that fascists come to slaughter us."

Adam was impressed by the tattoo on Gary's chest; he knew that this man acts desperately to save the oppressed, colored population. They spent a long time talking and contemplating until Robert returned when Philip guided him in.

Robert was carrying a heavy bag on his back, apparently bringing all his valuable stuff with him. As they entered, Christopher was about to leave empty-handed, but Adam was reassured about the possibility of his success in the future.

Gray glanced at the two newcomers and left without a word. After his departure, the room was quiet for a few minutes. Adam was brooding deeply, so Robert and Philip decided to sit on the floor, without disturbing him.

Robert whispered in Philip's ear: "Where are we going now?"

Philip: "We will finish some unfinished business, and by midnight we'll go to the Port Town. There is a guy who can pass us across the ocean safe and sound."

Robert: "Ok, shan't we go and take care of your small business?"

Adam said softly: "I fully understand your condition Robert and I'm grateful you're not asking questions, or I would better say you don't ask now. But it's time to join your family. Many years have passed since then, neither of us is like before, I'm not your childhood master, and you are not a kid anymore. But the time for the reunion is close. The first thing I want you to do is to communicate with Nadia, tonight. You know, Nadia and her twin brother, Alexi, are imprisoned in Alucine jail and need our help. I'm sure that soon they will get killed if they don't expose information. In fact, the twins don't even know what is hidden inside their souls, and that's why they haven't imparted data yet. But we are running out of time."

Philip added: "We have to communicate with Nadia tonight. If she gets our message and trusts us, we will provide a condition in which she can talk to Adam, in a place where no one can even imagine."

We tried several times to make a connection through fire, the power that Nadia also owns it, but the connection was too weak to communicate via it. Unfortunately, Adam can't use his powers now, as he has kept them all for you and that's why all the connections we made until today were unsteady. Now, you must help us to make a stable link.

Adam: "The time for training hasn't come yet but you know, and you use your powers to some extent. Now, take our hands and communicate with Philip, in your mind. The Polish resistance has an important mission tonight; they have a spy there who can help us communicate with Nadia through something other than fire. A difficult, risky but entirely safe way."

Then he turned towards Philip and said: "Kisan told me to use the Taarnaar for finding the hatch to Gaalve, something I would have never done. I never took the Taarnaar down there and maybe that's the reason why I couldn't find the way. I know you've done many types of research about Gaalve in

Limora's library and I hope they would be of use when you find Gaalve."

Philip: "I don't know much about the underworld of Gaalve, Adam. But I'll try my best to concentrate and to trust my inner voices".

Adam: "When you get there, use the Taarnaar to summon something that you like. You have to keep a part of you away so that it could save you from death if you were trapped there."

Robert asked with wide eyes: "Die? Where the hell are we going?"

Philip looked at him and said: "We're not going on a picnic, we need to be careful." Then he turned to Adam and said: "I know what to do, but still I don't understand why Kisan said the fire is the key."

"I'm sure that dream wanderers don't know everything about communication through fire, he is not an exception and for sure doesn't know anything about Nadia's connection with the fire. Maybe he meant fire or something like that down there which leads you to the main chamber. Anyway, don't focus on communicating through fire. He was so furious and sullen that even didn't give me a chance for a further talk, but that small amount of information means a lot to us. We need to seize this opportunity and go on with your power and knowledge, Philip…"

Adam paused to make sure that Philip was listening carefully. "You know that the fake yellow pills kill people, so we need to hurry unless we will put her to death, ourselves."

Robert was freaked out; everything sounded weird, and now it came to the yellow pills which were used for making fantasies; the fake ones! He just hoped that all this would get done quickly. "I'm not ready for such things. I even don't know what you want me to do?" He asked in surprise.

"Concentrate and try to see Philip in your mind, he will handle the rest of it; Support and help him to accomplish this mission."

115

Robert closed his eyes, but Adam took his hand and said: "Open your eyes and listen to me! Just remember not to swerves down there. If you get lost, we can't bring you back." Robert took a deep breath and said: "Ok. I'll do my best."

Philip made incantation and sticky liquid formed between his and Adam's hand, pouring of the ground like the water overflowing a glass. The liquid was spreading on the walls, covering everywhere. Adam closed his eyes with a deep concentration and joined them.

Robert closed his eyes, nothing happened. He could see nothing but darkness when suddenly he saw a hatch of light in the distance. It was then when he realized that he had entered another world. Though he was not walking, the hatch was coming closer. A great mass of light moved through him, and he found himself standing in front of a large tree, an uncannily huge willow tree.

The world before his eyes was the image of heaven. Right beside the tree, on a high hill, a narrow path started and ran down the mound. Wherever he turned to, an instant concept was illustrated in his mind, as if someone was elucidating them to him.

The path would reach an enormous gate. The first concept came to his mind was an odd sentence: "The Path which Simboos the Great, stepped into and created the Andium World."

He didn't know who Simboos was, but thinking about this name, a tall woman appeared in his mind.

The willow tree was dancing in the wind when he heard Philip's voice just behind him. As Robert turned to Philip, he found out that besides the magnificent tree, other fanciful landscapes also existed. Right behind him, amongst two long rivers, a mighty temple, decorated with red rubies and green emeralds, could be seen.

"Shrine of the fallen king, Merion."

These concepts were still meaningless to Robert, but the scenery was pleasant. On the horizon, there was a rocky wall, widened into the distance.

"The Great Wall" was echoed in his mind.

Philip: "be more predominant. Here is a bit different from where we live."

Robert: "I can feel it's a strange place. By the way, which way we should take?"

Philip pointed at a third path. As Robert turned towards it, warm, dry wind blew to his face. It was so disturbing that he covered his face with his hands. Its meaning was tragic. "The path in which, Feloma, the son of the Crystal wood's queen faced his fate."

Robert: "should we take the worst path among many better ones?"

Philip: "We're going to Gaalve; there we can find a way to communicate with Nadia through it."

Robert looked around, but couldn't find Adam: "Where's Adam?"

Philip smiled meaningfully: "He'll join us soon. I don't want to confuse you, but he's everywhere and nowhere. I don't know how he does it, either; but one thing is clear, Gaalve is beyond his power, and that's why we're here to enter that doomed hell. Adam's mind has a special condition, and as soon as he enters the Gaalve, they will be aware of his presence. That's why he can't step inside it."

Robert had a bewildered look around: "Jesus Christ! Somebody wake me up, please. Alright, let's go to that damned Gaalve…"

They started walking down the hill. Though they were still in open area before the gate, the pleasant weather and green surroundings were replaced by stuffy sky and yellow and withered leaves.

Robert: "From above it was like verdant heaven, but the closer we get, the more it turns to the wreckage."

Philip: "natural principles do not exist here. You absorb the energy from where you are. Up there, the willow tree spread the sense of vitality, that's why everywhere you looked was green, but here beside the human fear and terror, it differs."

They looked back once more, the huge willow had lost its leaves and towered bare into the red sky where the bright sun was no longer visible, and the azure gave its place to hazy and smoky one.

Robert: "If I knew my soul could get lost in a place like this, I would never come here! I was living my life bro."

Philip said with annoyance: "This is the easy part and you're nagging. What would you do when we reach the burning dark?"

Robert smirked and said: "I'll put it out."

Philip patted him on the shoulder and said: "It's not as easy as you think. Don't you see, a mighty power like Adam Heber's dies away before the mysterious forces of the underworld, let alone yours boy!."

He continued on his way and shortly after Robert followed him. The gate was larger than it seemed from afar. Philip took out a shiny necklace from his pocket, a pendant, with a green jewel floating at the heart of it.

It was the Taarnaar, Adam Heber's treasure, with a green jewel, belonging to wisdom, beyond the distant world. Looking at it, Robert felt pulses of life in it; a beating heart inside the green jewel was talking to his mind. Philip wore it around his neck, turned to Robert and said: "Welcome to the Gaalve."

Then he stepped into the burning darkness of the underworld. Robert, followed him bewildered but determined, and both disappeared into the shadows.

CHAPTER FIFTEEN
THE YELLOW DREAM

The heavy footsteps of several soldiers, passing through the long corridor, could be heard in the distance. They stopped outside the Alucine Prison's warden office. The secretary welcomed them politely. Six officers, in dark green uniform, were escorting three men, wearing black suits.

One of them was quite chubby, with semi-bald hair and fair skin. His two well-built and chic companions entered the office after him and stood aside. The secretary guided him to another door, opening to colonel Vasily Petrovic's office, the Prison's warden.

As he entered, Petrovic welcomed him, and said, "Mr. Jones! The authorities had announced your visit. I would be grateful to help you."

Jones looked around the splendid office and said, "Contrary to what I've heard, it doesn't look that bad here.", And sat down on the brown leather couch across from colonel's desk. Petrovic ordered coffee on the phone, then turned his smiling face towards Jones and asked, "How may I help you?"

Jones took out a letter from his pocket and put it on the desk. It was stamped as 'Top Secret,' signed by the high authorities of war ministry of EFE[3]. Petrovic started reading it immediately. The letter made it clear that the demands of its bearer should be carried out with no hesitation, in any possible way.

---

[3] Europe for European

Scratching his chin, Petrovic said, "Well, authorities had mentioned that you are coming and I should comply with your demands. I'm at your service."

Jones: "I want to meet two of your prisoners successively, Alexi and Nadia Sokolsky. You keep them here, right?"

Petrovic leaned back in his chair and began swinging it from side to side: "Under normal circumstances, the two do not exist, but since I have to cooperate with you, I should say, they're here. Particularly and segregated from other prisoners. When would you like to see them?"

Jones: "As soon as possible."

Petrovic picked up the phone and spoke in Polish. His secretary entered the office and received commands from him in the same language. Petrovic turned to Jones and said, "Lieutenant Berdaric will guide you to one of the special interrogation rooms where you can meet the twins."

Jones stood up: "I appreciate your help.", and left the room along with the secretary without hesitation.

Accompanied by his broad-shouldered bodyguards, Jones was walking through dark corridors to reach interrogation room.

Nadia was the first to be summoned for the umpteenth time. They dragged her in and seated her on a chair before Jones. Her left eye was blackened, and numerous bruises were on her frail body. She was resisting with her spirit, as long as she had lost much of her strength. Just a few days ago, two guards had beaten her to death. Her condition was so fatal that Poland's resistance had lost hope on her survival and sent a secret message to Adam Heber through Western Europe's front. However, it never reached him, since the Western front condition was critical; they were hit heavily by the enemy and had lost many of their links. So transferring messages among resistance in that crisis wasn't possible.

"Such a pity! Why should a young girl like you be imprisoned here?" asked Jones indecently.

Petrovic was overhearing the conversation. Nadia looked at him with her right eye but did not say anything. Jones put his leather briefcase on the table and searched for some confidential documents. Then he went on: "I'm here to take you to the Northern Alliance; both you and your brother. You'd better tell me the truth, so I will be able to help you more. Everything is ready to move you to the Northern Alliance, and you can live a peaceful life there."

Nadia, unimpressed, said: "If you wanted to help us, we wouldn't be sitting here. We would already be on the way. I cannot help you, sir."

Jones: "Do you both have the same impression? You and your brother   I mean."

Nadia: "We're innocent and imprisoned because our parents worked for the UPNO ..."

Jones smirked and said: "Do you really think you're here because of these bullshits? I don't think so, and you shouldn't either. Let me explain it to you. You are here because of a briefcase and confidential documents inside it, which are related to a secret order called Half-Dream. It was the core of resistance movements against the New World Order. I've read the idiotic story of you and your brother in your files here! Many of those who know you, have affirmed that you two possess unknown abilities, it doesn't really matter! Let's consider you have this powers, would you be imprisoned in such a dreadful place for three years, just for having these abilities??. Top secret documents about half dream order were in that briefcase, and the guy is carrying it burned parts of them before being arrested. He knew he was being chased, that's why he was trying to destroy them. This proves that the Half-Dream Order was not a small, regional group and was linked to resistance cores in different zones through connections it owns. However, the dark side of the case is those documents at hand. Some of them were fully burned, some were partly destroyed, and a part of them was intact."

"What do all your stories have to do with my brother and me?" Said Nadia with disgust.

Jones pointed his pen towards her with narrowed eyes and said: "Exactly. The list contains names of those who have a key role in the order, and among them, your names are under alias 'Sokolsky Twins.' Before realizing the relationship between you and this surname, we had no reason to be worried, but how many Sokolsky twins exist in Poland whose father had been in the central circle of resistance? The unsolved part is back then when you were only nine. So there were two possibilities. Either these were fake identities used to cover main members, or you possess privileged qualifications, enough for nine-year-olds to be members of the central resistance."

Nadia turned her face away and stared at the mirror wall, where she knew Alucine wolves were auditioning their conversation. Jones went on: "I don't see any coding in these documents, and nothing is concealed by the author, which is proved by the evidence extracted from the letters. Therefore, the first hypothesis is improbable. Now, I want to know what made you so significant and valuable for the Half-Dream Order. In fact, you are trophies at the hand of Northern Alliance and United Europe, against the insurgent resistance. I guess this much is enough to make you talk."

Nadia looked at him and laughed hysterically. "A bunch of stupid dreamers…" she said, but she had the vision now. A stream had begun deep in her mind, making her aware of the things going on around.

Jones looked at the CCTV in the interrogation room, took a piece of paper out of his pocket and wrote something on it. Without anyone noticing it, he placed the note behind his leader bag, in front of Nadia and pushed the paper towards her. "They're going to kill you and your brother. Join us, and we will save you." The note said.

Nadia looked into Jones' greedy face, knowing that the Northern Alliance is also going to turn them into war slaves. She made up her mind and started shouting: "I want to go to my cell! I want to go back to my cell!"

Some guards hurried in and took her out of interrogation room. Jones, with a disappointed look on his face, pocketed the piece of paper before anyone could see it.

The guards shoved Nadia in her cell and left. She cringed in a corner, thinking about all they had been through. She thought about Jones words. Now she knew why they were imprisoned there, an order called the Half-Dream, resisting against the new forces which had raised to the power. To her, the game was over. She was filled with rage and grief, thinking about Alexi, whom she hadn't seen recently and had communicated through taps on the prison's wall and coded short messages.

Nadia wished her parents had been alive so they could live just like good old days. They were murdered dastardly, and all hopes for future was gone forever. She couldn't even cry because of the recent punch in her left eye and the pain it caused.

Nadia looked at her hands, thinking of the special power she owned and had to use them as soon as she could.

She had to burn…

She was so tired and weak that fell asleep; it was midnight when she woke up to a weird sound.

A stranger was standing behind the door to her cell, staring at her through the small hatch. Whenever she was beaten and tortured, the same eyes would come to visit her and bring her some food to give her strength. Now, he was there again. Nadia could only see his worried eyes who looked around from time to time, making sure that nobody is coming over.

When he made sure that Nadia is alert, he pushed in a small tray from the lower hatch and left immediately. It was long past dinnertime, around one in the midnight. Nadia didn't know the exact time, but the heavy silence of the prison was its proof. Something odd was about to happen. Instead of food on the tray, there was a yellow pill, a half-filled glass of water and a note: "Take the pill."

Nadia didn't trust the other guards, but this one had helped her from time to time. She thought it was a painkiller for her eye, so took it with a sip of water. A few minutes passed; she felt warm insides, and a pleasant feeling filled her body.

Nadia stepped into the realm of the dreams. One of those fake yellow dreams…

CHAPTER SIXTEEN
THE DREAM HALL

Philip and Robert passed through a huge gate which looked more like an entrance into a subterranean cave. They set foot on the dark border of the Gaalve. The further they went, the darker it got, nothing could be seen but ascending dimness. After a few steps in that dreadful zone, Philip took out the Taarnaar from his pocket. That radiant, luminous jewel was shining like a star at night sky. Philip put his forefinger on the pulsating green jewel and immediately a white beam radiated into the surroundings. Only then, Robert could see the world around him, which was wallowing in stifling darkness.

There was a narrow path in front of them, running along the ridge of a black mountain, but its depth was not distinctive. Now Philip knew why they couldn't make their way through, without the Taarnaar. Kisan, though scant, had made a great contribution to their mission. Behind them, all they could see was dark walls to the infinity; it was as though magic had separated this hideous part of the world from another side.

They looked around and found out they were amongst two gigantic walls extended to the infinity. At the end of this path, a red, narrow cleft could be seen in the wall before them. They had to go about one mile to reach that cleft. Darkness and silence had created an eerie atmosphere, and Robert preferred not to break that terror's quietness. He thought to himself some mysterious creatures must have been resting in the deadly peace and darkness beneath them…

Philip said in the lowest possible tone: "We will enter the limbo between the Andium and the Gaalve. Without the Taarnaar, we would have fallen into the darkness or we couldn't find the entrance at all; that is why nothing commutes here. Things will change as we pass through it. The guidebook said so; then we have to watch our every step."

Robert nodded and looked at the view above. Despite what he had imagined, they were going up. Formerly, he believed the "world beneath" would be underneath their feet; but the Gaalve was not down there, it was extended to somewhere above its entrance. He thought he must have dizzy due to the mysterious power of that place and was losing his conscious little by little.

While Philip could feel a shadow chasing them in limbo, they reached the cleft. As they stepped inside, Philip rotated and rubbed the Taarnaar in the back. A silvern drop fell out of its green jewel and floated in the air. It was connected to the Taarnaar via a tiny, slender ray of light.

Robert: "What's that?"

Philipe: "It's a teleport. It will bring us back to this point in a blink of an eye." Then he raised a brow: "At First, it may look convenient, but as soon as we find and contact Nadia, they will notice our presence and will come for us. Without this, we would be in trouble."

The cleft was at the end of a cave, opening into the Gaalve. They had to cross the cave to reach it, and without the Taarnaar's power, it was like staring at endless darkness.

Philip sat on the ground, behind a large boulder inside the cave and said: "it's time to use your soul. Split it into two parts, so that you can get away from this hell with one part if another one got trapped."

Robert, asked anxiously: "What should I do exactly?"

Philip shook the Taarnaar slowly in the air. A surge of energy encompassed him, took a part of his soul out of his body and moved it to a corner. From where it landed, a dark shape raised and came towards them. Robert took a step back; he couldn't believe what he was seeing.

It was a huge, black dog; a black Labrador with abnormal big muscles. Robert asked ironically: "Does everything here have to be big exaggeratedly?"

"This one is exceptional," Philip answered with a smile and touched the dog's head and face. The Taarnaar had regenerated his favorite dog to which he could give a part of himself in order not to be fully wiped out in that unknown place.

Philip: "Even in the real world, he is big; the biggest dog in the real world, called Borak. I found him when he was a puppy. I was on a mission in North Africa at that time and saw a group of children trying to hang him. People there, don't like dogs, so it is not an unexpected scene. I cut the rope and brought him down. He was weak, and well, he was just a puppy, shaking in fear. He bit my hand and escaped into the bushes behind the trees. I didn't see him again until a few years later when I was languishing in the jungle, and he saved me. He took me to the nearest village on his back. Well, it has a long story, maybe I tell you the rest one day. Now you have to create something; something that exists and belongs to you in the real world."

Robert thought, but nothing crossed his mind. Philip took two small pills out of his bag which they had to take before entering the Gaalve. Holding the Taarnaar tightly, Robert closed his eyes and thought about a sword which he had seen a few years back, an old memory that he couldn't even recall its place and time. He believed that a sword would be more useful than a dog down there. Blue flecks were coming towards him from all around the cave, gathering together and joining at the center of his concentration and turned his imagination into reality along with a shining light.

It was a sword, with a beautiful curve, ended in a golden hilt. It looked wide and short lightning-like flashes scattered from it, every few moments and faded out quickly.

Philip raised his head, looked at the floating sword which it's dazzling beauty could charm anyone. "How did you made it? Do you know what it is?" said Philip with wonder.

Robert, staring at the sword, said: "No…" and took it. Suddenly, a blinding light emitted from the sword, as if it had found its rightful owner.

Philip recognized the sword immediately. Adam had inherited it from his late master, Felokimoos. They didn't have much time and every second meant a lot to them, so he decided to defer his curiosity regarding the sword to another time. He took out a bottle which contained blue potion and said: "Each of us has to drink from this." Then he pulled out a doodled map from his pocket and read it under the Taarnaar's light.

"When we leave here, we will see a village. The distance is less than two miles. Then we will go to the mansion in the main village where is the place for mysterious tasks. I couldn't find anything useful about it through my researches. All I found was that resistance core knows that yellow pills are linked directly to this mansion, but what this link is, we don't know yet.

This potion will change our appearance to locals, all you have to do is not to look at them, especially into their eyes, just follow me. Diamons have a strong perception of intruder's presence."

It was the first time Robert heard of Diamons who were the ancient inhabitant of the Gaalve. As soon as they drank the potion, the white of their eyes turned completely black, their nails darkened too and they got taller.

Philip gave his cloak to Robert so that he could hide the sword beneath it and left the cave with Borak. Robert accompanied them and soon after, found himself in a different world.

The Gaalve's red sky, made their hair stand on end and relentless terror assaulted them. In the distance, they could see an enormous stone tower on the peak of the mountain which with no doubt, belonged to the dark lord of this realm.

Robert felt like the sky overhead was nothing but an immense illusion as if a fearsome image was painted on the ceiling above him. Far from them, on the left side of the cave, there was a mountain range with a river of fire alongside it, and its widest branch passed right below the Shadow Citadel.

Philip started walking ahead, and Robert followed him. Borak was walking behind them out of the rocky road, keeping a safe distance. Soon, it was time for their first experience. They were standing on a hill where they could see a massive fire on the top of a huge mansion located right in the middle of the village. Its blaze was blue, burst from time to time, and receded once again.

Robert pointed to the fire, but Philip lowered his hand and pointed to somewhere before them with his head. A group of Diamons, wearing long rags and carrying heavy gunnies on their backs, was getting closer to them. When they were passing right beside them, Robert heard them whisper, rather than speak, since their lips were covered by something like a muzzle.

When they passed Robert and Philip, one of the Diamons stopped, turned back and looked at them. Robert could feel that look from behind but preferred not to look back and kept on walking. The Diamon also continued on his way.

The more they went down the slope, the more vibrant Diamons became, in a morbid state. Robert didn't feel good about the way they lived, as if the dark lord, was beside them like a shadow. A life full of fear and humiliation. It was habit or surrender, Diamons always lowered their heads, and due to this, they all had humps. Without a doubt, it was the result of constant horror and abidance.

At long last, they reached the village. There, they could see the immense fire. Everywhere was filthy, but no stinky. It felt like all the happiness had drained in this part of the world. Passing this realm of illusions and reaching the beautiful Andium seemed tough.

The touch of a hand startled Robert. A Diamon was staring at his face, but in a short while, he recognized Philip's voice. He was so lost in the surroundings that forgot they had disguised themselves.

Philip pointed to a stone house behind them. It was different from the rest of the houses with two hefty armed Diamons, guarding its gates. From time to time, some Diamons entered there with full sacks on their backs and left with empty ones. There was no window or hatch, and the only entrance was the main door where the guards let others in and out by sniffing them. The fire was burning right on the top of this building.

Philip: "We cannot risk. If they notice our presence through smelling, everything will be over. I didn't expect these guards." The weather changed unbelievably quickly. In a few moments, the wind was blowing so fast, sprinkling dust into their faces and the clear sky turned overcast, covered with heavy, dark clouds. They stood there for a bit.

Philip: "I guess here is the destination and the fire is what Kisan had warned Adam about."

After a while, something came to his mind. "We can make a fake argument and enter in the middle of the commotion."

Robert looked at him, but didn't have any idea, in fact, he couldn't think, so he accepted Philip's suggestion without hesitation. They reached the entrance, and while they were waiting for the best opportunity, something worse took place. A tall, dark creature was getting close as if he had sensed something was wrong. The creature was sniffing the air continuously, when it saw the tiny silver thread right before his ugly face, covered with the muzzle.

Philip put his hand inside his pocket and held the Taarnaar tight in his fist. The dark creature lowered his head and looked at them, but despite what they expected, he followed the silver trail to the Gaalve's entrance. Philip was not sure whether he had seen it or not, as he was still sniffing the way the two had come from. He was fortunate that the creature took the opposite path and was gone. Philip had heard about the Gaalve's creatures but didn't know this one. His presence scared the Diamons to death, and they stood aside in fear, which showed that he was higher in both position and power. Finally, the right moment to enter the mansion arrived when three Diamons were entering the building with full sacks on their backs. Philip pushed Robert. He stumbled upon one of them, and the three fell over one of the guards. Soon, chaos ensued. The enraged guard took one of the Diamons and pushed him against the wall, while the others tried to intervene; it became an epic scene of mayhem and disorder. Diamons tried to defend the three helpless ones and guards were harshly countering them. It was the best chance for Philip and Robert to enter the mansion, accompanied by Boorak.

Upon their entrance, Robert realized the building is completely different from what it seemed from outside. It had a high ceiling, more like a warehouse and instead of walls, shelves had partitioned the space. Some blue cylinders with pale light were on these shelves. Seeing the building from the outside, they couldn't even imagine such a vast space inside it, as though the area had stretched in there. As far as they could see, there were rows of shelves. The red sky had illuminated a part of the arch…

A group of Diamons was moving among the endless, huge shelves, delivering their sacks to the chiefs of each sector and then leaving the place. At the center of each section, there was a white sphere linked to shelves by bright, narrow beams of light. Utter silence ruled there, and the only echo of water dripping in a big cellar could be heard from afar.

Philip and Robert continued on their way with consternation and in silence. Philip knew they have to find the chamber of

131

dreams, but his thought was trapped in a disturbing ambiguity and didn't know which way to go. The red sky above them was gradually faded away, and the ceiling of the immense mansion was immerging in the dark.

Suddenly, Robert stopped. Before him, there was a small, ugly creature looking at him. It had a feeble body, whispering something under its breath.

Philip: "Don't worry. It's a Pern and has nothing to do with us."

Robert was staring at the Pern. It had big eyes, which against his short height, was suitable for searching and finding items. After a while, the little Pern went on its way. Philip knew that Perns had important tasks in the darkness. Based on the information he got from Limora's library, he knew that Perns work on dreams, but he didn't know what they exactly do, so he decided to follow the little Pern.

The creature moved among the shelves without any attention to them, it rounded a wall and disappeared into the distance where they could hear some murmuring from behind the wall. The Pern was leading them to their goal unintentionally. The Taarnaar was brighter which assured Philip that they are moving in the right direction. The chamber of dreams was some steps away, and eventually, they reached their destination.

They turned around a curve, passed through a short doorframe and entered a big hall. The name didn't fit its magnitude and vastness. A huge hall where astonishing happenings there, had amazed them both.

Rows of metal chairs were installed there, with aisles between them. There were no windows, and only numerous candles had lightened that illusory spot. From the holes on the high, domical ceiling, ghosts with a human face were coming down slowly. Perns, waiting with prongs, seized and seated them on the metal chairs.

With blue orbs floating before all of them, they had greedy looks at Perns who were searching inside their heads rapidly. Seeing this, Philip found out the link between yellow pills and this place. The blue balls illustrated what they had desired, while Perns could dig through their minds for major information without any prevention.

Robert: "What should we do now?"

"Nothing. We'll wait here."

"Wait for what?"

"When someone takes the fake yellow pill, something will happen here that we should realize it. The Taarnaar has Nadia's track. Adam linked all of you to it since you were kids. As soon as Nadia enters here, the Taarnaar will notice her presence, and we'll do as well, or at least this is what I think must happen. There are many people here. We cannot, and we don't have the tool to check them all one by one."

Philip glanced at Borak and added: "Go and search for Nadia." He knew it is in vain, but they had no other choice.

A few minutes passed with the same flow when something interesting happened. A Pern put an orb before one of the new customers, its pale blue color turned into red, and the Pern retracted immediately. Phillip, excited and stressed, took the Taarnaar towards it, but nothing happened. A few moments later, a winged creature appeared and dragged the poor ghost away violently.

"What was that?" asked Robert.

"A wretched, unhappy guy who had taken a fake pill…" said Philip.

"Now I realize why fake pills kill people. Son of the bitch, they treat their victims like this"

"Exactly. Also, there is something I didn't know. The yellow pills permit Perns to inspect and steal important data. Now imagine a member of the resistance, uses one of those pills. Valuable information will be in enemy's hands. That's why

Adam had forbidden use of dream pills. I'm sure this information will help Adam in facing enemies and their tricks." A long time passed, meanwhile, other red orbs appeared and moved Philip and Robert, but nothing happened. They were losing hope, and the effect of the potion they had used to change their appearance was wearing off.

Robert: "Our presence here is wasteful, or maybe Nadia hasn't taken the pill tonight. We would better go back before it's too late."

Philip looked at him without saying anything. Borak was prowling among the chairs; Perns were focused on their job and just reacted to those creatures coming around to drag away the unlucky ghosts. El Corp was selling unbridled evil to its customers.

Philip took out the Taarnaar to get back via its teleport feature. It was then when an orb turned into the red a few rows away and instantly; the Taarnaar was lightened, engulfing the orb by its green rays of light. Perns retracted with scream and Philip yelled: "That's it, Robert! Get ready!"

Both started running towards the ghost sitting on the chair, and Phillip held the Taarnaar close to the red orb, floating in the air. The Taarnaar got brighter, and its bright light filled up space. Robert took his cloak off and covered the Taarnaar and the orb to lessen the light, but its light emitted even from beneath the cloak.

Robert felt someone behind him, he grasped the sword and turned back. It was a Diamon, who was looking at him and the happenings, in amazement. Robert's sword flashes scared the Diamon, so it ran away and disappeared horridly. Philip looked around anxiously. The Taarnaar could be seen from afar since its light was much stronger, even it had covered the ceiling above them.

"Soon they'll find out we are here and send Karoups after us. Be careful." Said Philip.

"What the hell are the Karoups?" asked Robert.

"They were disciples of dark arts under one of the Andium's rulers. Nobody knows their real name, but since they followed the dark arts and learned it from Karapan, they are called Karoups. Adam taught me this part of the Andium's history."

Borak ran fast towards them. In that chaos, Perns left their posts and were running away and unleashed ghosts were moving around, trying to get away from the Taarnaar's bright light.

A group of winged creatures passed them overhead. Philip followed their movements and said: "There they are; they're coming for us. Be very careful, Robert. We have to buy enough time for Adam to communicate with Nadia, just be at hand so when Adam finishes, we teleport out of this hell."

A few ominous moments passed until two dark figures entered from the doorway and went straight towards Robert and Philip. They had smart eyes and seemed more intelligent than Diamons and other creatures there. They also were more of a fighter than the two silly guards were. They had four hands while standing on two legs with a slightly bent back and swaying long tails. Two of their hands jointed to their bodies and looked more like a blade, while the two others were on their chests. They could move with agility to catch their prey and tear them apart.

Robert attacked them in rage. His courage startled the two Karoups as he was the one who started the combat, not them. Robert pressed the sword handle and the sparks on its blade scattered in the air. He screamed and swang the sword like a whip. Dazzling blue light emerged from it and went straight towards Karoups and cut everything between him and them. Chairs overturned and fell between the two sides.

Philip went closer but had to retreat. Five Karoups came down between Philip and Robert and attacked them aggressively. Philip released an invisible surge of energy from his hand and sent fiercely to Karoups, which crumpled one of them on the spot.

A harsh battle ensued. At a breathtaking moment, a Karoup decked Robert on the ground and was about to pierce his flank with his bladed hand when Borak went to his aid and jumped and pushed Karoup away. As time passed more Karoups arrived at the scene. Eventually, Robert and Philip retreated and decided to teleport. Philip jumped to grab the Taarnaar with one hand and stretched forth his other hand towards Borak and Robert. Before leaving, he broke the red orb before Nadia with a kick; her ghost was awakened now and escaped out of Karoups sight.

Philip shouted: "Now...!" And a white light engulfed them all. Swirling in the combination of white and green, they returned to the first place; the entrance of the cave.

Philip hadn't reached the ground yet when a dark, merciless hand grabbed his neck and with a hoarse voice said: "You filthy rat! You think we wouldn't realize you broke the rules and trespassed this forbidden land?" and threw him harshly to the cave wall. Apparently, the dark lord had noticed their presence; he had made every effort to ensnare the intruders, and now he had found the trace. That tiny silver thread of the Taarnaar hadn't been missed from their observant eyes and had tracked them to the source. Philip and Robert were very fortunate that instead of following them down there, it had waited for them at the entrance of the cave. The chief of all Karoups under the command of the Shadow Citadel, called the Life Stealer, was there. He had no name himself, but due to his unbounded cruelty, had a prominent place to the Shadow Citadel's steward.

Encountering Robert, that beast was astonished. He couldn't face Robert's terrifying mental power, as he thought some negligible spies trespassed into the Gaalve. Robert took the time and without hesitation attacked the beast, slashing its

136

armed figure with his sword. He could hear unrelenting pounding which meant other Karoups under Life Stealer's command, were getting close, as it had summoned more forces. Robert hardly bore enemy's strike, gathered his power and hit the ground with his sword. A blinding blue glare filled the space and parts of cave's ceiling collapsed among them. It gave Robert enough time to carry Philip who was injured, out of Gaalve with Borak's help. At this very complicated moment, the beast grabbed Robert's cloak and unbalanced him. By entering the forbidden zone, even the Life Stealer had violated the rules.

He hit Robert heavily on the head with his sledgehammer hand, and all he could do was to defend himself with his sword. Once more dazzling light sparks glittered from its blade.

The Life Stealer knew Robert was just a sidekick and Philip was the key person. He had to reach his main prey and seize that dazzling, blinding jewel, the Taarnaar, and bestow it to the dark lord of Citadel.

Therefore, he kicked Robert in the stomach and tried to hold Philip's neck when suddenly Borak attacked him, and both fell from the sharp slope into the deep darkness. Robert humped Philljip on his back all alone and looked down where Borak, a part of Philip's soul, had just fallen into. Other Karoups, standing in the cleft of the mountain, didn't dare to enter the limbo and all they could do was howling and crawling.

The journey back and the last two miles seemed to be the toughest part in Robert's whole life. An irritating illusion bothered him all the way back. With each breath, he was waiting for the beast or other creatures to return from the dark down there, though he had seen fall of the Life Stealer and Borak himself.

He kept talking: "Philip, please, say something, for heaven sake, are you fine…"

Finally, they arrived at the gateway where he could see the large willow on fire. He knew that was just an illusion and desperately, cried Adam Heber's name. While dimness was surrounding him, Robert tried to keep his eyes open among that deep terror, and not to surrender to darkness. But it expanded more and more and even swallowed the burning tree.

A few moments later, he opened his eyes in the room where they all had been before. Philip, lying down, could hardly breathe while Adam was looking at them in utter shock and anxiety. As the outer world and the liquid between them disappeared, Robert's sword slipped and fell on the ground.

CHAPTER SEVENTEEN
THE SERPENT KING

In the cold dusk of last days of autumn in 2059, a black limo was crawling in a mountainous road towards a fortress, built at the heart of Switzerland's Jungfrau Mountain. Locals called it Devil's den as it had appeared overnight. Since then, the local government had forbidden roving about that area.

The car moved up towards the main turn of the road, then entered a private gravel road, reaching the gates of that fortress. There were no guards around, and it was getting dark. As the car reached its destination, huge, steel gates were opened, and through a big entrance, the car went into the main lot.

The very first scene that grabbed the attention was a few parked private choppers and a vertical plane in the corner of the broad, snow-covered courtyard, belonged to the Northern Alliance. The limousine stopped right at the steps of the hall. Two men in black suit and mask, hurried to the car to welcome and guide the high-ranking guest of their lord towards the main room.

A tall, thin man, wearing the United Europe fascist's uniform, got out of the car. Medals and stars on his chest indicated he was one of the few higher ups ruling over Europe. He glanced at the snowy peaks, put on his hat and slowly climbed up the stairs. He passed the hall and entered a semi-dark room. A hearth had lightened the room. He could not recognize those present in the room, but William Noland.

The leader of the Northern Alliance was standing there with pride, drinking whiskey with his comrades. Noland saw him by chance and welcomed him with buoyancy. "General Adler! I'm glad to see you again."

Hearing the name 'Adler,' all the people in the room fell silent and turned towards him. Now he was the center of attention. The new lord of Europe had joined them.

Noland guided Adler towards the window. Enjoying the scenery of sunset on the mountain, they started talking.

Adler: "I thought I'm the only one who was called up."

Noland: "Well, I thought the same, but guests are here from everywhere. That guy, standing in the corner, is Lucas Oliviera, Marco Monte Corrales' right-hand man. The old general couldn't make it, and instead, he has sent his closest commander. Lich factories owner was also invited. Both, rich and military men are here; I was wondering what a dangerous combination they can make." He quaffed his drink smiling.

Adler turned towards the mountains reluctantly. The sun was setting behind the tall mountains. Everyone in the room was enjoying the foods and drinks, but Adler. He was thinking about a man, whom he had been looking for inch by inch. Adler had dogged the whole Europe, but couldn't find a single trace of him. He was thinking about Adam Heber and the resistance, which was getting stronger more and more each day. Although Adler had the whole Europe's military power and strength, a concealed terror wouldn't leave him alone. He knew that a real threat, much greater than a bunch of names and imprisoned twins, is lying in wait.

Adler looked at people in the room who were the most powerful ones in the post-war world. They had gathered there, jubilant after their great triumphs, enjoying themselves with no prudent. Adler was deep in his thoughts, when another door opened and four tough guys, wearing masks, entered. Following them, a tall man stepped into the room.

The broad-shouldered man was over 7 feet tall, taller than any other one in that room, stood before the guests. His eyes were

140

determined, and whomever he looked at, unconsciously showed honor and reverence for him. His bony face and long forehead gave him a compelling look. This rigidness, coming from somewhere beyond human prescription, affected guests profoundly.

The man glanced at attendances and beckoned to them to sit at the luxurious dining table. Adler chose the closest chair to him, on his right side and stared at his penetrative eyes but as their eyes met, the man's look shook Adler's soul like a battering ram which made him look away.

The man doffed his snow cloak from his broad shoulders to sit on his majestic chair, with ease. What he wore looked like anything but clothes. As if his muscular body was made of sturdy alloy and muscles. Adler was close enough to see his massive arms and steel streaks on his flesh and skin, emitting amber light. Slow, subtle movements could be seen on his shoulders, as though a creature was slithering there. The man touched his left shoulder and movements ceased at once.

The man started to talk when the condition was fine. His voice was sonorous and deep, and despite the friendly atmosphere, it shivered everyone around the table.

Shagad, Adam Heber's greatest enemy, was hosting the most influential post-war world men.

His voice echoed in the room: "I'm glad to see you all after a long time. Now that our dreams are fruitful, there are still people out there not yielding to us and want to spoil our accomplishments and premier ideology. You guided those mislead people lost in their ignorance and superstition, towards an unexpected development.

Yet, there is one question left unanswered; with all the power and facilities provided to you, why that ragged, rebel man and his followers are still out there? Why should I get factual information about the Half Dream Order and Resistance activities all over the world? It is embarrassing how these rats are sabotaging right before your eyes, and you do not even notice them."

Adler said softly: "Sir, we have found and destroyed numerous branches of the resistance. The largest one was active in Spain, which had been fully eradicated. We have some clues regarding their activities in North Africa, but it's of no value. We should ask our partners in the Northern Alliance, why despite their advanced information systems, they were not capable of finding a single trace of the Half Dream Order mobster."

Noland, quite calmly, said: "We have not lost hope on their detention, but I emphasize that this core is not centralized at all. Each resistance works independently from the central core, which makes it difficult to find clues. They're like a tough virus; tiny, leeching our energy and the power that must be spent on developing our true ideals. Confronting this tough resistance is not an easy task. Captivation of their leader is your will, but their concealment makes it hard to achieve. I'm glad that we have General Marco Monte Corrales's representative here. He could explain why the Southern Confederation is refusing to cooperate with security forces of the Northern Alliance and United Europe. We have information that proves their loose legislation, lead to fearless activities of resistance members in regions, under Southern Confederation control. So they plan to sabotage our vital hubs and energy recklessly."

Lucas Oliviera, who was impressed by Shagad's charisma and influence, stood up like a student reciting to his teacher and said: "Initially, I want to relay General Monte Corrales message." He took out two letters from his pocket; surrendered one of them to Shagad and started reading the other one.

"From General Marco Monte Corrales to the Nobel Shagad,

Considering the frequent contacts from the Northern Alliance and United Europe, for the Alliance of Free Latin America to join the 2042 convention, I would like to announce our approbation with the terms and conditions of this convention. We promise to aid and support the Northern Alliance and United Europe in providing information and security and prevent the misuse of our land and resources against these two entities. I should note that the Southern Confederation believes it's not the right time to join 2042 convention due to the high sensitivity of handicapped and terminal diseases patients' eradication with cost-cutting purpose, and rejection of LGBT[4] rights, in lands under Alliance of Free Latin America leadership.

With all due regards,

General Commander of the Southern Confederation."

Shagad frowned and said: "Just like a bunch of schoolboys, you put the blame of your incompetency on each other. Time is passing, and if Heber swings into action earlier than we do, we will get into serious trouble."

He struck the table with his fist, and shouted: "Do you know anything other than debauch?"

Noland who was taking a sniff of his whiskey at that moment put his glass on the table and sat still on his sit out of fear. Shagad glanced at the audiences with such a heavy and intimidating look that forced them to lower their heads.

Shagad's pet wolf entered the room and sat beside his master to be by his side when he is provoked. The wolf sat on his hind legs and looked at people with fiery eyes. Shagad petted wolf's head and said furiously: "I gave you power and wealth, but I won't let you get away with it. You owe this to me, and I will get it back from you but not with generosity... you will pay it back with your life. I'll peel back your skin alive and feed you to the King Wolf."

Then stood up and tore Monte Corrales's letter apart aggressively. He turned towards Oliviera and said: "give my

---

[4] Lesbian, Gay, Bisexual, and Transgender

message to your master. Either you'll join us or I will break the gates of your land and turn your green farms into red streams of your women and children's blood."

Oliviera could wet himself right there out of fear, but Shagad left the room suddenly. Adler hurried after him and said: "Master, declaring war on the Southern Confederation is not a good idea. If we do so, they won't ally us."

Shagad turned, grabbed Adler's throat and pushed him against the wall: "Shut up Adler. I have to go through another war all because of your incompetence, while you are following me brassily and barking like a contemptible dog. Get the hell out of my sight and pray that your people find Adam Heber and bring him to me. Otherwise, you will pay a heavy price for it."

That nightmare-like banquet in the cold night was over, and all the guests left Jungfrau fortress as fast as they could.

After that meeting which ends very quickly, the lord of the fortress didn't even accept his business guests, as if he had invited them, just to humiliate them.

Shagad was looking over the sleeping mountains from a room on the highest floor of the fortress, trying to break through Adam Heber's mind from afar, but his effort was in vain. His servant, Charlie, was standing behind him wearing a chic suit and a red bow.

"Lord, as you ordered, Professor Primius has arrived here undercover and has requested an audience." Said Charlie.

"Tell him to come in.," said Shagad.

Charlie bowed and left. A few moments later, an old man with short hair, carrying loads of documents entered the private lodging of the Serpent King. As soon as he spotted Shagad before the window, he bowed and said: "Your Highness, my colleagues and I are working on the project that I explained it to you in my letter. Tonight, I'm here to give you more details."

Shagad, humbly, invited the old man to sit and said: "I read your letter, professor and I'm interested to know what your plan is. I'm also working on a project very similar to yours, with a different approach, but I'd like to know more details regarding your project. If it attracts me, I will shell out the whole cost of it under one circumstance, and that is the entire project shall be done under my direct supervision. I'll provide you with every necessary equipment you may require.

The old man put his documents on the table and pointed to them reverently. Shagad bent on the table and read the name on it; the BRAIN Project. He was curious: "go ahead…"

Pirimus said: "Your Highness, this project works on a structure which connects all brains to one another, we have reached a type of immortality, for this…"

Pirimus took a long time to explain all aspects of the Brain Project while confronting Shagad's smart questions. The more time passed, the more Shagad was enticed to bring this revolutionary project into action.

It was midnight when Pirimus finished explanation of the project fully to Shagad, and in return, Sahagd promised him immediate support on it.

After professor left, Charlie entered the room and found his lord looking at the mountains again. "Sir, I can arrange another fake meeting with Heber, if you want."

Shagad turned towards him, with a smile on his face: "He won't be harvested again, Charlie. But this time, I have special plans for the Dream seller."

CHAPTER EIGHTEEN
THE THUNDER RAGE

Adam was anxious and reached Philip who was lying on the ground. Robert was still confused and unable to stand on his feet due to the heavy blows of the Life Stealer. His sword was in a corner.

Adam: "What happened?"

Robert bent and dragged his sword closer. "They had set up a trap for us. When we returned, Karoups's commander was waiting for us. We fought, but at the end, Philip's dog and the commander fell down the valley."

Philip was not fully conscious; he had frowned and seemed to be in pain. Adam put Philip's head on his knee and wiped his sweat away with his garment. He turned to Robert and said: "You did a good job. The connection was made, and I relayed all the necessary instructions to Nadia."

Then he looked at Philip's face with grief. His friend and companion was in serious trouble.

A few moments passed when Philip hardly and slowly, opened his eyes but he couldn't talk. Adam found out, though his eyes were open, he could see nothing but darkness, while his mind was still in a challenge. He was staring at the ceiling and searching for something beyond the dimness.

After a while, Adam said: "We must hurry. Nadia and Alexi are in danger. We have to go to Port Town, take a P-1 through a dealer we have and then go to Africa."

Robert helped Adam to move Philip. He could now move his hands and legs and even stand on his feet with their aid, but mentally he was utterly forlorn, not able to talk and was passive.

Robert asked worriedly: "what will happen to Philip?"

Adam: "We have to wait. His soul has fallen somewhere beyond our imagination. I have no idea about that place. Why you weren't more cautious?"

Robert shook his head and said: "We couldn't do anything. We were careful indeed, but they knew we were there and had set traps for us."

Adam: "It's all my fault, but I had no other choice as it was the only way of connecting to those kids. If they knew how important the twins were to me, for sure they would kill them, so I had to use an elusive way."

Philip gave moans time to time and calmed down again or whispered: "Shadows... shadows..."

It took them only a few seconds in Gaalve, so they waited for the darkness to fall. This part of the town wasn't equipped with street lights, and it lacked New Life City 's brightness and nightlife, so it was best to move as the sun sets. Port Town was close, but Philip's condition and his disability to walk on his own had made it difficult to reach there. While they were waiting for the sunset, Robert explained everything about Gaalve. Adam was mostly amazed when he heard about the Dreams Hall.

The sword was also enticing to him; the sword, which was no longer bright in Robert's hand.

Adam: "Where did you get it from?"

Robert explained how he had summoned it through the Taarnaar.

Adam: "Do you know what it is?"

"No. but Philip said it belongs to you and you had inherited it from your master, Felokimoos."

Adam took the sword in his hand, raised it and looked at its sharp blade. It was indeed his own sword. He whispered: "The Thunder rage."

Robert: "You call it by this name?"

Adam: "It is called The Thunder rage. It belonged to my master, then to me, and now, it belongs to you."

Robert: "It is still yours."

Adam smiled and said: "When the Taarnaar gives you something that belonged to me, it means, it's no longer mine. My master didn't forge it, but how he acquired it has a story that makes my hair stand on end. That place in the distant land is called the circle of fire where the border of reality and dreams are expanded. If you step into it, you will need an iron will to return, unless you would be lost in its convoluted shadows."

Robert: "Just like the Gaalve?"

Adam: "Not at all. That place is beyond the Andium's definite borders. There is nothing there but great walls with unknown barren behind it. Illusions will fill you, and it will take the spirit of life away from you."

Robert: "It's a terrifying place, isn't it?"

Adam: "It depends on how you describe fear. For me, it might be walking in an unknown desert with no hope of a return; but someone else might be brave enough to have a one-way trip to discover the unseen."

Robert: "One-way trip? Then how did your master return?"

Adam: "Felokimoos never claimed that he had reached the place where we call the Big Mystery. You know, when you pass the wall to a specified extent and reach the barren, you will see a light in the distance. No matter how far you go, you'll never reach it. This pale light is called the Big Mystery. You will go on and on until you'll be out of your mind and lost in the middle of nowhere. Before my master, many others have tried to discover the biggest riddle of the Andium, but they never returned. Nobody knows what is going on there. Let me give you an example." Then he took a small stone, put it before him and said: "If the entire Andium and Gaalve were this stone …" He took an empty can and covered the stone with it, then continued: "this can would be the great wall, surrounding the dream world on every side. It took me ages to learn about it. We don't know what is beyond this wall and the terrifying barren, but a light in the distance that you will never reach it."

Robert: "Is it somewhere like the limbo between the Andium and the Gaalve Where Borak fell into it?"

"Exactly, but far bigger, scarier and much more mysterious. Felokimoos once told me he reached a steep hill in that desert which ends in a valley, illuminated with light as pale as moonlight at night, but only the valley not anywhere else. When he went down, he faced an exciting story. The place looked like wreckage and seemed to be abandoned for a long time. He saw a creature there, which he hasn't seen before. It was tall and wrinkled, without eyes or clothes. Its only possession was the Thunder rage, which fell into my master's hand by chance. Felokimoos said its figure was like a human, wandering around. Since it had no clothes on to hold the sword, the creature put it down to go inside a hole in the wreckage to drink something like water. Felokimoos who found himself in danger since he had nothing to protect himself, made a brave choice, left his shelter and stole the sword. He did it only to disarm that creature, but as soon as he grabbed the Thunder rage, something weird happened. Holding the sword in his hands, my master could see the desert brighter than before. Out of fear or maybe common sense, he climbed up the valley immediately. Now he could see things that there wasn't any trace of them before seizing the sword, the desert was filled with wanderers like that creature, and the sky was full of lightning. He couldn't go further and decided to return, and with the help of Thunder rage, he went back to the Andium. This story engaged my mind for many years. Who were those creatures? Was it possible to reach the distant light using this sword? Unfortunately, I never had the chance to find the answer to these questions.

Life assigned me more critical tasks. Felokimoos never returned there and was hoping that I could solve this mystery one day. By telling you this narrative, I don't mean to burden you with it, but to tell you where the Thunder rage has come from."

Adam returned the sword to Robert and turned his uneasy eyes on Philip. He was worried about his old friend and fellow who was struggling with hardships.

As the darkness fell over the streets, they departed and headed towards the suburbs. Though Philip could walk, he needed Adam and Robert's constant assistance, while his heavy weight and hulking figure, made moving forward more difficult. He didn't say anything or didn't show any reactions, just stared at them like a dull guy when they called his name.

They reached the very last street of the town, and the only thing lied beyond it was desert, the terror of the post-war world and bandits who lived in the slums and had everyday struggle to survive. The Port Town was not far, but they had to make their way through the debris of war and barren ground towards the east. They had five more miles before them, and since no cars passed at that time, they had to go on, on foot.

Behind them, huge skyscrapers of the New Life City were flaunting; while before them was only darkness. In the distant, a gleaming light was flickering and showed them the way ahead.

Adam raised his head and looked up at the starry sky. The stars were twinkling, and a cool breeze was touching his face. Philip, with all the energy left in his body and lowered head, was going forward, while Robert was there to help him through this endeavor.

151

Adam, holding the Taarnaar- the darkness splitter- in his hand, whispered words with heavy estrangement. He looked up at the sky from time to time, which grabbed Robert's attention, and he tried to follow Adam's look. They had not gone so far, but Philip could not make it, and Robert knew his condition is worsening.

Adam: "Stay here with Philip. I know a dealer in Port Town's black market; he might be able to help us. Please, lend me seven Platiums."

Robert took a bag full of Platiums out of his big sack and gave it to Adam. He thanked Robert with a kind look on his face. He had to leave Philip and Robert as he could not risk Philip's life, so he left them in the debris and headed towards the Port Town alone.

It was about midnight when he reached a small neighborhood in the deserts of the Port Town. As its name suggested, it must have been a port town, but there was no sea nearby, nor vibrant in this dim and quiet city. Adam groped slowly in the darkness and had to stop from time to time to check the alleys. Eventually, he recognized a door. At that moment, a strong wind started blowing, scattering dust everywhere.

He knocked and waited. The electrical light was not expected in such area of the town, therefore when the light was on inside the house, he was amazed.

A few seconds later, an old man with green eyes opened the door and recognized Adam instantly. Without a word, he came out and looked around carefully, making sure no one was around. Then he invited Adam in.

He put the lantern on a ledge and asked Adam to sit. Adam looked around the simple room and said: "Hope you are fine Tortoise?"

Everyone called him tortoise since he carried out his customers' order very slowly but steady and finished the job with their desired result. He said: "I'm fine, Mr. Pernie. It seems that charlatan made you a super crossing card to pass the border."

Adam smiled and said: "It wasn't as useful as you think. Delaponte is a deceitful guy, and all he delivers in exchange for the money he receives is pretenses. He put me in big trouble at the border. I will work with someone else for this type of works I have."

A small electric generator in the corner of the room grabbed Adam's attention, as it was extremely expensive. He had three of them back in White Pasture and used them for lighting there. The old man followed his look and said: "I know I should bestow bounteous hospitality to my best customer under lamp light, but even this lantern light at midnight, is not sensible and wise Mr. Pernie."

"I know, and I'm not here to throw a party. Find me a plane; no matter if it is for rent or sale, I'm ok with both. Which one do you prefer?"

"What matters to me is my profit, so I'd rather prefer the second way. I only have one flying machine left, it's a bit old, but usable and can carry five people. Comparing to its usage, the price is fair. It's not anti-radar, so you should fly at low altitude in the Northern Alliance, and it burns more Platuims than other machines."

"I want it.," said Adam.

"Twenty Platiums."

"Fifteen."

"Not less than seventeen."

"Alright, I should accept, as I'm not in good condition." Said Adam.

Tortoise nodded and said: "I know you're in trouble unless you'd buy a brand new one from the factory half this price, but it's black market and our customers pay for whatever they want with satisfaction."

Adam knew, even a flying carriage would be a blessing in such situation. The old man grabbed his lantern and asked Adam to follow him. The next room was full of jumbles. He opened cylindrical hatch embedded on the floor, under an old dirty rug which looked more like a sewage hatch followed by a ladder going down the hole.

Adam followed the old man down the ladder and reached corridors that were like mazes. Tortoise tried to confuse Adam by taking him into different corridors. Finally, they reached his warehouse. It seemed like all the sellers of forbidden goods had built this underground warehouse, to prevent others from reaching their merchandises. He had a little bit of trust in Adam and for selling an old flying machine; he had no choice other than taking him down there. They entered the warehouse and Tortoise guided Adam towards the end of the hall where the flying machine, bigger than a minibus, was covered with a piece of cloth which he dragged away.

When the dust subsided, Adam saw an old P500, his giant salvage vessel.

"A Platium would be enough fuel for a two-month constant flight, so if you like it, please pay for it now."

Adam took out a bunch of shiny Platiums from Robert's bag, separated seventeen of them and put the rest of them back in the bag.

They were both satisfied with the deal they had just made.

Robert was sitting by a ruined wall, having Philip's head on his chest while his physical condition was worsening. Robert covered him with his own clothes to protect him from the dust and waited for Adam's return. It seemed like time was passing too slow when suddenly a dark object appeared in the sky above and landed before them.

Adam had taken the P500 outside the warehouse through hidden hatches, with Tortoise's assistance. He got off the plane, hurried towards Robert and said. "This is all I could find."

Robert was quiet. "Help me put him in the machine." Said Adam.

Robert helped Philip to stand up and placed him on the back seat. Adam wore the P500 pilot hat to head towards Africa in the bright, starry night with high speed since Philip's condition was getting worse every moment. They had to pass longitude of the Atlantic Ocean with P500, far from enemy's eyes. Therefore, they took off in the old-fashioned and long-nosed P500 with no lights on and disappeared into the night sky.

CHAPTER NINETEEN
WHITE PASTURE

Driving the P500 was easier than what Robert thought. Its steering wheel was just like the outmoded jets. A sensor was embedded in the pilot's hat to convert concepts in his mind to electrical commands for piloting the machine. Production of this type of smart vehicles had been limited after the war. Only those from wealthy class use these tools for their own welfare. They had a very low-altitude flight, passing the ocean. Robert glanced at Philip from time to time and then rest with closed eyes. The view of the vast, endless ocean along with a quiet and gloomy flight would make anyone drowsy, including Robert. He couldn't help sleeping as his eyes were heavy and eventually fell into a deep sleep.

He woke up with the plane's shudder as it landed. Adam's sore eyes showed his exhaustion. They landed somewhere between the courtyard of an old fortress and the northern hillsides of a mountain, fifty kilometers from the northwest of Douala. Robert could see the Mount Cameron rising before them.

Adam: "Finally we arrived."

Robert looked around; he could see the fortress's barbicans in the fog, but not the fortress itself. Tropical trees had surrounded everywhere.

Robert: "Where is the fortress then?"

Adam pointed to a narrow path passing through the trees: "It's not far. The bailey is vast, but we are in the safe zone now, and nothing can threaten us." He said as he was getting off the plane and added, "Help me carry Philip in."

Robert humped Philip with difficulty who was groaning with closed eyes. He followed Adam in the narrow path towards the fortress.

They walked through the winding path of the fortress's yard. It took them some minutes to the fortress, facing to the sea, appeared. Light fogs and rain forest had covered everywhere, but the towers loomed out of the trees. As they reached the tall gate, Adam stopped and looked up at the walls of the keep; no light was on inside the fortress. Then he opened the gate with a flick of his finger.

As he stepped into the hallway, huge torches were lit; as if the fortress was welcoming its master majestically. Here was the territory of infinite forces and Adam could use his powers, with no fear of losing them. Robert was amazed to see an entirely different Adam Heber inside the fortress. Until then, he was an ordinary man with no specific power, but here, he was the living God.

The first person, who noticed their presence was a girl with blonde hair, wearing a long nightgown, standing on the stairs of the great hall and looking at them. Her eyes met Adam's, and he held her in his arms. She was about fifteen, with round face. Her bright skin was glowing under the torchlight.

"My dear Nilsa…" Said Adam, as he was holding her close.

Nilsa wrapped her arms around his waist and held him tight. "I'm so happy that you're back, father. I had nightmares the whole time that you weren't here, dark nightmares…

Adam kissed Nilsa's forehead and said: "you didn't have to wake up now honey; we would see each other in the morning." Nilsa noticed Robert and Philip's presence and stared at them so that Adam also turned and looked at them. She came closer; "Robert, the lonesome boy…" said Nilsa with no introduction, then she bent down and touched Philip's forehead.

Robert smiled and said: "Hi! I guess the fortress's residents know me, though I've never been here before."

Nilsa glanced at Philip and said to Robert; "it seems like you are the only one, not familiar with this situation!"

Robert didn't get her point but carried Philip to the stairs. No strength was left for Philip. Other residents woke up by their voice and Mariana was the first to talk to Adam anxiously, seeing Philip's dire condition. Delrise and Kalahi ran to Robert and helped him to take Philip to his bedroom. Adam left Mariana with Philip who was in a deep sleep like a child. He only hoped that love would be the solution to this severe problem.

Delrise and Kalahi were the two coloreds, in charge of the fortress, and being aged, Adam entrusted them with the responsibility of most perilous tasks, except for the Half Dream order.

"Robert will spend the night in my room. Prepare him a room in the morning," said Adam.

"Of course sir," Said Kalahi, and added "Goodnight."

The two left. Adam also asked Nilsa to return to her room on the highest floor of the fortress, then touched his bed and said, "As the old saying goes, nothing is like one's own bed."

"Of course I've left all I had behind and came to Africa with you. I guess I have to get used to beds in here. But, I think we have so much to talk about, right?"

Lying down on his bed, Adam said: "Yes, about many things but not now. You can sleep on that big couch. Our main task will begin tomorrow."

Robert: "Is she your daughter? I didn't know you have a family."

Adam: "Yes and no."

Robert was surprised and asked with a smile: "What do you mean?"

Adam rolled over on his side and answered: "She's my step-daughter. Her father entrusted her to me, fifteen years ago, when he was dying, and she's been living with me since then. I love her more than myself."

"When she called me by name, I thought everybody knows me. Later, I found out only she does."

Adam's mind was half-awake, whispered: "She's different from others and sees things before the rest of us do…"

He hadn't finished his sentence yet when he fell asleep.

Robert was staring at the high ceiling and listening, but when he saw Adam is quiet, turned to him and found him asleep.

Putting his hand under his head, he tried to sleep. The dawn was close.

As soon as he closed his eyes, he saw familiar darkness before him. Though it was dark, Robert felt like he knew it. Above him, lights could be seen, but where he was standing seemed to be dark and gloomy. Robert was standing on the ridge of a deep horrifying precipice and a few meters beneath him, a creature was struggling not to fall from a crack in the cliff.

A few meters above, he could see Borak on a ledge. It was also trying to save himself from falling into the deep darkness. Suddenly, he realized that the dimness beneath is related to the Life Stealer who was trying to return to the limbo between the Andium and the Gaalve, after that fall. Both were striving hard; Borak for escaping and hiding, the Life Stealer for saving itself and killing Borak. The dog jumped and climbed a few meters high. Robert was trying to hide his glittering sword, so he took off his cloak, covered his sword and tried to lessen his distance with Borak.

The Life Stealer had noticed his presence and without hesitation, changed his direction towards Robert.

Filled with terror, Robert started to climb up the cliff, but the steep slope made it difficult for him and the Life Stealer was getting closer, fast.

While Borak had reached a wide area, which was like a shelter to him, the Life Stealer was close enough to Robert and reached out to his ankle, but Robert jumped higher and kept the distance. The enemy was jubilant, confident about his triumph over the prey.

Robert decided not to run away anymore, as he knew slope would make the scape impossible. He unsheathed his luminous sword, its sparkles scattered all over the place and filled the soaring darkness. The Life Stealer stopped there, trying to fortify himself. However, Robert didn't give him a chance and with the very first move of the sword, sent a whippy thunder towards him.

The Life Stealer leaned against the rocks on his right and dodged the attack. Robert was about to use his sword again, when the muscular Life Stealer, jumped over Robert, trying to tear Robert's throat apart with his coarse, yellow teeth. At that very moment, a flare lit up above them. The Life Stealer turned to find the source, but it was too late; a bulk of white light hit him, and he fell into the hollow down there. Robert also lost his balance and was about to fall, when suddenly a hand grabbed his collar and lifted him up.

It was Adam Heber who had saved him. Borak howled and reached them through dark, sliding ledge. Robert respired deeply, while he could hear the Life Stealer's deafening roars who was falling into darkness. Adam looked at Borak, petted its head: "Your soul was about to perish in the shadow for good."

Robert breathed deeply: "I never thought you could step in here."

Adam: "I may not able to set foot in the Gaalve but here, I can. Tell me, Robert, What happened? Why did you fall? Where is Philip?"

Robert: "You've already seen it. We were fighting this devil when suddenly Borak attacked it, and they both fell. I went down to save Borak, Philip is not feeling well, and he is thrashing out of pain."

Robert could feel he was faltering saying the last words and couldn't utter them correctly. Adam gave him a hand to stand up and said: "Let's go up. We must take Philip with us and get out of here."

Robert felt dizzy and couldn't realize how the three of them went back. But then he saw Adam, distressed, bending down and calling Philip as he was unconscious and breathing with difficulty.

Robert was confused; he believed that the Life Stealer's forces would reach them at any moment. He could see them in the distance, coming in the groups and gathering around the cleft; but they didn't dare to step into the terrifying darkness of that limbo.

Adam: "Didn't I tell you how to do it? Then what did you do? What the hell did you do there that harmed Philip?"

Robert faltered again, he held his head in his hands and tried to explain everything even though he was stammering, but he couldn't. Borak came close and licked his face with affection. Robert lied down on his side and could see Philip's health condition was worsening. Adam was trying to aid him and shouted at Robert: "What did you two do?"

Robert: "We did what you asked us to do."

Adam stood up and said: "I didn't ask you to kill yourself! Didn't you use the instructions I gave you? Where and how Philip came to this?"

Robert stretched forth to get help from him; Adam left Philip and hurried to Robert's aid and asked; "What's wrong with you? Why don't you answer?"

Robert: "I don't know why I'm stuttering…"

Borak went over to Philip and smelled him. Robert, desperate, could see it out of the corner of his eye.

"Tell me where did you go and what did you do? Unless I cannot help him. Talk to me, Robert… talk to me" Said Adam in a gentle tone.

Something passed through Robert's feeble mind. He knew Philip was not all right but didn't know the reason why, when suddenly that horrible scene evoked his unconscious mind.

Robert: "Borak… Borak. Philip is prostrated because of Borak's fall… but he is here now, Borak is here."

Adam: "Yes, I know, however, it's not the reason, it is the Gaalve. You didn't follow my instructions there."

Robert: "No, Borak's fall is the cause. We divided our souls and placed them in our mind projections like Borak and this sword to prevent from being totally lost in here. He must get well now… I saved Borak; I saved Philip's soul from death… he must get well…"

He was trying to look at Borak and Philip, but Adam turned Robert's face towards himself. Robert tried to turn to them and make Adam understand where the issue was, but Adam didn't let him and asked articulately: "What did you do in the Gaalve? Tell me, Robert. Whom did you talk to instead of the key person?"

As if gunpowder has exploded inside his mind, Robert jumped backward and looked at Adam like a burned child who dreads the fire. Adam was standing between Philip and Robert.

Robert: "You dispatched us there, why do you ask what we did. I'm telling you, the problem is Borak, not the damned Gaalve!"

Adam stared at the ground desperately, rubbed his forehead and said: "I thought you would help me save Philip. But you're worse than my enemy! I should have trifled you and left you in that filth you were living. You're a useless person Robert."

Then he raised his head and looked directly into Robert's eyes who was shocked and offended by the words he was hearing from Adam, a guy whom he hadn't fully trusted yet. He was hurt. Suddenly a touch of disappointment invaded him, as though he was trapped in a bone-chilling cold, abandoned in the darkness, but his mind didn't let him break.

Robert wanted to cry and tear Adam apart with his sword, but he knew that he wasn't strong enough to do so. He moved his lips and uttered unintelligible words.

Adam: "What did you say?"

Robert roared: "Who are you?" He knew it wasn't him who asked this stupid question, but his mind.

Adam answered with nauseating laughter. "Who am I? I'm Adam Heber, the Dream Seller! The savior of the mortal men, your master! You know who I am!"

Holding the sword tight in his hand, Robert asked the same question in louder, intense tone. The sword started to shake while scattering its sparkles into the air.

Robert knew that the demon had seized his mind and was trying to break free.

Robert: "You're not Adam Heber! He cannot come here. And...also Philip, it's not him. Borak's fall caused his indisposition, and now that Borak is here, he must be fine. No, you can't be Adam Heber. He, himself sent us here; knowing why we were here and to whom we were supposed to talk."

Adam looked him in the eye with poignant hatred and rage. A heavy silence filled the air.

A voice shouted in his mind: "Shagad! Shagad!" And he was startled with a shake. Adam was standing beside him, looking at his eyes.

"I saw him… I saw your enemy in my dream. He generated a dream for me to find out about the Gaalve and whom we talked to, there." Said Robert desperately.

Adam touched Robert's forehead and said: "I know, I felt his presence and I knew he had come for you. The steward of Gaalve is in good relationship with him naturally, and I guess Shagad has acquired important information from him. He also generated fake dreams, to get more data from you."

Robert, filled with terror said: "I didn't say anything to him… I didn't say anything…"

"I know, Robert. Your mind was well prepared and didn't let you give up and break. I also helped you, but as it was Shagad's dream, I couldn't cut off the connection. I couldn't do anything, but help you resist him by making you stutter in your speech, or giving you instant consciousness. It was a narrow escape. I never thought he would go into action so fast; otherwise, I wouldn't let him penetrate into your mind. I'll do it now, but remember, this danger will remain in your mind potentially."

Robert whispered the name Shagad and asked: "Who is he? How did he find me?"

"Through the traces that were left there, from you and Philip's mind. Your connection with him down there brought our enemy to you." Said Adam.

"I will tell you who he is. You'd better wash your face now, it's almost morning, and we have so much to do."

CHAPTER TWENTY
THE CALM BEFORE THE STORM

Robert was still bewildered. Though he had been through many perplexities since he had met Adam, he could hardly think how close the enemy was to them. He believed that they had broken free from danger, but now he knew it lies in wait for them. On the other hand, Adam was in a challenging situation. Things hadn't proceeded according to his plans, and only luck had taken them this far.

Their success or failure was hanged by a thread, while Shagad was chasing them like a shadow.

Robert pulled himself together and left the room. Standing near a small room, Adam was staring at the ground and rubbing his chin, while an old man was talking to him. The news didn't seem to be good.

Without Robert, noticing her, Mariana came to him and said: "Good morning, Robert. Let's have breakfast; everyone is waiting for us upstairs."

"Good morning" Robert replied and looked at Adam again. Mariana noticed it, grabbed his arm and led him to the room.

Robert: "How's Philip?"

Mariana: "Not fine. He was delirious the whole night."

Robert: "I don't know how to save him. But I will go back to the Gaalve to find him if it works."

Mariana: "Let's see what Adam's decision is."

They entered the room where an old, big dining table surrounded by wooden chairs was there, Delrise and Kalahi were setting the breakfast table at the corner of the room.

Mariana: "no one serves food here; so help yourself."

Robert shook his head and thanked Mariana; "no one has ever served me food all my life, I've always been on my own."

The breakfast was milk, fried eggs, cornbread, and apple. Adam, Nilsa and the old man joined them.

Adam stepped forward and said: "Let me introduce Mr. David Baldino" then pointed to Robert and added "David, this is Robert, Robert Delmar."

Robert shook hands with the old man. Seriousness resulted from after war days, could be seen on his face.

"Your father was a brave man; you look very much alike." Said Baldino.

Robert looked at the old man, without saying a word; in fact, he didn't know what to say. Memories he had about his family dated back to many years ago, muddled and time-worn.

Everyone sat at the table to have breakfast.

Adam: "Spain's resistance has faced serious troubles, and David is handling the situation. We need to reach Peloma very quickly; we'll depart this evening, with David."

Eating breakfast, Nilsa said: "Last night the Serpent King was here and was looking for a soul he had lost."

Mariana burst into tears and left the room.

David: "What happened?"

Adam explained to him in a nutshell, afraid to mention where they had lost Philip.

Nilsa seemed very weird to Robert. He constantly looked at her, but she kept on talking unknowingly; she knew that Shagad had penetrated Robert's mind, but she was too young and Adam had only taught her the very basic lessons.

Adam left the room after Mariana, as she wasn't feeling well. She was sitting on the stairs landings outside and crying.

Adam: "I do my best for Philip to get well soon. Look, I cannot go there, but I will help him find the way out."

Mariana sobbed and said: "He's dying, Adam. Didn't you just hear Nilsa? Shagad is after him."

"I know dear, I know. But Philip is not amateur. Without a doubt, he's trying to find a way to save himself."

Mariana couldn't help crying, she wiped away her tears with her blue dress and said: "You mean we just have to stand by and hope for his return? I cannot bear it, Adam. Help me go there."

Adam put his hands on Marina's shoulder and said with deep emotion: "People like you can't go there; I cannot risk your life."

Mariana: "But Robert said he would go there."

"Though he's strong, he's still young. Shagad's tricks could overwhelm even the most experienced ones. Moreover, I cannot send just the Taarnaar to Gaalve, and you know that Shagad wants it more than anything. Let's give ourselves sometime; I'm sure Philip can make it."

Mariana: "I know that Philip has cringed at a corner, waiting for you to help him. We can't leave him alone until he dies there, Adam."

"Of course we won't leave him alone Mariana, just be patient."

Robert left the room and went upstairs. He could see the coast of Guinea from the windows. It rained the whole night and made the weather so fine that tempted Robert to go out for a walk. Nilsa joined him and said: "It's always like this, it rains and because of those white stones, we called here the White Pasture."

Taking a deep breath in such clean air, Robert said: "This place is beautiful, and in such a dark world, must be a treasure."

"That's right."

Robert asked her excitedly: "You see the future, right?"

"No. sometimes I can see a few minutes beforehand, and sometimes I notice things that are not common and others can't see or feel, just like last night."

Robert said: "Yes, last night."

As they were walking, they reached behind the fortress. Nilsa was moving a few steps ahead, so Robert looked her over. She was a simple girl, wearing black, cotton pants and calf-length boots. Suddenly, he felt a movement on his right side. A huge Labrador that Robert had met before jumped out of bushes. The real Borak was there, standing between him and Nilsa. Borak had an unfriendly look at Robert as an unwelcome guest. Nilsa noticed it, turned around and hugged Borak's neck, which was taller than her. "Easy, Borak. He's a friend."

Robert nodded unwillingly and said: "Oh yes, we have met before, in the Gaalve."

"I hope you treat our other pet better, cause it won't behave as nice as Borak did." Said Nilsa

Robert smirked and said: "Nice? With this grimace, he would swallow me!"

Nilsa: "What would you do if you see the Wing King?"

"The Wing King?"

Nilsa: "Yes, the king of birds and the last of its species. No mate or sample, but it's my father's one and the only..." she said the last sentence with a smile.

Robert smiled and pondered. He knew Adam is not Nilsa's birth father but enjoyed the pleasure she took in him. Robert could feel a strong bond between Adam and his close retinues, just like a close family, but with no blood relation, a relationship that Robert had always longed for, yet never owned.

Robert: "Can I see the Wing King?"

Nilsa: "Oh, yes. However, I don't think it would be here in the bailey. Let's go up; we'll have a better view from my room, we may find it in the sky. It usually doesn't show up during the day and may come at night just to sleep on the barbican. I haven't seen it since my father was gone, sometimes, I think to myself that it goes after him."

Robert tried to touch Borak's face and communicate with it, but it retracted its snout and went. They reached Nilsa's territory, a room in the highest floor of the fortress which was full of antiques from the pre-war world and bunches of history books were at its corner. Her bed was next to a big window opening to the Guinea Gulf. Robert was looking at stuff in the room when he noticed Nilsa, going out of the window to get to the gable roof. He followed her immediately, and both reached there. They were sitting up there, and Nilsa was searching in the cloudy sky above to find a trace of the Wing King. It seemed simplistic to Robert to find it in the vast sky when suddenly his eardrum was shaken with Nilsa's cry of happiness for finding it. Adam's favorite pet was on the way to their hideout from a distance. At first, it was a small black dot flying from the Mount Cameron. Gradually, got bigger and bigger. A huge eagle was screeching and flapping towards them.

The Wing King hovered above the fortress and landed smoothly a few meters away from Nilsa. Robert was thrilled; The Wing King was an enormous eagle, bigger than any other birds he had ever seen flying in the sky.

"It's even bigger than the flying machine!" said Robert.

Nilsa: "Yes. I told you it is the first and last of its species and also my best friend."

The Wing King neared and glanced at Robert with sharp eyes. Nilsa drew closer to it and caressed the bird's beak. Robert, who had always relied on his inner powers, didn't' know how to overcome his inherent fear of this huge eagle.

"Can I pet it too?" he asked with hesitation.

Nilsa: "of course if it's only petting."

Robert: "What do you mean?"

Nilsa: "Don't even think about riding on it. The Wing King won't even let my father ride on its back! Hmm, I was just kidding you, as I remember no one has ever done it, but Adam.

Even I won't try it, as my father has suggested me not to do so."

Robert: "caress would suffice." And standing behind Nilsa, he got closer to the eagle and hesitatingly moved his right hand towards it, yet the Wing King pulled his head back. Nilsa took Robert's hand and placed it smoothly on Eagle's beak, along with her hand.

It was such a wonderful feeling, for a young boy, who had spent most of his life lonesome, with no companion. Nilsa could sense Robert's pleasant sensation.

She wrapped her hands around its neck and said: "You can also do it."

As Robert held it, the Wing King moved its head harshly, which upset him. At the same time, he stumbled and was about to hit the ground when suddenly a dense air surrounded him and prevented him from hitting the ground, just like the one in New Life City when he was falling from the eagle statue in Salvation square. Once more Adam saved him, and before Robert could realize, Adam appeared before him like a magician.

"You saved my life again? Thank you." Said Robert, in amazement.

Adam: "You are not supposed to die in my house, son! Don't get too close to the Wing King; it's not tamed like Borak."

Robert: "I should have been more careful. But this time Nilsa deceived me..."

Right then, Nilsa yelled from the top of the tower. "Are you alright?"

Robert: "Yes, dear Nilsa! Thanks to you and your plumy friend."

Adam bent and held out his hand to help Robert stand up and said: "Let's get in. We need to talk to David."

Once Robert touched his hand, they vanished and emerged into Adam's room. David was leaning over the table and looking at dispersed papers when he jumped suddenly by the ear-splitting sound of the two appearances. Seeing Adam and Philip, he took a deep breath and said: "all your mysteries aside, but your scary emerging is something else."

Adam apologized with a smile and said: "We don't even have time to take the stairs and we should depart quickly."

He asked them to sit before his desk and he, himself, sat on a stool and started to talk: "We're not in a good situation, and no one proves trustworthy enough that we can count on him, that's why I decided to ask for Robert's help."

David: "It's a right decision. As I said, Spain's Intelligence service had traced the resistance to the main members. They arrested three of them, five nights ago, and only Martin could pull through. To prevent laying bare of our continuum by arresting one member, we used coding, but still, the risk of being identified exists.

Martin had a message for Sara Herbod before leaving. He also informed me in a message that the enemy has detected two of our radio stations. Therefore they had to evacuate them. That's why we have lost connection with major parts of the northern and east Europe. We continuously transmitted a message in Spain, using "Free Doves" code, to chase away other members. However, by losing two stations, I doubt many of them could receive it. They were supposed to shelter in safe houses if the radio connection wasn't made in two days consecutive."

Adam: "What news do you have from Poland?"

David: "Last week I received an encoded message. The Polish resistance has found out that Nadia and Alexi are supposed to be transferred from Alucine to the Northern Alliance territory. They couldn't find out the reason, but they know it will happen shortly."

Adam: "They think we're going to attack Poland. Europe is not as tenacious and powerful as the Northern Alliance. Or maybe it's a trap to make us act sooner."

Adam took a deep breath and brooded. David lowered his voice and said: "We cannot risk Adam. If they transfer the twins, we will lose the chance of saving them."

"Can't we do what we just did some minutes ago?" Robert asked with hesitation.

Adam looked at him and said: "You mean to disappear and emerge there?"

"Yes, yes!" Robert said excitedly.

David leaned back and stared at the ceiling desperately.

Adam: "No Robert. I can only use all my forces in this fortress, not outside here."

Robert: "But why?"

Adam: "Because I've restricted this place, none of the forces that I use will infiltrate outside or die down here, so I can keep them for you. It's a little bit complicated, but I made a decision which is directly linked to my forces, based on that I can no longer use them. I must hand them over to its rightful owners before they come to an end. This decision is my best weapon in facing our bloodthirsty enemy. We should be divided into two groups. I'll go to Helena with the P500. You and David go to Peloma and Herbods I will join you there. After saving Peloma, you will come back here, then Robert and I will go for Nadia and Alexi."

David: "When will we depart?"

Adam: "I will leave now. You go tonight to reach them tomorrow. We will meet tomorrow morning near Mr. Herbod's house. I'll find you there." Then he stood up "thanks for helping me in these dark days."

David said: "my pleasure, even if I don't live long enough to see the Serpent King's downfall with my own eyes."

CHAPTER TWENTY-ONE
TOWARDS DANGER

After the meeting, Adam Heber left the White Pasture for Vietnam to reach Helena by midnight.

David Baldino and Robert would arrive at Spain in the early morning, and last members of the lost circle would join the Half Dream order.

Mariana felt terrible when Adam left. She lied down beside Phillip's bed, and Kalahi checked both of them to make sure they were fine. The Wing King was gone, and Borak was not around. Nilsa went back to her room, and there, she was watching the heavy rain from the window.

Robert was walking in the old corridors, waiting for the right time to set out on their trip. The fortress was much larger than it seemed. In the nested corridors, he reached a door made of black stone; it was heavy, tough and oddly alluring. A longing to know what was behind that door was streaming in his mind. Such circumstances reminded him of Shagad and the probable treat from his side. He opened the stone door with cautious and looked inside.

A narrow corridor, lead him to a round room, with five stone tables, placed in a circle, and at the center of them, there was a small stone stand.

A mysterious green light was penetrating the room from a source in the walls. Robert was walking towards the tables, but as he got closer, a power from the opposite side prevented him from going forward, and the room before him got dim and gloomy. Instantly he realized there was a barrier between him and the tables.

Around the room, there were five rows of benches by the walls like staircases, parallel to each table. The atmosphere was mesmerizing, and suddenly Robert felt sleepy.

Suddenly Baldino appeared right behind him and asked: "What are you doing?"

Robert: "Hm? Nothing. I was just walking around when I saw this room. It is tempting, isn't it?"

David raised his eyebrows and said: "I don't know."

Robert: "the green lights inside walls or this huge dome ceiling, looks like a conference room, but much bigger and more attractive, but I don't know why I can't get any closer."

David: "I think it's among Adam's mysteries. Come now, we have to move."

Robert was surprised and asked: "Now? We were supposed to leave at night."

David, leaving the room, looked at him and said: "Well, it's nearly midnight…"

Robert: "But… I entered this room five minutes ago. It was just evening…"

Kalahi who had just arrived was standing outside the room and hearing their conversation, said: "Excuse me sir, but the middle part of this room retains people inside, in a way that they won't realize the passing of time. It's a kind of defense system."

Then he turned to David and said: "Lady Mariana has prepared some equipment for your journey."

David nodded and said: "Okay, thank you. We are coming; you can go."

Kalahi bowed and left. Robert and David passed through labyrinthine corridors and reached the main hall. There, Mariana and Delrise were checking the stuff they had prepared for them. Adam had asked the two ladies to prepare equipment for the second team, Robert, and David, based on the list he had given to them.

Mariana: "We'll transfer everything to the P1, and you should hand them over to Adam in Spain."

A few minutes later, they set out on a trip to Spain, in a smooth flight. Robert was looking around in search of the Wing King, but some minutes later, he realized it was too dark to spot a single light, let alone a flying bird.

They were both quiet during the flight when finally David broke the silence and said: "Mr. Delmar, I never thought that one day I would accompany you on a trip."

Robert: "to tell you the truth, I never thought I would be flying in a brand new P1 and going on an unknown mission! Two nights ago, I was resting in my bed, and now, I've left all I had behind and follow Adam Heber. I've seen many weird things in this short period; honestly, I never thought there would be other people out there, with unique powers just like me."

David: "for sure not everyone is like you. I don't have any superhuman powers. I used to work in the Spanish army, and after the Great War, I was the leader of the Southern Europe resistance, of course, a part of it. The day Adam talked to me, I never thought it would affect my whole life. Meeting Adam changed my life for good. We are a separate order, rising against this unbridled regime, just like a few others in this world. In the first place, we didn't want war since its consequences are certain and clear. But they deceived people who were tired of classism, poverty, discrimination, inequality, and cruelty. Worshiping idols who are our congener, hurled us into prejudice abyss."

He added: "Tricksters like Heinrich Adler deceived people with the promise of a better world, just like what occurred, first in the Northern Alliance and then in other parts of the world; a conspiracy and Shagad was behind it all. It was too late when we found the truth behind it. The monster we set free with our own hands is devouring us now, a devil in disguise of a Guardian Angel. I have no answer for the future generations, but regret; regret about the hand I gave them for setting up another fascist regime. Now I want to atone for my past mistakes. People like Adam Heber are rare, and in a world that all legends belong to ancient time, he is a living legend among us. Nobody knows his identity, and I don't even figure out his plans, but his words convinced me to have trust in him."

Robert said with a smile: "He hasn't talked to me yet as things happened successively and spontaneously; I just found myself in the middle of this adventure."

David looked at the dimness beneath and pointed to a district: "Everywhere is in dense darkness, no electricity, no health and medication, nothing is in its rightful place. People are struggling to survive, while a few others are cosseted amid stunning wealth, considering others as their jackals. Have you ever heard of the City of God?"

Robert shook his head: "no."

Baldino: "This city is a perfect example of our world and the living imposed on us. The best area of the city covers only ten percent of it, which has electricity, clean water, and full welfare services, which of course belongs to the wealthy people in this new world."

Robert remembered the New Life City instantly, a paradise for the Northern Alliance's well-off. Now United Europe was the same with a similar city for its affluent.

David: "As you pass the aristocratic part, the city is divided into different districts with huge walls, surrounded by guards, armed from head to toe. Gypsies live behind the very last wall. You should see the way they live Robert. They eat others' leftovers and live in utter filth. This is the cross-section of the revolution across the world. All Medias are controlled, and no one is allowed to have any opinion, which is in contradiction with the official beliefs, no matter it is religious, ideological or related to any institution. Nothing out of triumphant government's charter area is acceptable. They are against liberty, but they no longer need to fight anyone. People are bogged down in poverty and misery; they just struggle for their everyday life, not for freedom. Also, you're not alone Mr. Delmar and nor the only one. We're going where someone like you lives there ..."

Robert: "Yes, Adam has talked to me about four other people since our journey has begun. Nadia, Alexi, Peloma and..." He paused for a moment and thought about the old days when they were classmates in Douala school in Cameron. "... and Helena" he continued. "I wish to see them again. When the war began, we lost everything overnight; I thought I'd never see them."

Thinking about his miserable past, Robert sighed deeply.

David: "I know you've been through many difficulties, but it's just begun, Robert. We should be ready for facing more hardships. The storm is brewing."

They continued their flight in utter darkness, due to security state; any flying object was easily recognizable, as the number of non-military flights had decreased drastically. David turned off all the lights, even the lights in the aircraft cabin.

They would reach Spain borders in few hours.

CHAPTER TWENTY-TWO
THE END OF NIGHTMARES

The sound of a huge explosion was heard, Helena awoke to this sound and sat on her bed, assumed it was another nightmare. But soon she noticed that Tuan is also awake.

Helena: "Are you okay?"

Tuan: "What was that sound?"

Helena: "I thought I'm having a nightmare of the blast, it awakened me."

Tuan said: "No, no, I heard it too. It was like an explosion."

Tuan held his staff in his hand and left the hut. Helena followed him outside, to the glade and both kept their ears open. It had stopped raining.

Helena: "Maybe it was Green Hats' ammunition?"

Tuan: "I've got the same concern as you do. If the sound has reached here, it means something bad is happening."

Helena: "But it is well past midnight. Normally there should be nothing going on there at this time."

Tuan shook his head sadly and said: "let's go back to the hut." They hadn't moved so far when another enormous explosion filled the mountains. Uncertainty gave its place to anxiety. Something was going on down there.

Tuan: "You stay here. I go to ferret out, and I'll be back before the dawn."

Helena: "let me come with you. This won't do at all."

However, Tuan resisted and headed back to the village. Helena's mind was locked up on that dark, lonely night. She believed that villagers were engaged in a harsh brawl with green hats, but she didn't know whether to stay or to go back.

Suddenly she felt a dark presence in the surroundings, far from her hut, so she lowered her head immediately and looked out through the loophole where she could see two men in black, standing there, looking around with eyes that were shining in the darkness.

Helena was terrified; she had never seen such creatures before. They were inspecting the huts, so she had to be quick. Otherwise, they would reach her hut before she could do anything. Helena looked around for the right set of circumstances to run away safely. But it was too late, as one of them had noticed Helena's hut. She sat down next to the hut's door and hunched her shoulders.

The two black creatures were as tall as a human, but their behavior wasn't ordinary. They wheezed instead of talking, and their bright eyes would frighten anyone in that darkness. Getting close to Helena's hut, one of them bent down, as a movement behind the trees aroused its curiosity. Someone was among the trees, looking back at the dark creatures.

The stranger: "There is no room for you here, dogs of Darkness…"

Helena raised her head and looked at the man through the window; he was coming towards them steadfastly. There was no fear in his eyes, and as he was moving forward, he raised his staff.

The stranger: "Go back to abysm where you turned up from…"

One of them who was close to him said: "Are you scoffing the Dark Lord's wolves, you asshole?"

The man came closer and stood there, surrounded by more dark figures or so-called Dark Lord's wolves, which appeared from among the trees. He looked around carefully and mumbled with hatred: "Tonight, I'll teach you a lesson that you'll take to heart…"

Five or more wolves jumped towards him at once. He hit his staff to the ground, and a white light spurted out of it, creating a barrier of light between him and them. Hitting the barricade, wolves moved back, but he pointed his staff at one of them, and red ball of light hit its face and knocked it down.

The wolves receded. The man was frowning and yelling while hitting one of the assailants in the back. The creature fell to the ground with a broken spine, half-dead and howling.

Helena felt she was dreaming but put herself together to run away in that chaos. As she left the hut, another dark creature jumped out of the trees and barricaded Helena from scape. It happened so quickly; she was frozen as if she has seen a ghost. As it bounced towards Helena, a bolt of lightning reverberated in the air.

The mysterious man teleported himself behind the creature, grabbed its neck and along with a dazzling thunder light demolished him into powder. The man brought his hand forward and crumpled the two other raiders with the light emitting from his hands.

Howling, the wolves escaped and disappeared into the dark forest, as they knew there is no chance of their victory in that battle. The man looked around carefully, and when he was sure that all of the raiders are gone, he turned towards Helena and said: "It was a dangerous night. Come on Helena, let's get back to the village."

Helena, gasped in horror, asked: "Do you know me? Are you the Dream Seller?"

The man smiled, shook his head and said. "No, I'm the local guard."

Helena: "But how did you find me?"

The man: "Do you think that our leader would leave his valuable treasure unguarded? Pointing to Helena: ". I'm Sertis. I've been looking after you since the very first day you came into this village, at a good distance. Today when Mamalan informed me about the impending danger, I reached you immediately. I just wonder where did these wolves emerge from."

Helena: "Wolves? But they looked just like a human."

Sertis: "They only resemble us, but they're not human. Many years ago, an evil guy created them, and now they serve him. They are called Wolf Pack as they move in groups, and unfortunately, they just nourish human souls. But what were they doing here?" he was deep in thought.

Helena: "We heard the explosion. My friend went down to see what was going on there."

Sertis tied his long black hair behind his head and said: "Ah, yes, I heard it too. It must be the Green Hats. Let's go. I hope nothing has happened to your friends, but I will help them as much as I can."

Sertis found the road, using his staff's light and Helena followed him down. They headed towards the village through the narrow path.

Although they could not see the village yet, they could feel unpleasant signs; the smell of gunpowder and smoke had filled the air, Helena could see a thorny redness in the sky and the closer they got the more murmuring they could hear. Eventually, they passed the last turn, and the village appeared before their eyes.

All the way down the mountain, Helena was agitated, thinking what she will see when they would reach their village? What she observed now, portend what had just happened to her favorite village. She was staring at the scene with wide eyes. The huge elm tree at the center of the village was broken, and the wooden huts were burning in fire. There were no soldiers around, but villagers had gathered around the square's grand stone, wailing. Helena unhanded her hand from Sertis's and hared off to them. Everywhere was devastated. Some people were on the ground, and nothing could be done for them. The big tree was burning, and the wind was carrying its ashes everywhere.

Tuan and Hong were sitting at a corner, crying in one another's arms.

Mamalan...

Helena's heart skipped a beat. There was no trace of her stepmother; she felt sick with apprehension, which told her to make her way out of the crowd to reach the square. Sertis was moving alongside Helena when finally she faced the heartbreaking scene. It was too much for her that she couldn't even stand on her feet. Helena was shocked and got down on her knees, wailing.

Mamalan, the Grande dame of their village, was lying down on a stone and had closed her eyes forever, while the flames of burning cottages were lighting her face. Helena threw herself on Mamalan's breathless body, lamenting and asking the cause of her death.

Sertis looked around and noticed a flying machine, which belonged to the Guardians of life's leader. Adam Heber was sitting next to the P500, staring at the ground. Sertis took Helena away from Mamalan's dead body and carried her in his arms to Adam Heber. Lassitude overcame her sobbing.

Tuan and Hong reached them and stood behind Sertis, crying. Adam stood up, wiped away his tears with his cloak and looked at familiar faces.

Sertis bowed to him and said: "I saved her right on time."

Adam nodded his head in respect and said with a lump in his throat: "But I was late..."

Helena was sitting beside Sertis, with lowered head. Adam bent and held her close to his heart. Helena looked at his grey eyes. Now, with no doubt, she knew who the old man was. She remembered everything; He was the one who saved her life by standing in front of the bombs, barricading them and the one who took her to this village afterward. Now the Dream Seller had attained his treasure.

Adam: "Do you remember me?"

Helena nodded. She was too shocked to speak.

Adam: "I'm here to take you away from here."

Helena only looked at Hong and Tuan who were still crying.

Adam: "They are not in danger anymore."

He whispered in Helena's ear until she calmed down.

Then he left Helena with Hong and Tuan to say goodbye. He asked Sertis to talk to him at a corner.

Sertis: "I'm so sorry Adam. I know how dear Mamalan was to you, but I couldn't defense both Helena and the village at once."

Adam sighed with sadness: "I know Sertis."

The local guard was lower than the main leader of the rank. Although they had much power, they were under the commands of just one leader, due to customs and deep respect to those customs. Now, Sertis was meeting his rank's leader after a long time.

Sertis: "I should tell you something, Adam. When Mamalan told me about Helena, I went after her quickly. Up there, the Wolf Pack were looking for her. I had never seen any of those demons around here before."

Adam was distressed and said: "condition has gotten messy. I don't know how they found out and came here. But time is against me Sertis. I have to go back immediately and fulfill those unfinished, critical businesses. I'll send a message to the rest of local guards using the Taarnaar and ask them to come to your assistance. You'll control this chaos until I come back here."

Sertis: "Should I use my powers in front of the ordinary people?"

Adam looked at him with his powerful eyes and said: "Not only use them but also destroy the Green Hats where ever you confront them. This command also applies to the Wolf Pack. I have to go now Sertis."

Filled with grief, Adam flew to his next destination, Spain, along with Helena. Mamalan's face was before his eyes for hours, and when Helena fell asleep, he cried in silence for the Grande dame of the village.

CHAPTER TWENTY-THREE
A HERO AMONG WOLVES

Herbods began another day in fear and distress. The family spent two harsh days, Since Juan Pablo Alvarez had seen Peloma and Hana on the seaside, also the time was passing too fast, and the chances for escape were ceased to retain.

The beautiful Sarah was sitting on the blue couch, listening to the longcase clock ticking in the room. Her mind was obsessed with the news David Baldino gave her a few days ago. Martin, her childhood friend, true companion in hard days and the only love of her life, was exposed to arrest and fusillade at any moment. Cantabrian was not safe for them anymore. She was thinking about the possible ways of escape from the Wolf Pack of Spain. A group of Neo-Nazis extremist had called themselves the Wolf Pack. It was rumored that dark, semi-human creatures are roaming around at night and feed on the human soul. The unbridled terror they generated, caused the extremists to call themselves the Wolf Pack. Bribing the military officers was a possible way of escape, but there was no way out as the Wolf Pack were only satisfied by fulfilling their own moralities and institution.

Peloma reached the window and watched the yard furtively. It seemed to be calm and at peace, yet the heavy fog had still covered everywhere since last night, limiting the sight. She turned back and sat beside Sarah. It was almost two days that none of them had slept, but the semi- quietness provided them the chance of quick rest. Astera was sitting next to Hana in the basement, praying undertone. Daniel Herbod, the father of the family, had returned early that morning from a trip with no achievement. He couldn't find a middleman for transferring Hana. Frustrated with all closed door in his life, he was taking a nap on the coach on the second floor.

Peloma: "I feel uneasy; I can't calm myself down."

Sarah looked at her and rested Peloma's head on her shoulder. She touched her sister's hair and said: "Everything's gonna be all right, everything's gonna be all right …"

Peloma: "I always have this dream that our life is fine again. I don't believe that we would face any serious problem."

Sarah: "I know. That's why we're all doing our best."

Peloma: "Any news from Martin?"

Sarah breathed heavily. "No news…"

Peloma: "What should we do? Should we go after him?"

Sarah: "Not now. Not until we are sure about Hana's safety."

Peloma looked into her sister's Middle Eastern beauty, she was about to say something but then decided not to. They could hear Mr. Herbod's footsteps, so she went towards him.

Daniel Herbod was a tall man, with hair that had turned white during these years, but were still luxuriant like his youth. He was thin and since he hadn't shaved, his grey mustache and beard, made him look older.

As he came down the stairs, the girls held him tight. They sat on an old, worn-out sofa, while Peloma brought three hot cups of tea. Daniel was talking to them, and his deep, manly voice gave his daughters constant indescribable serenity.

He told them about his trip and how frustrating it felt when he couldn't find the right person for Hana's travel and safety.

Mr. Herbod: "There's no time to waste. We've been living here for too long, and there's no good in staying here any longer. The neighbors might have seen Hana, and we cannot trust anyone."

Sara: "Why don't you call the main branch of the resistance? They can help us."

Herbod looked at her daughter with a meaningful silence.

Sarah went on: "The past is the past. Right now, they might be able to find a way out for us."

Peloma was astounded, listening to them in utter confusion not knowing what they were talking about.

Herbod: "We have talked about this before, Sarah. Losing my brother was enough for me, and that suffices me not to want to see Heber anymore."

Heber… Heber… the name rang a bell with Peloma, but her mind was too exhausted and engaged that she couldn't recall him.

Sarah: "Even the southern Europe resistance is connected and gets help from him. You were once best friends, how come you can't get help from him only once, for Hana!"

Herbod: "It's more complicated and more profound that you can imagine Sarah, trouble, and danger is everywhere he goes. How can I risk my dearest's life and hand Hana over to him?"

Herbod: "Many years ago, when Benjamin got killed, I decided to put Adam away forever to protect my family from any danger. Is it so hard for you to understand it, Sarah?"

Sarah: "I know the influence of Uncle Benjamin's death was so deep and negative on you. He was young and strong, but you can't blame Adam for it. You should accept the truth father."

Herbod: "No, I won't accept, I just want to forget it. Thinking about it makes me extremely sad. Why must a young man like him die for Adam Heber's sake? Why really?"

Sarah: "He himself chose his path, it was his own will."

Herbod leaned back on the sofa and stared at the ceiling.

Sarah: "Father… Baldino was here…"

Herbod was startled, hearing the name and yelled: "You let that dangerous man in? In my house? How did he know here? Oh, my goodness, what did he want?"

Sarah said with serenity: "I'm a member of the Spanish Resistance."

Herbod was squirming in rage and terror. He yelled: "You stubborn girl, what have you done?"

Sarah stood up and said. "Of course I know. Why should I remain quiet when the world is filled with oppression and injustice?"

Hearing the quarrel, Astera ran into the room and said: "What's happening? Why are you shouting?"

Herbod's face was red with rage; he turned to his wife and asked: "Astera, did you know Sarah has joined the resistance?"

Astera looked at Sarah with her eyes wide open: "No…"

She was speechless and wished it were just a dream.

Herbod was walking up and down the room: "We have to leave; pack your things, whatever that is necessary." And went to the door. He held the handle, turned to Sarah and said: "You single-handedly destroyed our family."

As Herbod opened the door to go out for gathering their stuff at a corner of the yard, he faced a man on the other side of the door who was about to knock. The man was in army uniform and made Herbod breathless; a heavy silence filled the air. After a few seconds, Herbod asked: "How can I help you, sir?"

The man looked inside the house, then turned his look to Herbod calmly and said: "We have to talk, very urgent."

Herbod: "what should we talk about?"

The man: "I'm Major Pablo Alvarez, the executive administrator in the 16th army established in northern Spain. Can I come in?"

Herbod looked at his family and let him in. Sarah took the pocket pistols from the drawer and strapped it under her clothes.

Seeing Peloma, both recognized each other. Alvarez stood aside politely and said: "I received a prompt message from the Execution Squad, for sending a team of investigators to this house. Your name was familiar; I had seen it on car documents this lady showed me, you must remember that night, near the lighthouse… "

Sarah was standing behind Alvarez, her hand was clenching the colt tighter, and she was ready to shot him in case of any misbehave. Herbod stood beside his hunting rifle and was ready for the worst case. Alvarez moved his hand towards his waist, and it was enough for Sarah and Daniel to aim their guns at him in the blink of an eye. Alvarez stopped as adrenaline shot through him.

Alvarez: "I just want to give the letter I've received."

Herbod nodded and signaled Astera to stay with Hana. Alvarez took the letter and handed it to Herbod cautiously.

Alvarez: "As you see, it's from Jose Martinez, a secret service administrator who is suspicious about your family. I think they've found out about your daughter whom you kept alive."

Hearing Martinez's name, Peloma said with anger: "Actually that dirty pig did it …"

Alvarez: "We have to hurry; I received this letter by midnight and tried to reach and warn you about the investigation team presence. I don't know when they will arrive, but they're coming. If you want to leave, it's time."

Herbod looked at Sarah and said: "Lower your gun." He put his rifle down and moved quickly to the underground hideout. Sarah turned to Peloma and said: "Go to the garage and prepare the van."

Peloma ran to the van. As she was about to start the car, she heard something. Some cars stopped right near their house. Peloma reached the garage window and noticed a few army jeeps, parking near the house.

Peloma went back to the house from the garage back door to inform others, but her father and Sarah were already aware of their presence. Alvarez looked through the window and said: "Damn it, they're here…"

Daniel ran towards the basement once more but hit the old table so harsh that all teacups dropped and broke. He informed Astera about investigation team's presence and asked her to stay in the shelter in silence. Then he shut the door behind him and covered it with an old rug. Alvarez went into the room and helped him to place the heavy table over the hatch.

Herbod looked at the major; he knew that Alvarez couldn't do anything more. Otherwise, he could easily sacrifice them for his own good. Also, his behavior and concern made them trust him somehow.

There was a rapid knock on the door. A soldier shouted: "Open the door!"

As Sarah was opening the door, a group of soldiers pushed it and entered the home forcibly. Behind them, a fat lieutenant, entered the hall, holding a gun in his hand. Without looking at the Herbod family, he glanced around the house and ordered his soldiers to search the house.

Herbod stepped forward and asked: "What is the matter, sir?"

He looked at Herbod arrogantly and said: "You would better hand over the handicapped one you've hidden here."

Herbod: "I don't know what you are talking about; we don't have a handicapped here!"

The lieutenant shook his head and said: "Soon we'll see." and lighted a cigarette.

Right at that moment, Alvarez came out of the room, which was right in front of the door. He was a high-ranking major and seeing him; soldiers stood at attention. Alvarez asked them to be at ease. Though the lieutenant was older than Alvarez, he had a lower ranking which forced him to drop his cigarette and stand at attention.

Alvarez pretended to be in ignorance and asked: "What are you doing here?"

Lieutenant, still at attention said: "We're ordered to search this house by the execution squad of the 16th army."

"I'm here for it, and I'll take care of that myself. You'd better take your team out of here."

Suddenly a voice came from the door and filled the room. "According to the law of free Europe, the secret service's command is prior to those of an army officer, so I am going to scour this house. By the way, may I ask what you are doing here during office hours, Major?"

Peloma was frozen. Jose Martinez had come to follow the case in person. Now, he was standing at the door, wiping his colt with a blue handkerchief. He puffed at his colt and placed it back in its sheath. With a fake smile on his face, he entered the house and stood very close to Alvarez. He looked him right in the eyes and said: "Well, I'm waiting. Why are you here early in the morning, while you must be at your office, major?" Staring at him with his wolfish eyes.

The very first thought came to Alvarez's mind was to hold him hostage, but changed his mind immediately. With a dozen soldiers present at the scene, that wouldn't end up well. He looked back at diabolical Martinez and replied: "I don't see any necessity to explain it to a compeer."

Jose Martinez was losing his temper. He always uttered word faster in such conditions: "According to the special decree of the army, secret service officers are prior to their compeer in the military, and you must know it. Now, you will answer my question, or I will arrest you right here, right now."

The fat lieutenant gulped his saliva; he never imagined a simple investigation would get so screwed up.

Suddenly Peloma said: "He's my fiancé. He's here to accompany my father to the headquarter to get permission for moving from this house."

Sarah, Herbod and Pablo Alvarez look at Peloma, but Martinez even didn't bother himself to look at her. To him, it was all disgusting words. He spat and turned to Alvarez: "Such a shame in the military! One of us is in love with an Asian migrant..."

Alvarez: "Beware of what you're saying, major."

Martinez receded a bit, but he was very suspicious of them. He dragged an old chair closer and sat backward on it. He noticed the pieces of broken cups and said with a grin: "You were in a hurry early in the morning!" and then ordered the fat officer to search the house carefully. Herbods were under great pressure and stress. All they had done to protect Hana could be lost at any moment. Peloma frowned: "I explained everything to you; I have already told you my sister passed away two years ago. You even called that hospital."

Martinez: "Your words didn't convince me and the documents were fake. The doctor who issued her death certificate was later accused of conspiracy and combating the Neo-Nazi government and was executed to a death squad."

Peloma said with hatred: "Why do you seek a young child's life?"

Martinez's stood up with his face filled with rage and shouted: "Because that's our ideology and I executed my own brother, why should I care about your infirm sister's life?"

At that very moment, a soldier entered the room and said: "Sir, there's something you should see." And pointed to the other room, where Astera and Hana were hiding. Herbod looked at Sarah, made her understand that it was time for taking action. They had to start shooting them rapidly.

Martinez went towards the room with greed. There were three soldiers and one of them managed to find the entrance to hidey-hole. Astera and Hana were hiding right behind that hatch, and soon they would face their fate.

Peloma implored Alvarez with her look, but he could do nothing either. Martinez stroke the door with his jackboots several times: "Well... what is this?"

Herbod tried to have self-control and replied smoothly: "A cellar which we haven't used for a long time."

Martinez shouted furiously: "Open it, now."

Herbod prayed that Astera hadn't forgotten to lock the door from the inside. He tried to open it, but the door didn't budge. He was a bit at ease and tried once more with anxiety, but it didn't work.

Sarah entered the room, and Peloma stood behind her. She was ready to shoot Martinez and any soldier on her way at her father's signal. Sarah knew she would get killed, but she and her father had made up their minds.

Martinez kicked Herbod aside. Too excited about his important detection, he seized one of soldiers' automatic gun and aimed it at the hatch.

Herbod yelled: "No!"

Martinez was laughing wickedly, releasing the breechblock when Alvarez attacked him and knocked him down right before he could shoot. Astera and Hana were in the cellar which looked like a big grave, and without a doubt, they would be killed in his shootings.

In a blink of an eye, a set of events took place, which was weird and bizarre to everyone. Martinez managed to shoot, but as Alvarez jumped over him, he had lost his balance, shot and killed two of his soldiers. Hearing the gunfire, the fat lieutenant and other soldiers rushed into the room, but Sarah started shooting and bridled them for some seconds. Then soldiers opened fire on them in return and pieces of walls and doors were thrown everywhere.

Alvarez punched Martinez in the face and took away his machine gun. Martinez's face was red with rage and yelled: "You traitorous pigs!"

In the midst of chaos, Peloma was beside herself. At first, she felt like being shot by a bullet, since she could see the house and its surroundings with all details from 100 feet above. She thought she was dead and was flying up in the sky, but then she realized that something was happening, something which was only in her mind, until that day.

She could see the army jeeps in front of the house, and two black flying machines, which were landing in the backyard. She had an unbelievable dominate over every details, feeling everything around her, water drops forming the fog and the slow touch of the wind on her face. She had no flesh, but in that darkness, Peloma could see everything so clearly. A part of her mind was engaged with the happening in the house. Without looking inside, she could feel where the people and objects are; even more lucid and fluent than the time she saw them with her eyes.

She could see Hana, clinging to Astra in fear. The rage rooted deep in her grew and Peloma was able to see how the wind inside the house was hitting the soldiers to the walls. A purposive hurricane was running like a bolting horse, victimizing the soldiers. Then, the back wall of the house cracked with a grievous sound, and a surge of rain and wind surrounded Martinez, thrust him into the sky as if he was as light as a feather. His very last scream was when the wind pounded him to the ground from 40 feet above, smashing his head on the rocks outside.

A dazzling light awakened Peloma. When she opened her eyes, she was in Heber's arms. "Calm down, just calm down," he was repeating in her ear.

The wind was still blowing, but less strong and Peloma was looking around in surprise. As if, an explosion had happened indoor, everything was smashed and broken. Half of the roof was gone, and broken pieces were outside the house in the distance.

Alvarez was stuck to the ground under Robert's power and was nearly suffocated by the pressure. Two or three soldiers dragged themselves to the door and ran away.

Baldino took hold of his chapeau so that the wind would not blow it away. He was standing beside Helena, where the building had collapsed and was looking at it, astonished. Sarah ran to Mr. Herbod and put his head on her lap. Martinez's blow had injured his ribs.

Adam held Peloma's face in front of his: "Look at me, everything is over. Just calm down. We're here to take you away."

Herbod pointed to Alvarez and with a fainted voice, in pain, asked Robert to let him go.

Robert took the subdue power away from Alvarez, and now he could breathe. Sarah took a soft part of the smashed coach, placed it under Herbod's head, and went to Astera and Hana. She looked at Alvarez and Robert: "Could you open this door?"

Alvarez was still rubbing his neck: "I don't think so."

Sarah shouted: "Mom? Open the door!" However, she got no response.

Robert came forward, put his sword in the crack of the cellar hatch, and with a slight move, dragged the door from its frame. Astera and Hana were clinging to each other and could not move out of terror. Sarah jumped in and tried to help them out of there. Baldino entered from the main door. Herbod said in sad and exhausted tone: "I don't know whether to be thankful or complainant. Thanks, anyway..."

Baldino nodded and went to Heber. It seemed tiff and acrimony between Herbod and Adam still existed, but at those moments of panic and distress, there was nothing to talk about. Adam turned to Herbod: "Daniel, we're here to help you. When David told me about your dangerous situation, we took quick action and hurried here." then looked around: "this house is no longer habitable, nor safe. Soon the army would be here again, bringing more forces. Please come with us to the White Pasture. Everyone would be safe there, and later we can talk more detailed."

Herbod was in pain: "As it seems we have no other choice."

Peloma was too shocked to pay attention to her surroundings, and it was the first time since all that chaos when Robert could see Helena with a bit of peace of mind. When their eyes met, they waved hands to each other and then looked back at the scene of the struggle.

Adam, with Robert and Baldino's assistant, carried the Herbods in the P-500, sending them over to the White Pasture. However, Adam and Robert had to get ready for flying to Poland on the P-1. The only one, remaining was Juan Pablo Alvarez who had saved Hana twice. Baldino and Alvarez knew each other afar, and Baldino's words about him convinced Adam. Saying that he was an army major and a member of the Spanish Resistance made Adam invite him to go with them. But the major refused: "Now that they know about me, they would come for my family and me. I'd better go to my old mother in Murcia State; then I try to contact the remaining members in the south. Maybe we could meet again."

Adam: "I wish you pass this hazardous road safely. We're in such a hurry that we can't miss two or three hours riding you there. Also, I know times matters to you, and you must meet your mother very soon. Let's say goodbye and hope to see you in the future."

The brave Alvarez disappeared in the fog, just the way he had come through it in the morning. As Peloma moved away, that heavy fog covering the San Sebastian neighborhood was gone and just then the amount of the ruins was revealed to the inhabitants of that area. Soon, security agents would rush into that place, to find out the secret behind that hazy, foggy morning.

Adam and Robert headed towards Alucine Prison in Poland to rescue the last members of the Half Dream Order circle, without wasting time.

CHAPTER TWENTY-FOUR
CLOSE ENCOUNTER

Robert kept on thinking about Helena during the trip. He asked about her from Adam several times and Adam, explained patiently, how he had gone to Vietnam to return her. He explained how they met unexpectedly, about locals help and their long-lasting friendship. He talked about Helena and her grief, which was healing, with his help. However, more than anything else, Adam was focused on what they were about to encounter and was flying at high speed to arrive before the dawn.

The Alucine prison was located somewhere in Belovezhskaya Pushcha forest, near former Belarus's border. Heber found that dreadful place, which was supposedly made for post-war gangsters, with difficulty. No lights diffused from it and no possibility of tracing it existed. Adam had to pass the longitude of Lesna Prawa River and look for that terrifying place. It didn't take him too long to find some traces of it in the darkness, so he landed the P-1 far from the Alucine prison and reviewed their plans with Robert once more.

It was simple; they had to reach the southern wall of the prison before the sunrise. Fortunately, the Polish Resistance had provided them the likely location of twin's cell, but there was a negative point in it. They found out that the twins were relocated every month, and were in solitary confinement in special parts with the least possibility of contact or aid from guards. Yet, they were always kept in the southern part of the prison intentionally, so that stink of sewage would offend the two.

Adam: "In our last communication, I asked Nadia to make small fire orbs by the end of the second night and send them out from the hatch above her cell."

Robert gave him a reproachful look: "And this is your bold plan, huh? What if her cell does not have a hatch, then how can she send us orbs? How on earth is she supposed to know when to start, while she is locked in the darkness? What will happen to her brother?"

Adam: "Well, we had no other option. What do you expect from me? At least we have a chance to find them faster. Anyway, we have to be ready for facing and fighting the guards. When we find Nadia, we can search the cells next to hers; they always keep them next to each other, for torturing them even more."

Robert; "Damn it. Are you kidding me? You risked Philip's life and mine just to tell her to send fireballs out of that fucking hatch?"

Adam replied solemnly: "That was not all, Robert. I talked to her, introduced myself and gained her trust. Then I taught her how to create a stable fireball and guide it. All these subjects mattered to me a lot. And about Alexi, I asked about him but, he is not feeling well enough to assist us in the escape."

Robert said desperately: "We cannot do this, we will lose everything, Adam."

Adam: "No, it's not how you think. I'm sure Nadia can make it. We will wait for the signals and then we should destroy the wall in silence and enter. There you'll incapacitate everyone with your forces, and we can leave just the way we went in. But if she doesn't send us any signals, we'll do the same and find them ourselves!"

Robert: "and what if I can't incapacitate all guards?"

Adam: "The answer is simple, we'll be fucked off!"

Robert turned away as he didn't want to see Adam's face in such condition. He could not believe how naive the old man was. As he turned his head, he saw a giant, black animal very close to him. He could even see the steam of its breath in the darkness.

Robert asked Adam quietly: "What the hell is this?"

Adam came forward cautiously: "I guess it's a bison."

Robert seized his sword, but Adam placed his hand over his and prevented him from taking any extra action. He went closer and reached bison's snout. He touched it gently and said: "Here is their home Robert."

Then said softly: "Good girl, go away. We won't hurt you, and you don't hurt us as well."

Robert: "You recognized her gender in such deep darkness?"

Adam shook his head: "No, but that small calf following her, told me it's a she."

In a few moments, the bison turned away and left them.

Robert said ironically: "she understood what you said."

Adam made sure that it is gone, then looked at Robert: "No."

Robert: "So, you were talking to her aleatory, and it left?"

Adam: "Exactly. For communicating with animals, you don't have to understand each other's language. Just be a human and respect each and every living soul in the body of nature. This is what you should learn the best before knowing how to use your forces." And smiled at him.

Robert: "You're driving me crazy. Let's get it done; I do need a one-week sleep."

Adam looked at the sky above: "I do agree."

They made their way towards the prison's tall walls. Unlike any other prison that has different protective layers, this one had just walls, thick, tall walls made of stone with chains of watchtowers close to one another for the safety of the place. They approached the southern wall to have a full view of the surroundings. This part of the prison had only one watchtower, and at first, they couldn't see the guard inside it. After a while, they were able to notice the guard napping in the corner of the watchtower, leaving that part of the prison off guard to any raid.

They were sitting there for a while when suddenly Robert was startled by seeing a small orb up on the wall, 10 feet away from the main wall, in the darkness. It didn't look like fire, but was coming out of a hatch above the walls and went off after a short while. This cycle kept on happening; it was time for the operation.

Adam stood up and whispered: "Could you keep the guard unconscious?"

Robert: "I'll try my best." And raised his hand and incapacitated the guard easily. They went forward to destroy that part of the wall right beneath the place where fireballs were coming from. Robert placed the point of his sword midst the thick stones, splitting them with a cracking sound. On the other side of that giant wall, there was an enclosure, which must have been the prison's courtyard.

They had moved the remnants outside and made sure that the rest of guards in another turret would not notice their entrance. As a matter of fact, it was lost amongst the deep shadows.

Before them, there was a fortress-like tower with tall walls, where the balls were coming from a hatch, embedded in it. They believed that Nadia must have been imprisoned somewhere on the second floor there. Slowly, they approached a door, opened it and entered a small corridor, separated from the main part of the prison by a counter-insurgency system. Two guards were sitting there, one was reading a newspaper, and the other was cleaning his gun.

Passing them was an easy as pie; as Robert incapacitated them as he did before. He kept his left hand before his chest and made anyone in his way, unconscious with the power of his mind. He could feel the number of the people he incapacitated, and suddenly he felt the number had gotten larger; they were getting close to that part of the prison where countless prisoners were kept.

Adam took the passkey from the table and went up to the second floor. It was considerably unprotected, and as they reached the second floor, Adam opened the first cell; no one was in there. He was about to take the key out of the keyhole when suddenly a red ball crawled out, from beneath the door, three cells away from them, and was floating in the air.

Robert pointed to the ball and told Adam with a smile: "There it is!"

But Adam didn't move. He looked at Robert: "Do you have control over your forces?"

Robert contorted his face with wonder: "I don't get you."

Adam: "It was clear. Can you incapacitate people selectively?"

Robert: "I don't think I can. At a certain distance, they will all be affected. Why?"

The ball faded out slowly, and another one showed up.

Adam: "I guess we're in trouble."

Robert didn't get his point, stepped forward: "Every living being here, is under my will, I can feel them."

Adam shook his head: "Everyone but not the one who is waiting for us inside that cell."

Robert was agitated and went closer, but Adam implored him in a low tone: "please come back, we have to leave here immediately."

Robert raised his hand with wonder. He was just two or three steps away from the cell, very close to Nadia and Alexi and couldn't help looking inside the cell before leaving there. He was standing there with hesitation between Adam's warning and the craving to reach the cell. The second ball faded, and the third one just came out.

Adam knew that in this cat-and-mouse game, they would be the prey. As the third fireball turned cold and vanished, the lights in that part of the building went off. Robert and Adam were looking around in utter shock and could see nothing but fading fireball and lightning from Robert's sword.

Robert hesitated, looked at the door and called in a low tone: "Nadia we're here. Can you hear me?"

The door fell open with a friction sound, as the last spark of the third ball was fading away. An amber ray of light covered the iron door, getting stronger at each moment as if the light source was getting closer to the door. Robert, apprehensive, was waiting to face that final moment.

Shagad, Adam Heber's greatest foe, came out of the cell slowly, in heavy steps. At that terrifying moment, there was no place for doubt. They had acted so naively. Robert couldn't believe he was face to face with him with a latched brain. He stepped back like an idiot.

The amber light was coming out of Shagad's robust, stupendous body and floating balls of light were lightening the room. The Serpent King was standing there, while he had tricked them in the worst possible way. Robert and Adam had lost hope like preys in the grip of hunter's claw.

Shagad was wearing a victorious smile and in a resonating voice said: "I expected more of you, Heber. You have come to fight a dragon with this clumsy mosquito?"

Talking about Robert, Shagad didn't even bother to take a look at him.

Adam: "I'm not here to fight you. But sometimes a mosquito can get over things, out of dragon's power. And besides, I see no dragon here."

Now Robert could see the nightmare of his coevals very closely.

His skin was made of steel; a mountainous figure, with amber glowing streaks.

He was so scary that its terror could penetrate into one's bones. On each shoulder, he had a viper, writhing and hissing in the air. At first, Robert thought he keeps them as pets on his stout shoulders. But as one of them attacked him, he found out they have grown on his body like a tree. Shagad used a cloak which serpents could be seen moving freely over his shoulder to terrorize and panic others even more.

Shagad turned his head: "I don't know why we should fight, Heber? Ha? I want the Taarnaar. Just give it to me and live the rest of your life in the world I've created and enjoy its blessings. You know you have lost this war, and I was the conqueror of the final battle. You couldn't even prevent it from happening Heber."

Adam had a piercing look at his wicked enemy: "the hands of a demon like you would never touch the Taarnaar again."

Shagad said in repulsive tone: "Meligulia5 is just a deceit. You still believe Mother of life has chosen you to preserve the best souls for Meligulia? Your master fooled you, just the way he was fooled. In his last days, before transferring his forces to you, Felokimoos, realized that all his life, he had faith in an absurd belief …"

For the first time ever, Adam put aside politeness and interrupted Shagad: "you are mad because though Felokimoos is no longer alive, his student still denies what you say, right? If Meligulia doesn't exist, why are you craving for the Taarnaar?"

Shagad:"Stop it, you old man! You don't even know what you're doing. We have been enemies for years, without knowing the reason behind it."

Adam: "I guess you have lost your memory Shagad. Don't you remember how you betrayed Felokimoos, after all, he had done for you? You just turned your back on him ungratefully."

Shagad: "He was just a stupid old man with rusty beliefs. I had no idea why I had to stay in his school and worse than that why instead of me, he chose you as his successor and offered you

---

5 Meli'ghu'e lia - meligulia

the whole power that once belonged to me? However, the power that you and your stupid master possess is like a lake, comparing to the ocean of my new powers."

Adam: "you know the answer to your question, better than anyone else. Look at the snakes growing on your shoulders or the huge mess you caused until now. He had realized your true nature; he knew that you are a wolf in sheep's clothing. He didn't even let you keep the Taarnaar and took it back from you."

As if being hit with an invisible quirt, Shagad grimaced. Robert could see the angrier he got, the more glowing the amber streaks became.

Shagad: "presence of an insidious person like you separated us! I have to confess he was acting foolishly and now, with my own rules in my life, even uttering the word "master" while addressing Felokimoos makes me laugh! I know his shattered soul lives in the Taarnarr. I wish he could see how powerful I've become and how I'm going to send his dearest back to him; there you can join him, count the seconds as long as I live and wait until you join that Meligulia, though it doesn't exist at all."

Adam: "Meligulia doesn't matter to me, at least now. I'm living in a world that I love it, but you have just ruined it in the worse possible way. I'll do anything in my power to take what you've stolen from the people back.

You let the magic and other forces into this world, which was too soon. We could live our own way of living, and there was no need to make an effort for saving others. You broke your oath and betrayed Felokimoos. Your punishment is to be destroyed, and not a single name shall remain from you in this world; people should get rid of you forever."

Robert was standing between the two superhuman and each time one of them started to talk, he turned towards him, just like a tennis ball passing from one player to another. He couldn't understand what they were talking about, all he got was that both were Felokimoos's students who had learned hidden knowledge from him, but Shagad was the first to use his learnings, while it was illegal until an uncertain point in time.

He had passed the red lines and made the two old friends stand against each other. Now each of them belonged to different schools, without having the power to destroy one another. However, Shagad was way better in using the forbidden forces and used his initiative, while Adam had spent the post-war years and the next fifteen years to harness Shagad's loose powers.

Shagad took a step back and smiled while looking down: "don't play dumb with me Heber. I will have it, no matter you give it to me or not. But in return for the favor, you did to me before; I'd like to share my new kingdom with you. You see, we're superior to them, why shouldn't we be the lord and they wouldn't be our servants? Those who promoted racism kill and crush their own kind with no mercy. Standing in my way, you are only making it a bit difficult for me, just a bit..." and showed the small amount exuberantly using his thumb and index finger.

Adam was sure that Shagad didn't know about his plans. He had kept them so secretive that even he, had to search the mazes at the back of his mind for reviewing them. He had buried them in the deep shafts of his mind while none of his friends and fellows were aware of the plans. Adam was afraid of one thing; he knew Shagad very well if he found out about the plan, Heber's last hope to pacify and stabilization in the world would be gone for good.

The reason why Adam and Robert were still alive in such a terrifying morning was exactly due to Shagad's ignorance, as he believed Adam could still use his numerous powers for warding off his attacks.

Adam was trapped in a small hall, while a part of his intellect was analyzing the path to scape his great foe. Adam was trying to keep calm and hide his fear from Shagad's alert mind. Sooner or later, Shagad would find out about his Achilles' heel, and that would suffice him to break them by his devastating power with no hesitation.

Turning his back to Robert, Shagad ignored him and started to walk in the corridor. He wanted to make sure that Adam is not going to hand the Taarnaar over to him and hit Adam's weary mind with a deadly blow, stronger than ever before. "I know you're here for the twins and also the dog you left in the Gaalve was roaming around exceedingly." Said Shagad with a wicked smile. Adam got what he meant. Shagad had seized that part of Phillip's mind which was left in Gaalve, tracked them down and found out whom they had talked to and what their propose was. Shagad didn't wait for Adam's response and stroke his broken soul harder. "I arrived here earlier than you. I had no idea why the two kids must matter to you. Killing them sufficed me. And you wouldn't reach them anymore."

He added mischievously: "I fed my serpents with their brain."

And looked at Adam attentively to see the impact of the grievous news.

Adam tried to keep calm, though he was broken inside. Without the twins, his plans would face serious trouble. He had to wait for so long to find people similar to them. But that would be too late to fight Shagad's loose forces.

Robert: "You killed them? You evil!"

Adam interrupted Robert: "Be quiet, Robert."

Shaged looked at Robert for the first time since they had met and was still angry with his resistance against fake dream he had set to break into Robert's mind for digging up information two nights ago. As their eyes met, Robert realized why Philip and Adam, do not count him a minor enemy.

It was then when Robert felt loose and was about to be swallowed by the serpents on Shagad's shoulders. Shagad's eyes cast shattering fear over every human being, which was the result of his strong will. Robert's whole power was nothing but a childish game comparing to Shagad's.

Robert was grappling with fear and hesitation when he heard Adam talking to him inside his mind, out of Shagad's sharp eyes. Robert could hear Adam clearly, but he looked at Adam to make sure about it. Adam was saying: "When he was at a certain distance from us, hit the floor with your sword so that the building collapse. It is our only way out."

Robert nodded slowly to show he got the message. But Shagad didn't go too far, just like a lion playing with its prey, before slaying it.

Adam was waiting, and as Shagad turned back, he signaled Robert and both ran into the first cell. Shagad returned and said: "You've chosen an undesirable place to die in." He walked quickly towards the cell, and a sword, made of darkness appeared in his hand, hitting anyone on his way with deadly sword-stroke. As he went closer, Robert got out of the cell and ran towards him; hitting him in the chest with the Storm rage. His sword was crushed and broken into pieces, but Shagad wasn't even scratched. He grabbed Robert by the throat, with hatred in his eye, lifted him from the ground and strangled him in a way that blood gushed out from his nose and mouth. He was left with no vital signs before he could even shout.

All at once, a dazzling light illuminated the surroundings and the building collapsed with a booming sound. Immediately, Shagad realized he had destroyed Robert's shadow. Adam and Robert made the best of this chance and jumped off the building from 10 feet high, while the building collapsed on Shagad. They had enough time to get away from the predicament, so they ran towards the flying machine in the darkness.

Behind and far from them, Shagad roared angrily, made his way out of a wall, and broke it like a blade of grass. Prison's area was crawling with his guards, and his hungry wolves, blind with rage, were chasing Adam and Robert.

Robert sent a surge of light behind like a whip, cutting down the trees and leaving piles of lumber on the enemy's way. Escaping Shagad was a miracle, but Adam knew that he was not there, just for murdering which gave them the chance to escape serpent king. They flew on the P-1 at highest speed.

Shagad, enraged by their flee, slew two of his guards with the dark sword. The Alucine battle was over, without having any accomplishment for either side. Adam had lost his two valuable men, and Philip was also held captive in the Gaalve by the Dark Lord of that realm. They had to return to the White Pasture, while Adam was thinking of a way to recompense the loss occurred in his plan.

He was profoundly despondent and sorrowful. He couldn't save Nadia and Alexi and was imagining how Shagad must have tortured them mercilessly and with cruelty, before murdering them. Adam's silver tears rolled down his face. It was the first time Robert saw him crying…

CHAPTER TWENTY-FIVE
THE FOX OF POLAND

As soon as Nadia swallowed the yellow pill, she felt dizzy. She could feel sweet dumbness which she was longing for. She dragged herself to a corner of the cell and wearied, fell asleep immediately.

The very first feeling she had was well-being, her eye wound was gone, and after three constant years of agony, it was the only time she was free from mental and physical pain, in a peaceful place. Her surrounding was a glass room that looked like a hollow globe, full of moving fire streaks. Some parts of it got thin at a time that Nadia thought it might notch, but a stream of cold, bright fire flowed over it and covered the area smoothly.

She could see a big image outside as if two people were talking, but it was not explicit. One of them was holding a big, green shining object like a sun before the wall and after a while, the wall got entirely luminous. Nadia could no longer see behind the wall. Suddenly, an object which wasn't there up to that moment started shaking in the middle of the room.

The image of an old man started to shape, got more vivid, and stopped shaking. The old man in the room, looked at her: "Hello, Nadia. Do not fear. I won't hurt you as others did. You must remember me; I'm Adam Heber, your childhood master." Nadia nodded two times; she didn't know whether to talk or not, so she just confirmed with a head nod. The old man used to have long black hair, but it turned as white as snow now. His hairline had also receded, while the remaining hair was smooth and Nadia was wondering that the beauty and elegance of those grey eyes, was ignored due to his long, black hair.

Adam: "I'm happy that you remember me. I have to confess that I've aged a bit… by the way, I'm so lucky to see you here. I knew you were up to something but didn't expect you to receive this connection truly."

Nadia: "I don't get all these things… I don't know how I reached here. Where am I now?"

Adam: "Right now, you're in a part of the Gaalve which is not under our control. Nothing is arbitrary in here, but some of your friends outside here made our connection with dedication and sacrifice. They can't keep this connection stable for so long, so let's get right to the point.

We know you and your brother, Alexi are imprisoned. How is he doing?"

Nadia sat in a corner: "He is not good really, but we're both alive."

Adam: "Of course, of course, and it's so nice. I tried many times before to get in touch with you, but you were not prepared to make it."

Nadia was amazed: "Yes, exactly, I could hear some voices in my head, but I couldn't realize what they were saying."

Adam: "Anyway, the connection is made now; we don't have much time. My friends and I will come to save you."

Nadia: "When?"

Adam: "we will reach you in forty-eight hours. Now listen to me carefully. The prison, in which you and your brother are, is guarded closely and our undercover man couldn't be of much help to your scape, so I decided to do this mission in person. Two nights from now, you should make fireballs and send them out of the hatch on the ceiling near the dawn so that I can get where they exactly keep you; leave the rest of it to us."

Nadia was flustered: "I don't know how to do that! I mean how to move them."

Adam went closer and sat before Nadia: "Give me your hand." Nadia placed her hand on Adam's: "You must pay attention to the ball you make. When you perceived its dimension entirety, you can direct it with pressure. Let's try it…"

Nadia, made a fireball, using her empty hand. As Adam had just said, she was able to feel every fiery inch of it and moved the ball.

Adam: "as we are in your mind, we do not have limitations of the outside world. After this connection, try to make more balls and control them in the remaining forty-eight hours. It may be difficult at first, but practice makes perfect and also remember, finding you at the shortest time is very important to us. If you don't make it, finding Alexi would be so tough. Do you know where he is?

Nadia moved her attention from the ball: "Yes, he's two cells away from me. If you come into the hall from the main entrance, he is in the first cell."

Adam: "And do you know how many corridors end into the hall where you are?"

Nadia: "Yes. There are two, one at either end. Alexi is at one end, and I'm in the middle, but cells are too small, with no air conditioner. I guess they're trying to kill us slowly and gradually."

Adam squeezed Nadia's hand affectionately: "No, my dear daughter. Everything is going to be fine very soon, and you'll be released from this pain. I'm sorry I couldn't help you before. I had so much to do before this and not fulfilling them would make the rest of my work, meaningless. It is time for companions to get together. Let me tell you how proud I'm to live in a world where people like you live in it. If your parents were alive, they'd be proud of you and Alexi."

Her eyes were filled with tears but didn't let them trickle down her cheeks. Suddenly the luminosity in the corner of the room faded away. Adam returned and with a glance at the wall, found out the time of their short meeting was over.

Nadia stood up immediately and looked at the scene in surprise. The white sparkle was gone, the wall returned to its previous state and streams of cold fire covered it once more. Adam returned and looked at Nadia, trying to say something, but he decayed just the way he had appeared in the room.

As if an invisible hand grabbed her from the back, it pulled her out of that peaceful atmosphere. She was back in her cell again while a ball of fire was burning before her eyes. She was not dreaming this time, and she knew what she had seen was real. Nadia touched the bruise on her eye; the old pain was back once again. The chance given to her was until second dawn, so she started practicing the skills Adam taught her for guiding fireballs. She could see a spark of hope and was preparing to leave that hell.

She spent that whole day practicing until midnight. Nadia had no control over fireballs at first, but she was getting better gradually. After a long day of endeavor, she felt tired and sleepy.

On the other side of the Atlantic Ocean and with the help of Poland resistance, Adam had managed to choose the right time for connection. Things were concluding fine, before reaching the toughness.

Twenty-four hours after the first connection, Petrovic, who was sitting in his luxury office, faced an unexpected scene. The guards reported entrance of two black flying machines to the prison yard. Petrovic rushed out immediately; it was then when a tall, robust man got out of the machine. Neither Pterovic nor his guards had ever seen someone like him before. Jones, the security officer from the Northern Alliance, had recently left there which made Pterovic think they were back for another interrogation, but as the man stepped out of the machine, he encountered the worst nightmare of his life.

Strapping Shagad was standing there, staring at the rainy clouds, which had filled the sky above. His one look was enough to petrify despicable Petrovic.

Very quickly and without saying a single word, he led Shagad to his office and stood there with crossed arms, offering his chair to him.

Shagad sat down haughtily and waited for his guards to join him. Petrovic would break at any moment under his black look. Shagad didn't even bother himself to inform Heinrich Adler about his visit. He had found the reason behind Philip and Robert's presence in the Gaalve and was informed about the twins' existence.

In a short while, Shagad was standing behind Nadia's cell. She was still weary since last night and was lying on her dirty, dampened bed, when suddenly he opened the door, went straight to her, grabbed her by the neck, raised her from the bed and pushed her against the wall in rage.

The serpents on his shoulders were craving for Nadia's brain. Shagad penetrated her mind with his cold eyes. Breathing hardly under his grasp, Nadia disclosed her mind to Shagad, with no chance of resisting his will. Now Shagad could set his trap.

Their close encounter came to an end without a single word. Nadia was lying on the ground and could hardly breathe when Shagad left the room and beckoned to a guard to grab Nadia and drag her out of her cell. She could see another guard had already taken Alexi out of his cell, hauling him on the floor.

One of the flying machines in the prison yard was ready to take them to the Jung-Frau fortress. Shagad had decided to take care of them in a safe place in person. He would do anything to keep the twins out of Adam's reach. It was untimely to kill them, since he hadn't found the chance to elicit the whole data from her mind, regarding the Half-Dream order. He had to get prepared for welcoming the gatecrashers. Later, he would have enough time to deal with her.

Nadia could hear Shagad giving orders to his guards. He asked them to leave the southern wall unguarded so that his enemies could enter the prison with no barrier and difficulty; he ordered them not to interfere with them at all since he wanted to make sure that Adam would not give the Taarnaar back to him. He could enfetter him and soften his resistance through evil tricks.

They forced Nadia into one of the flying machines, which was bigger and was used for Shagad's guards. Alexi could see his twin after weeks. Her devastated and shattered look, shocked him: "Where are they taking us?"

Nadia: "I don't know. I just hope this nightmare would be over."

She lost her last ray of hope as they were leaving and her childhood master couldn't be of any help to them.

It was then when one of the prison's officers took an old, long-range transmitter out of his locker. First, he made sure that no one was around, then turned on the device with cautious: "Do you hear me? Can anybody hear me?"

A few seconds later, a voice could be heard: "Yes, audible and clear. Tell me your code."

Officer: "A2. Get me through Balzakich quickly."

"Please wait."

A few breathtaking moments passed when a woman answered: "Report."

Officer: "They're taking the twins away."

Balzakich: "How? Where is their destination?"

Officer: "In an advanced Thunderstorm. I guess it's a carrier."

There was silence for several seconds.

Balzakich: "Do you still have the magnetic bomb we gave you for the 'Deer' mission?"

Officer looked fluttered, and said: "Yes."

Balzakich: "Fix it under the cabin of the twin's flying machine. Make sure it is fully attached to its body."

The officer was standing there with his eyes wide open and couldn't believe his ears.

Officer: "But it was supposed to be used for a prearranged mission. Next week, the army generals will be here for a visit, and we can destroy them all, at once."

Balzakich: "That mission is no longer our priority. Roland, do it right now or shoot yourself in the head, you knucklehead."

Officer: "ok, ok! I'll do my best."

Roland turned the transmitter off. He couldn't carry it along, so he put it back in the locker, took the magnet bomb out and hid it under his army overcoat. He ran down the stairs and waited there for the right moment. While Jung-Frau guards were conveying their two prisoners, Roland reached the Thunderstorm. It was so enormous that no one could see the window which faced the yard. He switched on the disc-shaped bomb and held it close to the body of the flying machine, with agility. The bomb was attached to the machine successfully, and Roland speeded away from that area. As he was going back, he saw the twins were settled near the back door of the machine, on safe seats.

Roland hurried back to his room, turned on the transmitter and waited to report the exact route of the carrier. The Thunderstorm took off and flew away in silence. He pressed the function key: "A2 is reporting. Passengers headed towards the southwest. Do you copy?"

The man on the transmitter said: "Copy. Over."

Roland turned off the device and rested assured.

Far-off, a group, in partisan uniforms were riding old, gas motorbikes at high speed. A woman who had covered her face with a brown kerchief was at the forefront, holding a device in her hand, which showed the bomb's coordinates on the flying machine. The Thunderstorm was a few miles away from them, and as the radar indicated, it would pass them overhead. The woman modified their route as much she could to reach the Thunderstorm at the right time and place.

Ten minutes later, she saw her target in the distance. On her order, those who were riding in the forest stopped. She got off her motorcycle and pointed her radar at the flying machine. Although they had tried to anticipate its route, the machine was still far from them and deviating to the left side.

She was determined and pushed the bottom on the radar; a second later, the flying machine was surrounded by light and crashed. Balzakich said in a rough, solemn tone: "We should go to the crash zone before army men can find them."

The pilot was killed instantly when the bomb detonated, and the autopilot was controlling the plane, but since its crash was certain, the emergency hatches were unlatched, and the rest of the passengers were ejected by ejector seats. Alexi and Nadia, along with three others landed under a parachute canopy. Nadia was too confused to know what was going on and just realized their landing when she felt wind and raindrops on her face. The guards were in utter shock but due to their master's training, knew what to do.

Nadia landed on a tall branch of a tree while Alexi fell facedown to the muds.

It didn't take the Polish Resistance team of thirty, too long to find and kill the three Jung-Frau guards. They lost five people in the process, but at least they accomplished the mission assigned to them by the Poland resistance core. Balzakic knew that the Thunderstorm machines are equipped with parachute seats, so her plans proceeded.

Nadia could only hear vague voices of joy and pain. It was a tremendous achievement for The Polish Resistance over European Neo-Nazis, using smooth penetration of their spy, which led to the deliverance of two important members of the main Resistance; A task, which had to be fulfilled three years ago, but was postponed due to lack of organization and absurd negligence.

Eventually, three years of hard working and numerous sacrifices was fructified. But it was not over yet. A few days ago, they had lost their communication link with the resistance in the south of Europe, and they could not inform David Baldino of their successful mission.

On the other side, Shagad was waiting for Adam Heber in Alucine prison, setting up a trap, unaware of his significant loss.

Roland left the prison overnight to a safe house. Nadia and Alexi could rest at ease in Poland's fox lair, after three excruciating years.

CHAPTER TWENTY-SIX
THE DARK SEED

Wake up… wake up…

The sound was echoing in Philip's ear from afar. At one moment, when the time seemed to be still, he sat up and looked at the room in confusion, as if he was blown to the head. He thought he had been in a long sleep, so looked around closely to realize where he was. Philip tried to get up but lost his balance; He seized the bedsheets and dragged himself back to the bed.

As he was panting, he looked at the window. It was a day in autumn, and pale sunlight was beaming down the room. He listened carefully but everywhere was filled with silence. A few moments passed when he finally could stand up, leaning on the chair, beside his bed. He felt dizzy, but little by little regained his lost power to move.

He reached the window; it was cold and gloomy outside. The mountain before him was in the mist where the fog rolled down its body into the valley, in the distance.

He thought himself to be a seventeen-year-old boy, but gradually he could recall things. A bunch of sloppy memories invaded him; an old bus in a war-torn desert, a cold night in the debris of a bright city, excessive darkness and a continuous whistle echoing in his mind. A fall; fall from a ragged edge into a deep, dark valley. Adrift struggle to reach the lights above, a cursed rage which was tearing his body apart, a pair of eyes, as dark as the worst nightmares with the shattering look... convulsing from head to toe, he was wakeful again.

He turned to the right and stared at the figure in the mirror. His hair had turned gray, and his stout figure was unprecedentedly lean and haggard; he was touching his cheeks when a voice from outside the room grabbed his attention.

The voice came closer to the door, and a woman opened it and entered the room. She was talking to Kalahi when suddenly they both retreated into silence. Mariana looked at him in surprise and couldn't believe what she was seeing. Kalahi went forward: "Mr. Vince! You're awake!"

Mariana came closer and hugged Philip. Her slim body appeared to be stronger than his bony figure. She caressed Philip's face: "You're awake! I cannot believe it."

Philip was puzzled: "What happened to me? How long have I been sleeping?"

Mariana helped him sit on the bed: "Don't you remember?"

Philip shook his head.

Mariana: "You have been unconscious for a month."

Philip calmly glanced at her. The look in his eyes revealed that he had no idea about what he had been through. Adam Heber's right-hand man couldn't recall anything now. Mariana tried to make him lie down again, but Philip resisted. He wanted to leave that room as a thought was annoying him. He was facing a dilemma of duty and time.

Philip left the room in his pajamas and looked around from where he was standing. Robert was down the stairs, talking to Helena. Once he saw Philip, he ran upstairs and held him close, but Philip was defiant, with no reaction. Robert had a quizzical look at Mariana, but she had no idea what was going on either.

Robert: "Are you okay? Do you remember us?"

Philip: "I guess I'm alright. I remember something, and I know you. Where is Adam?"

Mariana: "He left a week ago, but we don't know where he went."

Philip: "Are we in the White Pasture?"

Robert: "Yes, safe and sound."

Philip: "We... we were in New Life City, do you remember?"

Robert: "Yes. We went to the Gaalve together. Do you recall anything about it?"

Philip shook his head and then whispered: "Gaalve..."

Robert: "We wanted to get in touch with Nadia. We went there together, you and I. You must remember it."

Hearing Nadia's name, Philip looked at Robert. His mind was free, and he knew where they had been.

Philip: "What happened next?"

Robert: "We made the connection Philip. Let's go to the main hall, and I'll explain everything to you."

Philip and Robert went down the stairs slowly. There were people in the hall who distracted Philip. He first met Nadia and Alexi, and behind them was Helena with her golden hair, Peloma with her black eyes and the old David Baldino. They were all in the room.

As Philip entered, everyone stood up, except David who was napping on a chair next to the fireplace. Nadia was in a brown leather dress, and her eye wound was healing. Alexi was also recovering and looked much better, though still a little bit anxious and down. Enduring prison condition had nearly shattered him. Talking to her old friends, Peloma was apart from her family. Helena was also there and had found her childhood love, Robert.

Philip was restless; he couldn't figure out what he was seeing is real or a deception. While he was captivated in the Gaalve, fake dreams were made to deceive him. He had been tortured to death and couldn't distinguish a dream from reality. Nadia came closer to him and grabbed his hand in hers. She knew her rescue was through Robert and Philip's devotion.

Philip looked at Nadia's round, bright face and her long braided hair down to her waist. Alexi was standing right behind them, watching him with enthusiasm.

227

In that past steady month, Robert had the chance to narrate his stories with his old schoolmates, while Philip was worried; his mind had been brutally damaged.

People in that room were pleased about his wakefulness, and he could also touch the great feeling of living among a big, adorable family.

David Baldino woke up with the commotion in the room, moved his fedora hat on his head and said: "My Goodness! Philip, you're awake!" He stood up, went to Philip and embraced him with kindness. Then he took a step back, looking at Philip proudly: "I knew you could redeem yourself."

Robert was standing further, looking at Philip's skinny body. He knew that the condition was not as good as what others believed. He remembered his last encounter with the serpent king. Although the Fox of Poland rescued Nadia and Alexi from the Serpent's hand, Adam Heber had lost his last gamble. Mr. & Mrs. Herbod entered the fortress and went straight to Philip. Seeing him in such a miserable condition was off-putting to Daniel. Since their arrival, he always visited Philip, and this time he was awake. His old friend, an important member of the Half-Dream Order and the one who was directly engaged in disclosing of some documents and names, where his role was to prevent the members from being arrested and tortured.

Philip's look met Daniel's, while he was standing next to Astera at the door and looking at him in surprise. Mr. Herbod and his wife were disproportionate in appearance. He was tall, and Astra was short but, kind-hearted. Holding her hand, they both went towards Philip.

Daniel: "I'm so happy to see you after all these years."

Philip stuttered: "Me too."

David: "We have to celebrate this fortunate day..." uttering these words with delight and happiness, he asked Kalahi to leave the room with him. He wanted to arrange a small family celebration with Delris and Kalahi's help. As he was going down the stairs, he turned back: "Mariana, would you help us too?" gesticulating to Philip.

Mariana got his point: "Oh, of course." They wanted Mariana's helping hand to cook Philip's favorite food and make him happy in the best way.

Kalahi, Delris, David, and Mariana left the room; now the room was quieter and less clamorous. Baldino was a good conversationalist, and where ever he went, he brought joy with him.Daniel took Philip's hand in his: "We have so much to talk about, but it's better that you rest a bit now."

Philip touched his receding hair and neck: "Yes, I'd better do that. I'm so glad that all the ones that Adam wanted are here. There's no worry anymore; we can make a better world together. In such dark days, having a loving family is the best blessing."

They could hear someone running in the distance and getting close. Nilsa was the last person who came to Philip. She jumped into Philip's arms so that he was about to fall from the chair.

Nilsa: "Uncle Philip…" But she had a lump in her throat and couldn't continue.

Philip stood up from his chair and kissed Nilsa on the forehead: "My lovely Nilsa, I saw you glittering like a light above, in all my nightmares… I've missed you so much…"

Nilsa: "Me too, also Borak and the Wing King."

Robert wore a pleasant smile: "It's better not to tucker out Uncle Philip." And whispered in Philip's ear: "it's better that you go back to your room and rest."

Philip looked at him: "Do you know when Adam will be back?"

Robert: "I don't know. Nobody knows what's wrong with him; it has been a week since he has left."

Daniel helped him to stand up since he was weak and would lose his balance at any moment.

Robert: "Don't worry, He'll be back."

Philip looked at the ceiling and went back to his room With Daniel and Robert's support.

The sun was setting when Sarah returned from the forest with Borak, wet to her skin. In Adam Heber's absence and on Baldino's order, she was patrolling. Although the fortress couldn't be seen from the outside, Heber had insisted on guarding it carefully.

Borak shook himself off, and wetted the entrance, Sarah walked into her friends: "What's going on? You are all happy."

Nilsa answered with joy: "Uncle Philip is awake."

Sarah nodded considerately, then stood before the fireplace, took her raincoat off and blew her lantern out.

A few hours later, Adam Heber's new family began its celebration. They all gathered around a big table in a hall, in the fortress's second floor. They were all enjoying themselves with simple but delicately cooked foods. Robert was sitting next to David and Nilsa, near the door. Helena and Herbods were sitting in front of him while Alexi and Nadia were holding each other's hand and listening to Peloma, playing the violin. Borak was also there, lying under Nilsa's chair, placing his head between his hands reluctantly. Mariana and Philip were sitting at one end of the table with contentment in his smile.

Peloma kept on playing the violin for a while and finished with a heart-rending improvise. It was then when the lights hanging above the table were on. Kalahi looked up and said to Delris: "He's here…"

Robert asked in surprise: "Who's here?"

Kalahi said with happiness: "Mr. Heber. Whenever he is in the fortress, all the lights turn on mysteriously."

Right then, the door opened, and Adam Heber entered the room, calmly and serenely. He looked at everyone, but stopped at the moment he saw Philip.

Everybody stood up, and Adam greeted them kindly. They spent the rest of the night eating and drinking.

Robert was holding Helena's hands, talking about the past and Helena was leaning back in her chair, listening to him like an arrogant flower. David and Adam were sitting close to each other and speaking in a whisper. The feast was over; everyone was waiting for Adam Heber to tell the reason why he had gathered them together. But without caring about their will, he said: "I'm tired, and I'll go to bed," then looked at Philip: "We need to talk Philip, come to my room please." and left.

The fortress inhabitants were delighted and gleeful due to the peace they had obtained after what they have had through all these years.

Mariana kissed Philip on his lips, and he left the room.

Adam was sitting on an inlaid stool, staring at a picture hanging on the wall which was illustrating an old man on a stone seashore, with his back to the sea storm, looking at spectator out of that frame. The heavy rainstorm was falling, but he was trying not to weigh down and be strong.

Adam was lost in his thoughts when Philip knocked on the door: "Come in."

Philip entered and closed the door slowly behind him. He was in a long gown with his hair tied back, wearing a fake smile. He went closer and sat on the chair before Adam. He wasn't at ease.

Adam: "How did you return?"

Philip bit his lips and shook his head: "I don't know. I found myself here when I woke up."

Adam took out his red notebook from his pocket and skimmed it: "I don't want to upset you, Philip. There's no doubt in your loyalty, you've been my best and closest companion during all these years, before and after the war, but the plan I have is so critical that I ever fear myself to review it. You should understand my concern and sensitivity."

Philip was listening to him carefully. Adam continued: "you know better what you should do If you truly don't remember how you got out of the Gaalve."

Philip drooped his head and took a deep breath, then stared at the old man's gray eyes: "No, I don't know how I got out of there."

Adam nodded. "You were captured by Shagad. He tortured you and managed to reach much information. I don't blame you, Philip, as you did your best."

Meanwhile, Philip had unclear images of his endless struggle to escape the utter darkness and Shagad's stroking power. Though he was miles away from those memories, both in time and distance, he could feel the deadly pain of those dark nightmares.

Philip: "What should I do now?"

Adam: "Do what you have to do, I don't want to voice it about you."

Philip stood up with tears in his eyes and a broken heart. He knew what Adam meant, and he was right; He was worried about the serpent king's penetration to Philip's mind. One month in that dark realm sufficed Shagad to enchant Philip's mind, hide there and read his thoughts at any time.

Adam had just lost his most intimate companion and could no longer consult with him. One month! It was too late to scour his mind; Shagad was probably waiting for a chance, somewhere out of Adam's sight, to gain useful information.

Despite all the mistakes Adam had made in the past, this time he wouldn't make a hole for Shagad, even if it costs the separation from his closest companion.

Adam embraced Philip exhausted and sad about the upcoming: "Go to South America. Go to the free lands of Golden Eagles. It's time to rest."

Philip said with a lump in his throat: "How can you ask such a thing from me? I have been by your side for thirty years and struggled the enemy who shattered me at the end and sent me to a compulsory exile."

Adam put his hands on Philip's shoulders: "you help us get rid of this evil enemy forever, as long as you stay away from us."

He was thinking about Shagad's deception and the tragedy, which was about to destroy his plan's root and branch. The information he gained access to, about Nadia and Alexi could cost their lives, but with Balzakich's great luck, she saved them from that deadly hazard.

Adam: "You can take one of the flying machines and, about Mariana… the decision is yours. She can stay here as long as she desires."

Philip couldn't help crying and tears stream down his face. The game was over for him.

The next morning, Adam's decision shocked everyone. The fortress inhabitants saw Mariana and Philip off in tears and staggered as the two headed to South America in a flying machine.

Before they leave, Mariana hugged Astera: "I guess fate doesn't want us to stay together like those good old days and now that Philip is determined to go, I'll accompany him, and consider this war is over."

Philip had spent the whole night to convince Mariana to stay in the fortress's security and safety, but Mariana couldn't ignore the dictates of her conscience and made up her mind not to leave Philip alone.

Robert was looking at Adam, more somber than before. If they were a bit luckier, Philip could also stay with them. As Philip was holding Borak tight, Robert thought about the story he never had the chance to hear from him, the story of how Philip and Borak had met and the deep connection between the two, which now he had to let go of it.

A few minutes later, the P-500 flew away. The Wing King was whining a heart-rending mourn at the heart of the mountain, grieving his best friend's parting. He flew over the fortress until it was utterly out of sight.

Robert was staring, following P500 in the vast sky. Then he turned to Adam: I fully understand your grief". Adam took Robert's hand, and in a split-second, they were teleported to the room on the high floor of the fortress.

Adam: "My sorrow has no end and losing Philip is also among them now, but I can't pay a heavy price in this battle... My mind has recently been obsessed with a malaise."

Robert: "What makes you sad Adam?"

Adam: "Take my hand to feel it with every fiber of your being." And put forth his hand, waiting for Robert to hold it. With a short hesitation, Robert placed his hand on Adam's and all at once, everything around them started to change.

Robert saw a small boy, running around and playing in the vast grain fields in Kansas State of former America while the wind was blowing in his straight, silky hair. In the city, called "People of the Wind," on a warm summer day, those gray eyes and the shape of his face... It was Adam Heber's childhood.

The scenery was too old; there were no traces of flying machines or rusty electrical grids that were spread everywhere, like enormous ghosts in Robert's age.

The pictures changed rapidly, presenting Adam in his youth in Robert's mind.

Then another image appeared, which Robert had never thought could even exist in Heber's life.

Adam was a drunk, middle-aged man, holding a bottle in his hand, looking at the woman dancing before him. The bar was full of carouser men, gathering around that woman. She was the hooker to solicit customers for the barkeeper with dirty dances.

Robert could not breathe as he saw Adam's eyes were filled with lust, running on the woman's body with a craving for her, as if he had silence intercourse with her in his mind. Robert was saddened and couldn't figure out why Heber was showing his dark past to him.

The picture changed again. Adam was drunk and walking towards a small house where a red-haired woman was waiting for him. Adam fell on the wooden stairs of the house several times with a sound, which informed the woman of his presence. She came out worriedly and helped Adam inside. He was lying on his bed like a drunk boar.

Robert couldn't believe his eyes as he was watching the scenes in total perplexity. Another night and Adam was yelling insanely and the same woman, hiding her face in her hand, was crying. The tension grew, and Adam started beating her. The sight filled Robert with disgust, and he was outraged at this part of Heber's life in the past. In the middle of their argument, a little girl appeared with tears in her eyes, holding her hand-made doll and tried to stop his father, but Adam pushed her away with a kick. The girl was just five or six, and fell on the ground; her doll dropped down as well. She left the room as she was crying and hid in a closet. She could still hear them brawl, so held her knees, put her head on them while the tears were rolling down her face.

Seeing these footages about Adam's past was driving Robert crazy when suddenly a new picture shaped before his eyes; a younger Adam comparing to what he had seen so far. Robert could guess it was due to the life force. He was aged but looked younger concurrently. Trees and fresh lawns were surrounding them; the weather was fine and moist. Adam was wearing a long white cloth, holding a stick in his hand. He was standing before his old friend, Shagad; they were talking and getting ready for a fight. Sahagd was leaning against a tree and seemed young and proud, but there were no serpents on his shoulders.

Shagad invaded him, and Adam pushed him back with his stick. They both laughed. Adam: "I don't believe you could move such great amount of force!"

Shagad stood up with a smile: "and I don't believe you could ever ward it off! You're amazing Adam!"

They both laughed, but their fight escalated. Robert could see vividly that Shagad was sending unrestrained blows to Adam. However, none of them had supernatural forces and were fighting with their own strength. In the distance, a very old man was watching them. He could hardly open his eyes, and his long white hair was like a river down to his waist.

Suddenly, pictures came to an end. Adam was lost in his thought, and Robert was surprised, not knowing what to say. But Adam made it easier for him: "I don't know if these footages are real or not."

Robert: "How come you can't perceive?"

Adam: "Memories are divided into two parts. Those with origin are real and the rootless ones, which are just implanting; implanting of the dreams, inspiration or nightmares. I can differentiate real ones from unreal; anyone can! But I'm traumatized, I don't know if the rootless ones, once had an origin or not, like that woman and the girl. That memory has no origin in my mind, but what if someone has just manipulated the roots? It means I had a wife and a daughter whom I've forgotten and now I believe they have never existed before.

Or the memory in that bar has an origin in my mind, which means it existed. But I don't know if I have ever been this type of person in my life. I got into this mess since I faced Shagad. I can't figure out which one is real and which one is fake."

Robert: "So where is the problem?"

Adam turned and looked at Robert: "If Shagad had searched inside my mind and manipulated a memory from the past, a new memory will begin to grow like a plant, as if it existed in the past and as the time goes by I won't be able to control it or even to realize if it's real or not. Now, what if I had a wife and a child? Are they alive? Are they somewhere safe?"

Robert: "You can ask from those who know you for so long. They should know if you had a family."

Adam: "It's not that easy in my case. I live longer than ordinary people do. They may exist even before Philip was born and now I'm struggling with an utter turmoil in my mind."

Now Robert knew why even Shagad's name would convulse the enemies. He could not only fracture their bodies but also shatter their souls. The strongest person Robert had ever known was drooping before the simple but fatal game Shagad had just begun. A deadly virus had invaded Adam's mind, decaying the old man from inside.

Adam: "gather my fellows in the room; it is time to tell them the truth."

CHAPTER TWENTY-SEVEN
THE GUARDIANS OF LIFE

Many years back…

A thin old man with long, white hair was walking in the vast meadows; his surrounding forest resembled the heaven. He took deep breathes several times in fresh, humid air; it was time to make major decisions about final years of his life. Walking towards an old, small temple, he was wondering how his determination would change the world after him.

He went up the hill using his old stick to get to the temple. A group of students was practicing in the yard, but only two of them mattered to him. Two friends whom he had found in different parts of the world and discorded extraordinary talent in both of them.

Seeing him coming closer, students stopped training and bowed before their mighty master. It was getting dark; he bowed back and went to his small, humble room where he started writing something on a parchment.

Now it was time to talk to his cherished disciples, but instead of summoning the two, this time he went to them. He passed through a dark corridor and stood before the door to one of their rooms. The candlelight in the room made the aura hallucinatory; He opened the sliding door and found his disciple sitting and meditating on the ground, before the pure, shining jewel, which was on a small, wooden stand. He was so focused that didn't realize his master's presence; after a short time, the old man stretched forth his hand to seize the jewel, but suddenly the student caught his hand as if catching somebody in the act. When he pulled himself together, he saw his master and without hesitation bowed to him. Then he double genuflected and put his head on the ground before him: "I do apologize, forgive my impudence."

The master pushed his student shoulder smoothly back to make him sit at ease and smiled at him softly: "Were you roaming in it, Lancaster?"

The student knew that his master had realized his hidden mood and couldn't do anything but to confess: "Yes, master." and muttered "It has a kind of power which summons me. I feel a soft whisper in my mind whenever I look at the Taarnaar. In fact, he was prowling somewhere else but had decided not to reveal it to his master. The old man turned to him with a meaningful look: "The place where you are talking about is dark or luminous?"

He was in a predicament again as if the master could read his mind, but in a split-second, he dared to say: "a luminous one." Lancaster didn't want his master to know that he had stepped into Gaalve. Lying to him was like a cauldron as if his heart was filled with excitement and stir. He stared at his master to see the reaction in his face; the old man didn't seem to realize he was not telling the truth, he looked at the jewel and put it in the devil's hands: "You would better focus on the training I assigned to you. I'm really interested to know how you feel about it."

Lancaster had realized the mind games his master was playing, so he collected his thoughts and decided not to share what he deeply desired with him. His wicked feeling was longing for the jewel, a hidden force that empowered him to roam the unknowns.

With a short hesitation, Lancaster said: "It's beautiful and deceptive, and sometimes I feel like it's alive. You used to wear it around your neck but showed me a great favor by giving it to me. I don't know why you did this, but thanks for showing

240

this feeling to me. I was obsessed with it the very first time I saw it, and since then, I cannot stop thinking about it."

The master had a gentle and calm look at Lancaster, knowing his student was hiding things from his mind but decided to wait for longer. Suddenly he stood up and finished the conversation just as he had started it, so quick: "Take care of it."

The master left and closed the door behind him. Lancaster held the jewel before his eyes and stared at it under the candlelight. What he could see was unbelievable, motions at the heart of the jewel! He rubbed his eyes and looked again, but it was gone. He grasped it firmly and took a deep breath.

The master went to see his other disciple who seemed to be lazier than Lancaster; he was lying on his side and taking a nap. The master opened the door to his room with his stick. Seeing him, the student sat up and bowed to him. The old man asked his disciple to take a night walk with him.

A few minutes later, they were walking in the meadows around the temple and talking to each other. Felokimoos and Adam Heber were standing there, and Adam followed his master's look at the sky. Later on, this habit became Adam's second nature, and he stared at the night sky and the stars afar spontaneously.

Felokimoos: "I want to talk to you tonight, Adam. You know that you and Eden Lancaster have been the cynosure since the day I brought you here, two years ago. You two are from different social and financial backgrounds, but each of you has privileged qualifications. Lancaster is the only son of a rich family who was pampered all his life. But you were struggling for your survival and couldn't even feed yourself. However, you are both practicing hard."

Adam was listening with lowered head.

"Your enthusiasm for comprehending the life, just the way it is, gives me the feeling of accomplishment, but..." He paused, and then continued: "… But what matters now is that which one of you would be the leather of our rank in this world, after me."

Adam raised his head and looked at his master. Felokimoos was holding hands palm-in-palm behind his back, walking in slow pace: "you should learn the truth tonight, and I can be at ease with you more than ever Adam, though you are still a student, I do have trust in you and believe wholeheartedly that I can talk to you about certain things. Training you physically and teaching you the art of war is not the reason of your presence here, in this temple, though they are required to illuminate your soul as well, the most important thing to me is entrusting this rank to the righteous man.

"We are called the Guardians of Life, and we're the foremost branch among the rest of the guardians. As I'm getting close to my last days, my time on earth will be through, and also my duty will be over. I have to choose the next leader. Have you ever heard about the Guardians?"

Adam: "No, master."

"I've trained many students and each, befitting their talents, went back to their homeland to take over simple or important responsibilities. All of them were qualified, but not as much as you and Lancaster are. Leadership needs wisdom, intelligence and brave heart, which both of you, own. But something else matters to me the most which I prefer not to talk about it now. Despite my old age and loads of experience, I still doubt about how to choose the best one for this final, heavy duty." He paused and then continued: "You must have seen the Taarnaar, the jewel I used to wear. Has it ever arose special intuition and feeling inside you?"

Adam: "It was so beautiful and deceptive, but I believe there are certain things in our world which we should avoid them due to their nature; no matter how specious and pleasant they really are."

Felokimoos nodded with satisfaction: "Your passion for learning is comprehensible to me. You have been training with sword and spear, but from tomorrow, your main practices will begin, and it will be under my own supervision. Let's get back to the Guardians. In the world, full of ancient mysteries, no one could thoroughly understand how our seed of life perforates on this planet. We have a mysterious world; you will only perceive life's meaning when those mysteries are unfolded to you. Sadly, many people are unable to understand it; they live, just because they get used to it and they will do the same in the future. But if they only knew how precious and uplifting their lives are, they would try to make the best of it in the right way. There are five ranks among the humans, called the Guardians: the Guardians of fire who are the symbol of civilization and development; the Guardians of water, the symbol of health and well-being of the planet and its living beings; the Guardians of the earth, who stand for all the things relevant to intelligent life; and the Guardians of the dreams, which symbolize imagination and supremacy of human, and the Guardians of life who we are. These ranks are separated from one another and rarely get together for consulting. Each of them knows him responsibly fully and to the highest possible level unless a serious problem occurs."

"The seed of life was brought here from beyond the sky. My master told me several times that we owe this life to an alien type of life, which lives in a world called Meligulia. They are known as the Mother Nature, and their duty is to plant seeds in different worlds. They made Guardians to protect the life which we owe them."

Now things were getting clear for Adam, and he could guess the reason for his presence in that temple.

Felokimoos: "There are five jewels, and each Guardian has one which helps them reach their goals. Felonil is the ring made of vivid fire with its red ruby, in hand of Arosha, the Guardian of

Fire. Alanil, the bracelet with its pure diamond, belongs to the legendary Gloria, the Guardian of Water. Peron is the stick of Zoya, the Guardian of Earth. Hexaar is a dagger made of dreams, owned by the Gatekeeper of Dreams, Glidaar, and the last one..." he paused since he knew what Adam must be thinking of at that moment. Felokimoos went on: "The Taarnaar, the shiny emerald, is in the hands of the Guardian of Life, me!"

Adam stopped walking and looked at his master in amazement. Felokimoos also stopped several steps ahead. Their faces under the moonlight was a spectacular scene. Adam: "You are..." hesitated for a second and said: "So all these sayings are true!"

Felokimoos: "I have never seen Meligulia and its residents, but I know myself and other Guardians, so I assumed everything my master had said to be true. This is the mystery of our life on this planet. It may be hard for you to believe now, but if one day you join the rank of the Guardians, you will find it more acceptable."

Adam was confused. "But you handed over the Taarnaar to Eden."

Felokimoos smiled: "I test each one of you through something. I test Eden with the Taarnaar and you with secrecy. The jewel is nothing but a toy in his hands. He cannot use its powers and will neither believe these things to be true. From now on you will face the extreme temptation to give your best friend a hint of how precious the jewel in his hand is."

Adam: "You're telling me how you are going to test me?"

Felokimoos: "You two can't do anything with it right now as I am holding its key and I am the one who decides to whom it should be handed over."

Adam took a deep breath and was lost in his thoughts. The master had started a serious metal game with them.

Adam: "I don't see any factor in myself to make me a candidate for this position."

Felokimoos: "You are not supposed to see, it's me ..." he said the last sentence with a smile and continued: "I'm the one who chooses the next leader. Let's get back. Tomorrow I'm going to teach you the right way of living."

That beautiful moonlit night passed while indigestible thoughts kept Adam awake.

The next day, Felokimoos started to train his two senior students. Time passed very quickly for them.

The fall turned into the cold winter days while Felokimoos opened new doors of supernatural forces to Eden Lancaster and Adam Heber each day. Lancaster was still holding the Taarnaar and using new powers Felokimoos gave him, he challenged internal forces of the jewel. Sometimes, the Taarnaar emitted a bright light, which forced Lancaster to cover it beneath pieces of clothes in his room, but that also would not work and the light, even passed through Lancaster's body.

Adam spent a year full of vicissitudes under his master's supervision. Now, he knew life elements; sometimes he could hear the trees or feel a dragonfly flapping its wings afar. From time to time, he shrank away to see around him the way it really was not the way others would see. The whole time, he was struggling with the temptation Felokimoos had laid in him. Now he knew how his master was testing him.

Lancaster, his intimate friend, got more mysterious each day and preferred to be lonely most of the times and Adam could clearly recognize his unusual behavior. He was no longer the same old person. Lancaster was now more confident and without mentioning the Taarnaar's forces, kept on learning about supernaturals from his master with indescribable eagerness.

It was a fine spring day and exactly two years had passed since that night when Felokimoos and Adam had talked. There were no students there, other than Adam and Lancaster. The two were ordered to transfer all firewood outside the temple to the old warehouse. Felokimoos was out of the temple, and this time, he had taken the Taarnaar with him.

Lancaster was too anxious and irritable as he was mentally dependent on the jewel. Adam could feel his friend wasn't okay. Felokimoos had ordered them to move the firewood using their physical strength. A few hours passed, Lancaster put his load of firewood on the ground and called Adam. Adam was walking ahead of him, so he did the same. : "What?" Lancaster sat down on his loads of firewood and started to eat nuts.

He smiled at Adam: "I know the things which hearing them will floor you."

Adam wiped the sweat from his brow. "Well, why don't you tell me to drop my teeth?" and leaned against a tree to take a break.

Lancaster went towards him and sat before his friend: "I can see things!"

Adam pretended he was unaware of them: "like what?"

Lancaster: "Sometimes I go somewhere, not permanently, just whenever I want. It's sometimes dark and sometimes light, but I think there are two different places; something talks to me there and tiny, black, pitiful creatures ring around me."

Adam: "Stop it, man. You're scaring me. Eden, if what you say is for real, then you are going astray."

Lancaster: "At first, I was frightened too. I thought them to be evil, but they're not what they seem to be. I wanted to share it with you a long time ago. I want you to come and see there."

Adam stood up and put the load of firewood on his back: "No, thanks. I guess you'd better discuss it with the master."

Lancaster frowned: "No, I don't think he would let me go there. But I'm really eager about it. It's cool, isn't it?"

Adam shook his head and went to the warehouse. Lancaster stood up, but this time pointed to the load of firewood and brought it in the air.

Adam: "The master asked us to do the job with our physical power; he'll be upset if he realizes you are using your forces."

Lancaster: "Hey, you're defending him way too much. We're forty, stop acting like a kid."

"Maybe the master wanted to test me through this"; Adam thought to himself and subdued his inner temptation for saying anything. Lancaster kept talking about the things he had seen in the past two years until he reached the unpleasant part of it.

Lancaster: "You know, they are interesting with small horns on their heads. They are cheerful and are always dancing around the fire. However, once I saw an old chamber, and as I was getting close to it, they hid behind me out of fear. I could feel a mysterious power buried inside it, and those stupid creatures kept repeating Shigaat! Shigaat! It really scares me to go there alone, but if you come with me, we'll find out what is behind that chamber and moreover is that we can earn a lot of money through them."

Adam said tauntingly: "How greedy you are, man? Your father owns half of the factories in Wales, and you still think about money?"

Lancaster: "Where is the problem if we own Europe as well? You can do anything with money" and laughed out loud.

Adam put the load of firewood in the warehouse and sat in a corner: "You really need to talk to the master about it, Eden. It's not a joke."

Lancaster replied in a greedy tone: "No, I have to discover it myself. You know It is untouched, but the problem is that you can only go there using that jewel."

Adam grinned: "So that's why he took it away from you, and he may never give it back to you again!"

Lancaster: "Then I'll take it stealthily."

Adam: "Are you out of your mind? You know what you're talking about, Eden?"

Lancaster: "Oh come on man, I was just joking. You won't believe how much I've learned unless you see it."

Adam: "You're insane! We cannot use our powers during the daylight. What if someone spots us?"

Lancaster: "There's no one now. Let's duel!"

Then without alerting Adam, he sent the surge of force in his hands towards his opponent. It hit Adam's chest with a howling sound and hurled him some feet away. Adam stood up hurriedly and guarded.

Their friendly talk turned into a serious and rough fight. Immediately Adam realized his old friend was much stronger than he was and said with a smile: "ok, you won…"

But Lancaster seemed to have a hidden rage inside; his anxiety didn't let him end the battle. A black ball of hot bitumen shaped in his hands, which he sent straight towards Adam's face. Adam dodged his head without hesitation, and it hit the woods, next to the temple.

Adam yelled: "what the hell is wrong with you? You're breaking the temple apart!"

But Lancaster did it again, and this time, it hit Adam, and he dashed to the ground and couldn't breathe out of pain.

Lancaster: "They say Shigaat. But if I get to grip with it, the result would be a tuneful, beautiful name. Those dumb creatures call me with this name.

Adam was knocked down so heavily that he couldn't even hear Lancaster clearly; the blow was so severe that felt like being hit by a train. Lancaster summoned another black ball and stood over Adam with loose rage. As he brought forward his hands to throw the ball to Adam's face, a pile of wind hit him and threw Lancaster some feet away on the ground. Felokimoos was on the temple's porch, looking at his student's insanity.

As Lancaster saw his master, he got on his knees and bowed to him.

Felokimoos: "This madness will end right here, forever. You are no longer my student, Eden. Pack your stuff and leave here tonight."

Regretting his action, Eden Lancaster begged desperately: "Let me explain it to you master…"

Felokimoos had made up his mind and wouldn't accept a single word.

Lancaster: "Please master, I don't know why these all happened, please forgive me, master."

Felokimoos was determined: "You are going to leave here tonight, and the Taarnaar does not belong to you anymore."

Eden Lancaster said goodbye to his friend; the friend whom he had almost killed a few hours ago and left the temple despondent and regretful. It was the last time that Lancaster and master saw each other.

That night Adam told Felokimoos the whole story, and as he mentioned the name 'Shigaat,' the master clenched his fists and looked down in regret: "I should have been more careful about Eden… He had been to the Gaalve and was so lucky that he didn't open the chamber's lid. The Guardians of Dream told me that the Humans' fear called Ashaagaadaar lives there and breaches human's soul like a shadow. The lord of shade and horror is locked there by the Guardians of Dream."

Felokimoos had made his decision and chose Adam as the next leader to the Guardians of life. Later on, Felokimoos was summoned before the Council of the Guardians and was informed that the chamber's lid was open. With no doubt, it was Eden Lancaster, as he had touched the mysterious forces of the chamber with no mental barrier. It was probable to the council that someone among them had gained access to the mysteries of the Gaalve, but Felokimoos didn't even mention Eden Lancaster until he, himself could find out more about this issue.

Later on, they heard the name "Shagad"; both Felokimoos and Adam were sure that it is Eden Lancaster. A dark temptation that led an old friend and student to the well of naught and inexistence.

In his last days, Felokimoos bound Adam and Lancaster, which bothered Adam greatly for so long.

"As long as they both were alive, none of them could perish the other."

Adam felt ashamed about it, as he thought Felokimoos had realized how powerful that demon was and knew the fact that Shagad is much stronger than he is and feared that one day his evil powers could destroy the Guardians of Life. But later on, Adam understood the depth of the bond Felokimoos had created between the two old friends. It was their last chance for saving Guardian's council. The wise Felokimoos wouldn't be there anymore more to answer Adam's proficient wisdom and Adam was not the same naive person who wouldn't realize the reason why his master had cast this old spell between him and his foe.

Now Adam was thinking about the road ahead and the decision he had to make. He had managed to get all the members of the Half-Dream Order together, though the time they had lost, resulted in destruction and demolition of the world.

The final solution was before him now.

CHAPTER TWENTY-EIGHT
CONCEALMENT WAR

Adam was struggling with his thoughts when Robert knocked at his door and waited for his permission to enter. Adam let him in.

Robert: "Everybody is waiting for you in the main hall."

Adam: "Thanks, Robert. You go, and I'll join you."

Robert nodded and left the room.

Adam got close to the hall in short steps. Everybody was sitting there, whispering to each other. Adam glanced at them from the ajar door, but didn't go inside and instead, made a detour to the mysterious room of the fortress.

He closed the door behind and made sure that no one could open it from outside and looked at the five chairs, which were in a circle, across from one another. At the center of the room, the Taarnaar was floating in a water-like liquid, which seemed to be in a cylinder container, but in fact, that enigmatic liquid which was protecting the Taarnaar wasn't in any receptacle.

Adam put his hand in the fluid and without being hurt held the Taarnaar in his hand, Whispering ancient incantations, while the beating heart of the jewel could feel its lord's presence.

Suddenly, he found himself in a room where until that day no one had been there before, but a few mortals. There was a rectangular table with five chairs. Four of them were one-on-ones, and the fifth one was along table's tiny width, across from the rest of them.

Adam put the Taarnaar in the bulge before his seat, and as the jewel touched the edge of the table, it engulfed the jewel, and a string-like white light moved from the end of the bulge through notch over the four other chairs. As the light reached the other bulges, slight mist formed right above the junction and started to swirl and shine, forming vivid shapes; a ring of fire and a short dagger spinning in an aura of light. Then a stick from a living tree and eventually a bracelet made of pure diamond appeared.

Felonil and Hexaar appeared on the seats further from Adams. As the shapes formed fully, two men and two women, surprised at their sudden summons, emerged. Before Felonil, was Arosha, a robust and broad-shouldered man and it was hard to believe that he was over 300 years old. Across from him, the Guardian of Dream appeared in his dark cowl. Zoya and Gloria were sitting before their jewels, Peron and Alanil. All of these took place in a split second before Adam Heber's astonished eyes.

Those four were flaunting their powers to Adam exaggeratedly.

Arosha had appeared in a red garment made of fire, wearing a crown with blue flames. The Guardian of Dream, Glidaar, was covered with the dimness of his cloak, which was made of dreams, while the rays of light were beaming from his shoulders, creating a beautiful arc and returning to him. Zoya was in her green dress, made of the living nature with butterflies flying around her, while Gloria was putting white silk on.

Adam didn't have any notion of himself, but he was the Guardian of life and believed to look overstated to them just as they did to him.

It was the first time in the past seventy years that the Guardians were called up by one of them to the Guardian Council. The one summoning the rest would always sit where Adam was now, under their piercing eyes.

Not knowing where he was, Arosha was more confused than the rest. It took him a few seconds to realize he was called up to the council. He looked middle-aged, but despite his appearance, his sullen temperament was revealed as he looked at Adam Heber and said: "What happened? Why did you summon us? Let me see... who are you? Where is Felokimoos?" Then he frowned and said: "Glidaar, What on earth have you done to yourself, why do you look like this?"

Everyone looked at him, but without answering to Arosha, he turned to Adam: "Why did you call up the members?"

Adam: "Accept my apology, but I need your deliberation. I am Adam Heber, the Guardian of Life and the late Felokimoos's successor."

All the Guardians looked at the Taarnaar; the luminous jewel was shining before Adam, which was the symbol of all Guardians of life ever.

The legendary Gloria said in a simple but determined tone: "How may we help the Guardian of Life?"

She didn't call Adam by name intentionally since all of them were older than him and recognition of anyone other than Felokimoos was somehow hard for them. Adam could feel their arrogant behavior towards himself, but continued with his accustomed dignity: "In the days that many things have changed, the Guardians need to have more interaction with one other."

Zoya interrupted him: "This rule has never existed, and its recurrent is not necessary. Since each Guardian is fulfilling his own duties."

Adam wore a painted smile: "But that does not hold with the current situation. It might be better to enhance our interactions to prevent further damages and moreover is that this table and all these apparatus must have been made for the Guardian's consultation."

The Guardian of Dream: "and what would be the outcome?"

Adam put his hand on the table and replied in a calm manner: "Our life, just the way we knew it before, is being threatened by a common enemy and is about to be destructed and ruptured. I don't think any of you would consider today's world a suitable place after all those irreparable damages occurred after the war by our common foe."

Arosha was bored and impatient: "What common enemy? We're doing our duty in the best possible way and about that war; I should say it was inevitable."

Zoya was thinking about Adam's words and had different ideas from the rest of the Guardians. She already knew the extent of damages resulted from the war and the way it had taken the spirit of life away from the earth.

As the water was dancing splendidly among her clothes, the legendary Gloria said: "What do you suggest then?"

Adam was staring at the Guardian of dream and could see that Glidaar was glancing at the Taarnaar occasionally from beneath his cloak, but each time Adam looked at him, he looked away. Glidaar's face was not visible, and only from the movement of the cloak, Adam could feel his hidden look at the Taarnaar. What bothered him the most was the Guardian of dream's shattering look. Years ago, Felokimoos had warned him about the Guardian of Dream's unbridled and unpredictable behavior, and now Adam was meeting one of their greatest ones.

Gloria was still waiting for an answer, but Adam resumed: "Doesn't   the   name -Shagad the war bringer- sound familiar to you, respected Guardians?"

Guardian of Dream was outraged at the name; with a sad tone and hoarse voice said: "It wasn't Guardian of dream's mistake that one of Felokimoos's students met the Human's Bane. We were keeping that bane under lock and key, but can we condone Felokimoos fault for abandoning his student in the realm of dreams? We all know that he went to Ashaagaadaar's place without any mental barriers and that's how his soul decayed and was unified by the Dark's soul."

Adam: "that's hardly debatable the Great Glidaar. I don't want to blame anyone, but isn't it true that this evil spirit has gotten into a human body and is devouring their world like a huge bloodsucker? Shall we keep quiet and put the blame on each other due to our own imprudence? Like it or not, we are captivated by a disastrous evil whom we had raised."

Zoya said with wrath: "Never... we had never taken part in fostering this devil. I have always wondered has the Guardian of Life ever thought how they are going to compensate the mess they have caused in this world."

"That is exactly why I'm here," Adam said. "I'm here to put right what once went wrong."

Arosha: "And we're not supposed to pay for the mistake Felokimoos and your rank made."

Adam: "Of course you won't. But if the war breaks out, it will set fire to a quilt to get rid of a moth; then you have to face the enemy one by one or in groups. So, we have to shake the hand of friendship and be united more than ever before. The enemy who doesn't show mercy to the Guardian of Life would not do it to other orders as well, and I'm sure you're not going to join hands with this demon."

The last sentence had a kind of connotation, which made the Guardians think deeper. It was the first time that Adam could flaunt them by his power. The youngest Guardian was in a critical situation and was doing his best to change the condition to his own favor.

Adam continued after a short pause: "I want to meet each of in person. In our dark age, nowhere is safe and I'm afraid to share what is latent in my heart, here in public. Give me this chance..."

Gildaar objected immediately: "I cannot meet you in person due to personal reasons, my situation doesn't allow this."

But Zoya and Gloria accepted, and Arosha joined them subsequently.

Adam: "I will see you next week and thanks for taking part in this meeting" and said goodbye.

The symbols of the Guardians stopped shining and faded away gradually until they fully vanished. Adam looked at the Taarnaar, and as he raised his hand to remove it, Hexaar began to glow again, and when the rest of the Guardians left, Glildaar showed up. He looked around and said: "Good to see you're still here. I want to talk to you. Now that others are gone, I can talk to you more easily about the past troubles and the problems of our orders."

Adam invited him to sit, and he himself sat before him. Glidaar was still under his cowl of dreams and Adam could only hear his voice.

Glidaar: "We are sorry about what had happened in the past. Before anything else, let me explain something to you. Glidaar has disappeared since Serpent King emerged and I'm his successor. He did his best to protect the gates of the dreams, but in his last attempt to expand the dream world, he suffered from insanity to the point of no return, and nobody knows where in that dream world he might be now, or is he still alive or not. It was then when the Serpent King infiltrated to the realm of dreams wickedly and took the Human's Bane away. Now, I'm here to ask for your help. After Glidaar's fall and emerge of Shagad, my people haven't had a decent night of sleep. The gates of the Golden Limora has been locked, and the dignitaries of our rank are still waiting for Glidaar, the gatekeeper's, return."

Adam rubbed his face and said: "I would be glad if you could introduce yourself."

The Guardian of dream: "I'm Andowlin, one of the three main guards and after Glidaar's disappearance, I lead the rank."

Adam: "Why are you hiding the truth? Even the rest of the Guardians couldn't recognize you and still believe Glidaar is the Guardian of Dream."

Andowlin: "We honor boundaries of the dream land and the loss of our great leader who conducted this rank for four hundred years is unbearable. Moreover is that we still don't know what has happened to him which makes us so sad. It is so hard for many of my fellows to accept that our patron was the reason behind Ashaagaadaar's escape, and why the two happenings, occurred at the same time.

I keep on thinking about the simultaneity of Glidaar's fall and the escape of Ashaagaadaar through Felokimoos's student. Despite what I said at the presence of the five members of the council, I believe that our ranks are also as guilty as yours.

Now that you are asking for help, we want you to find about Glidaar's fate in return."

Adam: "How do you expect me to find information about someone who has disappeared many years ago?"

Andowlin: "By the Taarnaar. A relic of the previous Guardian is always kept in the Golden Limura. Since this city has never existed in reality and was built in the realm of dreams, these relics will remain there forever for future use. I used Hexaar several times, but couldn't find any traces of Gildaar; happily though it shows that a great part of Hexaar forces is still under the main Guardian's control, which means Glidaar is still alive. But the disappointing part is that as long as Glidaar is aboveground, other Guardians of dream won't be capable of using Hexaar's real power, and the dagger is practically useless for our rank. I spent a lot of time investigating about other quintuple jewels. None of them is as strong as the Taarnaar for finding a real Guardian. If you come to Limora, we could find Glidaar, using Hexaar and Taarnaar or at least we can find out what has happened to him. Then I guarantee that the real forces of the dream Guardians would be at your service to meet all your needs."

Adam: "As far as I know, Limora is the endmost land of the Andium, at the farthest point to the Gaalve."

Andowlin: "That's right. After Glidaar's disappearance, we moved all of our assets and installations there but observed all entries and exits. I have seen the traffic of people from your rank into the Gaalve several times but didn't warn them since you already knew about it. Moreover is that I was aware that after the Great War and the fall of the Dark King, Karapan, it was agreed that no force is allowed to haunt between the two realms. You violated this rule, but I believed something important existed there which someone had to see it, so I condoned this violation too."

Adam had realized that Glidaar's successor had found out about him, and his fellows sneaked and tried to penetrate to his mind several times, but each time an iron wall blocked his way. The Guardian of dream's mind was resisting any attempt at penetrating to it.

Adam: "I have to think about it. Anyway, I have to see you in person. Sharing what is latent in my heart in such an unreal room is too dangerous and counterintuitive. I get the chance to use the quintuple forces of the ranks to inform them about our crucial condition, and it's not wise to stay here any longer..."

Adam was not finished yet when Andowlin interrupted him: "What do you want? What are your plans for resisting Shagad?"

Adam: "I told you... talking here is potentially hazardous. Let me think about assisting you, and we can talk at a later time."

Andowlin: "I can train your people how to use their dreams for reaching their goals. Isn't it what you want?"

Adam realized Andowlin's acuteness since he had understood the meaning of "assistance" with acumen but preferred to keep silent. It was the first time that he was using the Council Room and had no idea what was lying behind its closed doors.

Andowlin: "This room is safer than what you can imagine. It is located in the heart of Limora where even its inhabitant can't find it."

Adam wavered for a moment "Andowlin can read my mind???"

"Let me make it clear. I don't care where the rest of the Guardians are heading to; Shagad's annihilation is my priority and won't share the information I have in such a place, see you soon." Said Adam and reached out his hand to release the Taarnaar from the notch when suddenly a powerful surge invaded his mind. He was not sure if it was coming from Andowlin or somewhere else, but it was delving his thoughts so recklessly that he was about to pass out. Adam touched the Taarnaar with all his remaining power and right away came down the mysterious hall of the fortress.

The Taarnaar was on the ground, shining strongly but its light diminished gradually. Adam took a deep breath, stood up and placed the Taarnaar back in the liquid, which only he could touch.

He walked through the corridors of the fortress in silence with a scrambled mind and reached his friends who had gotten together.

The room had different functions when people stepped inside it. For Adam who was the Guardian of life, the time extended while for others it was vice versa.

As he stepped into the room where his fellows had gathered, the look in their eyes was the proof of Adam's distress. Without any hesitation, Adam said: "I want only Robert, Nadia, Alexi, Peloma and Helena to stay in the room."

Mr. Herbod, Astera, David Baldino and Nilsa complied with his request and left the room, but before leaving, Daniel approached Adam and put a hand on his shoulder: "Are you sure you don't want help with that?"

Adam thanked him with a painted smile, put a hand on his and said: "No Daniel thanks."

As they left, Adam sat on a small couch before them with excitement in his eyes. Robert had seen many incidents prior to this, which made him feel a lot better than others.

Adam: "It's been fifteen years since I last saw you all together. My biggest concern was meeting you again, safe and sound. Once, you were all learning and playing together in a place not far from this fortress, and as your master, I witnessed your thrive. But during the last fifteen years, we all suffered the loss of those who were dear to us. Nadia and Alexi lost their parents; Helena lost her whole family just like Robert did. I felt the absence of their warm affection just as you did. To you, they were safe shoulders and loving parents, and to me they were kind, sincere children whose loss pains me day and night. Therefore, I gathered you here to get through the only way left for us together, the way, which your parents stepped into heroically and it's your duty to put an end to their unfinished tasks."

Adam told them how it all began. He told them about Shagad, the Serpent King and the pain humankind suffered from his arrogance and egoism. Then he talked about Guardian's council and narrated the story of Meligulia and the five ranks. He explained how those five befitted to be the Half Dream Order senior members due to their inner forces and how the survival of Guardians of life depends on their devotion. He talked about the long lost past, from Felokimoos and those before him to present and the future.

The five young people before Adam were gradually finding out the reason behind all those sufferings and the existence of unknown forces within themselves. He explained that all the human beings own such incredible powers, but neglecting it, they are consumed with everyday life just to fulfill their needs. He explained to them how the great enemy had faded their sense of urgency and humiliated the human values. He told them about the world which was gone and the meaning of love, devotion, and humanity though remained among only a few minorities.

He explained to them, as they walk out of that room tonight, they won't be the same person anymore and finished his words with the famous story: "When you come out of the storm you won't be the same person who walked in. That's what this storm's all about." [6]

The old Dream Seller had found his fellows and now looked intently towards the future when they will no longer be naive juniors but latent forces ready to confront the Serpent King. Adam could see his ultimate plan is shaping.

Talking to them took him so long until each, and every one of them was mentally prepared for the upcoming duties.

The time had come for teaching and training them as the terminal days meant a lot to Adam.

Adam was sitting in his room, thinking about the Guardian's Council. He had to convince them personally, to provide him with their powers. He must leave each of those five with one Guardian to learn preliminaries, and after that, he had to undertake the transmission of the forces himself.

Adam was thinking about the mysterious Andowlin, which had scattered his mind, and Philip who had been laid aside after all dedications. He pondered the memories in his mind, which were manipulated in his last encounter with Shagad, corrupting Adam's thought from within.

In the last days of autumn, Adam was thinking about his ailing mind rather than preparation for the battle, but couldn't find a way to relieve himself of this inner corruption.

---

[6] BY: Haruki Murakami

He kept on remembering hideous and tormenting memories and thinking about the person he used to be, about his family in the past, not knowing whether they were real or not.

Adam stood by the window and looked at the Wing King who was soaring aloft into the clouds with pride; Borak, far away from Philip, was gloomy and weary. He looked at Nilsa and Herbods who were roaming in the yard. He thought about members of the Half Dream order who were brooding deeply after Adam's talk.

On the other side of the ocean, General Marco Monte Corrales was sitting before the high commanders of the Southern Confederation in his black suit and lost in his thoughts. He had to be prepared for the decisive battle as the Serpent King had declared war on him and his confederacies and soon, a rising tide would hit the peaceful shores under his domain. The Northern Alliance had formed up and started troop movements, yet its break out was not obvious to them. He got stabbed in the back as his ex-confederacies had turned their backs on his pacifist people and him in the south, so he was waiting for news from a new ally impatiently.

He had realized with unshaken faith that joining the most menacing man, Adam Heber –as his enemies believed- was the best way. Maybe the wide resistance chain which had formed all over the world could protect the Southern territory from the new adversary. Corrales wished he had never been this dependent on the Northern Alliance and the European Neo-Nazis, but it was too late. It was time for the old, fat man to make the final decision; he had to make preemptive action to coalesce Adam Heber and the vast resistance.

In the distance, at the heart of the Jung-Frau Mountains, Shagad was holding the dream dagger, Hexaar, in his hand, rubbing its sharp edge to his face from time to time. He was brooding deeply just like the rest of his rivals. He had realized that Adam Heber had left him behind significantly since he had gathered his fellows, right before Shagad's sharp eyes. He was wondering which plan would endanger the existence of the rank he had newly formed.

Years back, following Glidaar's insanity, Sahagad deceived him and seized the control over one of the five ranks. And as soon as the Taarnaar summoned him, he attended the council, aiming to unveil Adam Heber's plans under Andowlin cover.

Now, he was the owner of the dream gates and had set up an extensive trap for his rivals.

As the sun set, Charlie, Shagad's loyal servant, knocked and entered the room obediently: "Master, she's here."

Without looking at him, Shagad said: "how about the guests?"

Charlie: "They are here as well, master."

Shagad: "lead her to my room."

Charlie, robbing his hands greedily, bowed: "yes master."

A woman's footstep could be heard, and in a few moments, a tall, beautiful lady entered his room. Just Before she came in, Shagad hid the dagger in an armoire and with just one move of his hand it disappeared.

She was a pretty middle-aged lady, who had designed her hair beautifully. Despite the great deal of poverty on those days, she was wearing expensive clothes while her shoe heels were also gilded.

She stood before Shagad and bowed to him. Shagad embraced her warmly: "Gilda! I'm so happy to see you, my dear daughter. Not a single day has passed without thinking of you or being worried about you."

Gilda: "Thank you, father. You summoned me in my dream, so I came as quickly as I could."

Shagad; "yes, beautiful lady. I've prepared a grand banquet dinner, and you will be the most magnificent guest there. Let's go down together."

They both walked towards the hall to join the guests. A murmuring sound was coming from the illuminated hall, and as the two entered, all dignitaries stood up. Shagad and her dearest daughter sat on the dais while a group of violinist was waiting on the stage to play for the European Neo-Nazi's fifteenth years of rising to power.

General Heinrich Adler stood up and turned towards the guests. He raised his glass for a toast and said in a stentorian tone: "Let's drink to the health of those who did their best to establish the new order."

The guests around the tables, raised their glasses as well, toasted and pledged their drinks.

The orchestra started to play.

Shagad was holding Gilda's hands in his and asked her about the dreams she had. Gilda: "I see the darkness by my side. Each time I fall asleep, a dark creature appears and looks at me wickedly."

Shagad had a meaningful look at her: "Does it have any symbol?"

Gilda: "yes, a green and glowing jewel which is ugly and seeing it makes my hair stand on end."

Shagad: "Why don't you keep these distressing thoughts away?"

Gilda: "My father's enemy is mine too, and I can't wait to take your command; I'm going to shatter its soul so that it would long for death."

Then she looked at the musicians: "come with me father."

Shagad and Gilda went down the stairs where the rest of the guests were enjoying themselves. Adler went to them immediately, kissed her hand and fawned over her: "A lady at the height of beauty…"

However, Gilda didn't pay any attention to him and made her way towards the musicians. She stood before an old man who was the best violinist in the whole Europe; as he was playing very euphoniously, he smiled at Gilda.

Shagad was standing behind her, waiting for a spectacular occurrence.

As Gilda looked into the man's eyes, his hands started to tremble. At the very first moment, he thought he is back to his youth, but then a strident sound was heard from his violin. A few of guests turned to look at him; he struggled again, but this time the sound was even more earsplitting. Almost everyone was looking at him now.

The old man looked at his own hands desperately; all he had learned through 50 years was gone with just one glimpse of her. The cold sweat covered his face, and as he was trembling, he repeated in despair: "I can't remember, I can't remember anything … I can't play it…"

Two masked guards dragged him out of the hall as he wa still shouting: "Sorceress! You sorceress!"

Gilda looked at those who were watching them; then she bent down and held the old man's violin, placed the bow on the strings and improvised beautifully with closed eyes.

Nobody knew what a tragic twist had occurred but Shagad the Serpent king. Gilda despoiled what the poor old man had learned all these years by one look, and while she had not touched the violin even once, she could play it in the most beautiful way.

While the guests were thrilled by the sound of the music, Shagad left them and went towards his room along with Charlie.

Shagad: "She mustn't find out about her real father. Charlie, you will serve her from today, and you won't leave her alone for even one moment.

Charlie bowed and left.

Shagad was going up the stairs of the Jung-Frau fortress with heavy footfalls, while his long cloak was dragging over the ground, making a rustling sound.

He had many evil plans to captivate the Guardians in his trap.

Shagad, Adam Heber and the rest of guardians were getting ready for the most difficult moment of their lives.

The concealment war was over…

www.ingramcontent.com/pod-product-compliance
Lightning Source LLC
Chambersburg PA
CBHW071135170626
46809CB00002B/626